FOREVER FINDS Us

A SMALL-TOWN WESTERN BILLIONAIRE ROMANCE

Greta Rose West

COPYRIGHT

PUNK
ROSE
PRESS

ALSO BY GRETA ROSE WEST

Wild Heart: Welcome to Wisper

Subscribe to the newsletter for this short introduction into the Cade Ranch world and for extra goodies and scenes. Sign up at gretarosewest.com.

THE CADE RANCH SERIES IN ORDER

BURNED

BROKEN

BUSTED

BRAVED

BLINDED

THE WISPER DREAMS SERIES IN ORDER

RIVERS BETWEEN US

STORMS INSIDE US

MOUNTAINS DIVIDE US

LIGHT BETRAYS US

MIDNIGHT SURROUNDS US

ROADS BEHIND US

FOREVER FINDS US

SCARS FORGET US

WYOMING LOVE EBOOK BOXSETS

LOVE AT CADE RANCH (Cade Ranch Books 1 - 3)

CADE RANCH IN LOVE (Cade Ranch Books 4 & 5)

LOVE IN WISPER, WYOMING (Wisper Dreams Books 1 - 3)

ACKNOWLEDGMENTS

To Peter Senftleben, my steadfast and unembarrassable editor, when your edit comes back with something like "I'm no therapist, but…" I know Reddit threads are in my future. Book 12. Dude. Can you believe it? Thank you!

MJ, Geri, Barb, and Kerry, thanks for beta reading and calling out my bad habits and mistakes, and for squealing when I really needed to hear it!

Thanks again to Laura for the blurb voodoo. And to the girls' group chat: I couldn't figure out how to put a meme in here, but just imagine there's one. Love you. Thanks for inspiring and supporting me and listening to me when I freak out and leave long, rambling voice messages.

To the lovelies who ARC read this book and helped spread the word: You are everyday magic. Thank you. I swear there isn't a day that goes by that one of you doesn't make me smile or laugh. The social shares and reels I find in my DMs and your words of encouragement are priceless to me.

If you know me, you know I can't live without music. These artists and so many others have been a constant carousel in my head for the last three months: Cowboy Junkies, Max McNown, GAI, Sam Barber, Penny and Sparrow, Chase Rice, Chris Stapleton, Zach Bryan, Jason Isbell, Ella Langley, Alex Warren, Journey, and The Smashing Pumpkins. Thanks for inspiring me every dang day.

And to my family: I do this for you. I owe any success I

find to you, and I love you. I beg you not to read this book, and if you already have, well then, Christmas is gonna be awkward.

To every woman who has desperately wanted something she didn't know how to voice, something that made her heart race and fall into her stomach. Something that made her want to drop to her knees, cast her eyes to the floor, and utter the words…
"Yes, sir."

TRIGGER WARNINGS

In this book you'll find angst and longing, love, hearts, and flowers. But you'll also find a blooming Dom/sub relationship and obedience. There is also power switching, light choking, spanking, punishment, withholding of gratification for amplified pleasure, consensual penetration with inanimate objects, and restraint during intimate moments. In the beginning of the story, a secondary character, a teenage girl, goes missing, and you will find talk of the loss of family members, emotional, verbal, and physical abuse from a parent, and of a family member who has in the past been addicted to illicit substances.

It sounds like a lot when I type it all out, but I promise that my usual humor and themes of strong and found family live within these pages too. And the HEA is utterly swoonworthy with a cowboy hat on top.

xoxo

Greta

CHAPTER ONE

BRAND

TEN MILES north of my childhood home near Wisper, Wyoming, I sputtered to a stop on Highway 20 beneath the shadow of Rendezvous Mountain and the shroud of utter darkness it cast over the Jackson Hole Valley.

As I tried to find my father's old mechanic's phone number on my cell, suddenly the glare from a too-bright flashlight tapping against my driver's side window made me drop the phone. When the SUV made a weird noise and my speed decreased even though my foot had been steady on the gas pedal, I pulled onto the narrow strip of dirt aligning the dark road, and now I hit the button to roll down my window so I could explain to the sheriff's deputy waiting for a reason why I had parked illegally on a normally busy highway.

Tonight, the way home was empty in all directions.

I couldn't see the deputy's face—she was tall—but the swell of feminine hips and a brown uniform gave her away. It was the same one my sister wore for work.

"What seems to be the problem, sir?"

"I don't know," I said, staring at the dash computer, hoping for it to give me a clue, but the screen was blank. The lights were on, but the damn car wouldn't move. "Engine trouble." I poked the screen, like that would make it blink back to life.

"Hm. Isn't this a new Explorer?"

"Yeah, it is," I said, and I leaned closer to my door and peered out my window at the officer now shining her light at the hood of my vehicle. "How'd you know that?"

"I've got eyes, don't I? Besides, you know how many cars and trucks I see on the job?" Finally, she looked at me, her light brown gaze traveling the side of my face and down my chest. She cocked a brow. "I'm surprised you don't drive a truck."

"I do. I bought this for my mother, but I have a truck too. An F350," I said incredulously, like I needed to prove my manhood by saying so.

"License and registration?"

"For my truck?" I asked, confused. Why would she want that?

"Are you tryin' to be funny?" She widened her legs slightly, hands on her hips now, inches away from a serious-looking Glock strapped around her tight thigh and a Taser holstered on her belt.

"No, ma'am." I shook my head. "I was just confused." I reached for the glove box and registration paperwork. "I apologize. It's been a long day."

"You're from the Sheridan area?" she asked, watching me closely, probably in case I pulled a weapon from my glove box. It wouldn't be unheard of in Wyoming.

"Uh, yeah. How'd you know that? Actually, I grew up right outside Wisper, but I've lived in Sheridan for a long time."

"The '3' at the start of your plate number gives you

away," she said, waving an arm toward the back of the car. "What brings you back?"

Loneliness.

"Family," I said, handing her the registration, and I pulled my wallet from my back pocket, slipped my license out, and handed that to her too. "Here."

The officer, who I now noticed had a kind of odd, quiet beauty about her with soft, wavy ash-brown hair and naturally rosy cheeks, took the ID from my hand. A lock of her hair had fallen out of the low bun at the nape of her neck under her deputy hat, and she waved it off her skin with my paperwork like a fan. She shined her flashlight over my license and glanced at my registration, and a little smile lifted the edge of her full, bare lip.

"Brand Lee. You related to Deputy Sheriff Lee?"

"Yes, she's my little sister."

She nodded in recognition. "Well, big brother, seems you bought yourself a brand-new, shiny lemon. That's gonna be a hefty tow bill this time of night."

"I'm aware. I was just lookin' for Mike Williams's number. I'll call him and have him take a look at his shop. Maybe it's just a loose hose."

I could've called the dealership where I'd bought the SUV. It was seven hours away, but the manager would've sent someone for me from the local dealership if I asserted my affluence. I wouldn't. I could've called the dealership owner on his cell, too, but I wouldn't do that either. I wasn't someone who kicked up a fuss to get my way. I never had been.

The deputy shrugged. "Whatever floats your boat."

"You're not from around here," I said, detecting a subtle nuance in her speech different than what I was used to in my home state, and it occurred to me that I was now interrogating my interrogator.

"No, sir. From Oklahoma. You comin' into town for Bax's wedding?"

"Yeah, among other things. You know my brother too?"

"'Course. Wisper's a small town. I'll see you at the ceremony. Your sister invited me."

For the first time, I focused on her name tag. "R. Fitts? Oh," I said, realization dawning, "R for Roxanne. You're Roxi? Abey's mentioned you."

The deputy bent at the waist. She leaned a hand on the edge of my open window, patted it twice, and handed me back my ID and registration, and her big, clear eyes took me in.

"That's me. I'll give you a ride to your mama's house. You can call Mike Williams on the way, but he probably won't get out here till mornin'."

"Oh, uh, sure. Thanks."

"No prob." She straightened, and I watched her in my side mirror as she walked back to her cruiser. I couldn't be sure because they all looked the same, but I thought she might've inherited my sister's old truck when Abey took the deputy sheriff promotion a couple years ago.

I also noticed she was taller than my sister who had been five-ten since she turned twelve.

Roxanne had the longest legs I'd ever seen, and they led my attention right to her ass, which, wrapped in her fitted uniform, was kind of doing it for me.

Rolling up my window, I found myself staring at her in my mirror as she opened her door and folded that lithe frame into her driver's seat, and when she was in the safety of her cruiser, her eyes stayed on my vehicle. She lifted her radio from her dash, probably to report that my new, sixty-thousand-dollar hunk of metal wasn't abandoned.

Dammit. Some gift. When I bought the car for my mother, I figured she'd like a shiny, tricked-out, four-wheel-drive SUV to go with her new house. Plus, it was safer than the junker she'd been driving for ages. Or at least I thought it would be until it landed me stranded in the dark, but there was no way I was going to give her the car now.

Irritation festered beneath my skin. I wasn't accustomed to my plans not working out, but self-sufficiency had always been more important to me than the need to voice my displeasure. If Mike couldn't find a quick fix, I'd wait until the start of business on Monday morning, and then I'd quietly let the dealership know that the luxury vehicle they'd sold me was defective, and then they'd scramble and stumble over their apologies and offer me countless perks and free shit to earn back my good grace.

I checked for traffic, of which there was still zero, and when I stepped out of the car, the crisp air outside was unmoving. There was a stillness and a soundlessness that set my jaw on edge, but it was just the quiet way of Wisper and something I'd have to reacquaint myself with now that I'd moved home.

Opening the back door, I grabbed my suitcase, laptop bag, and at the last second, remembered my water bottle in the center console, then dragged it all with me to Roxanne's truck. Until I could build myself a new house, the container I'd rented to store the rest of my furniture and household items would be delivered to my family's ranch tomorrow afternoon.

My first night as a returning resident of Teton County hadn't gone to plan. Was that indicative of my future here back in my hometown?

Goddamn, I hope so.

"So," Roxanne said, staring at the side of my face when I was seated next to her in her truck and had clicked my seatbelt into place.

"My family's place is about ten miles from here."

"I know," she said.

"Right."

She put her truck in gear and pulled out and around my deserted SUV. "Your sister says you sold your company and are startin' a new one here?"

"I did, Abey's right. Well, I sold the contracts I had up in Sheridan. Not the company itself, but it's similar, I guess. We're startin' over from scratch down here."

"That's cool though. A lot of people around here will be happy for the jobs."

"Yeah," I said, hoping I could find a solid crew in Wisper and the surrounding areas.

Starting fresh meant I didn't have the reputation here that I'd cultivated in Sheridan, but I hoped a few people had heard about some of the jobs we'd worked and would spread the word. A lot of the local crew I'd hired to help build my family's new rental cabins and houses last year had already started on some of the outbuildings on our ranch and the small inn we'd recently decided to add. Most of those craftsmen and women had inquired about future jobs. That was promising.

It was a point of pride for me, to bring good-paying jobs to the people of Wisper, jobs that would pay them enough to support their families. I had money now, had spent my adult life making Lee Construction a household name in Wyoming, but my brothers, sister, and I had grown up eating bologna and cheese sandwiches, just like most other farming families.

Other than the small handful of workers who'd already committed to working for me, I'd need to hire many more. I recruited my office manager to join me, paid her a hefty retainer fee to entice her to Wisper with me, but it was worth it. After working with Tabitha Ketterman over the last year, I didn't think Lee Construction could survive without her.

And my right hand, Sweetie Baker, was about to marry my brother Bax, so thankfully I'd have her steady support too.

Dammit. *Bea* Baker. Bax and my niece Athena had tried to drum it into my head to stop calling Bea by her nickname, but it was a habit, and one I couldn't seem to break.

What is that scent? A calming, warm aroma wrapped around me in the cab of the deputy's truck. It seemed odd to be riding shotgun next to a law enforcement officer and be tantalized by a fragrance, but it was kind of intoxicating.

It wasn't perfume—more like flowers and body heat, and it made my mouth water. The scent fought against my earlier irritation, trying to calm me, but calm wasn't something I often succumbed to.

Forced calm worked well in business, but real calm—inner peace—wasn't something I'd gotten the hang of. I hadn't found anything that could tame the wild anxiety I sometimes felt, especially when things were out of control, like tonight when the brand-new vehicle I'd bought died on the side of the road.

But something about Roxanne Fitts's truck and her scent leeching into my bloodstream had me taking deep breaths and my muscles relaxing. The knotted kink on the back of my neck I'd felt for the last seven hours on my drive to Wisper disappeared.

Discreetly, I looked for one of those dangling air-freshener trees, but didn't see one.

No, the scent was coming from Roxanne, and my eyes landed on the side of her face as she drove.

Her skin was smooth, but I noticed a few laugh lines around her eyes, and the way she draped her hand over the steering wheel gave off a nonchalant, laid-back air, but she swallowed, betraying her show of ease, and her throat rippled with the movement.

Was I making her nervous? She was the cop. She had the authority in this situation.

The movement led me to the hollow at the base of her neck, barely visible below her buttoned-up uniform shirt. A simple necklace lay there, with some kind of delicate charm. A small, gold cross.

Her free hand resting on her thigh twitched, and she tapped her fingertip three times against the outside of her leg.

"Abey said you'll be stayin' with your mama for a while," she said.

"Yes," I answered, startled out of staring at Roxanne by the sound of her voice.

She'd been talking to me, but it wasn't until now that I noticed the silky sound and the way it traveled around the truck cab, like heat rising from asphalt in the summer, making beads of sweat form at the small of my back. The soothing murmur reminded me of simpler times—long summer days and movie nights in the dark, entangled limbs, bodies entwined, skin slipping over softer skin.

What the hell?

"Hello-o-o?"

"Sorry. What?"

"I asked what your immediate plans are? Do you have a project lined up?"

"Oh," I said, stuttering to catch up to the conversation I'd zoned out of again, noticing fir trees and rugged land blurring out my window as Roxanne drove us down the road into higher elevation. "Yes, a new subdivision on the east side of town. It won't start until spring, so I'll have plenty of time to get set up here, but the county wants to tear down the old Teton Corner mobile home park."

"What?" Roxanne argued. "What about the residents who've lived there for years? They're your mama's friends. You're just gonna throw 'em out?"

"Of course not. They'll be offered one of the new homes. It's a low-income development. The county and state will subsidize."

"Oh."

"I'm workin' with the builder on a temporary housing plan while the homes are built, but there's only a few residents left. The trailers are old. They're fallin' apart. Those people deserve better." Thank God my mother had finally moved out of hers and into the home I'd built for her. Every night for the last several years, I'd gone to bed worrying that it might crumble down around her in her sleep. And then the guilt would set in.

I'd left. Built a life for myself away from my family. I stayed away because I had to. I couldn't have been the man I'd needed to be in order to build and run my company if I had the tribulations of my family's lives poking at me every day. And if they knew about some of the choices I'd made, they probably wouldn't have wanted me around anyway, and they probably wouldn't be welcoming me home now.

"Hm."

"What does 'hm' mean?" I asked. I hadn't had anyone around to question my decisions in a long time, and the way it niggled and buzzed under my skin surprised me.

"Nothin'. I'm pleasantly surprised by your answer."

Was this woman under the impression that I was a monster? I wouldn't have elderly people displaced with nowhere to go just so I could make more money. But I didn't say so.

Roxanne turned onto Old Fish Creek Road and it wasn't another mile until I saw the first sign for Spitfire Ranch at Lee Valley.

The cattle ranch was new, a joint venture I'd bought into with my older brother Bax and our best friend from childhood, Rye Graves. But the Lee Family part had been there for years. My father had tried to make a go at sheep farming and had failed miserably, but the land was rich and good, and alongside Spitfire Ranch, we'd started Lee Valley Cabins, a rental-cabin business that had already begun to bring in a profit.

Sweetie—dammit, *Bea*—had finished building the cabins for me last year, and this was our first open season. Already, Bax had told me we'd managed to enchant some of the families and adventure enthusiasts who had visited this summer and fall into booking ahead several years, and soon, the B&B-type inn on the property would be open to guests too.

My brother and Rye had big plans to tie the cabins to the ranch side of the property, and then my sister and her new wife, Devo, had started a community garden program that would help feed Teton County, and our renters would have the opportunity to participate in tending the garden and harvesting the vegetables if they wanted to.

If they were run well, any business ventures in the Jackson Hole area were bound to profit.

I'd remained hands-off until now, but it was part of the reason I'd decided to move back home. That and the guilt I felt every day, plus the fact that I missed the closeness my siblings and I once shared, had me itching to make the move for a while now.

I'd stayed away long enough. My father was gone. He'd

been dead nine years now, and his mean stain on our lives had finally faded. Mostly.

But there was something else. Something I'd been searching for, something I hadn't yet been able to define or find, but after several years of feeling this way, when the opportunity to move Lee Construction to Wisper came up, I thought maybe I'd find what I was looking for back home.

"Here we are," Roxanne said when she pulled up in front of the house I'd built for my mother. My little brother, Dixon, should've been living here with her, but he'd left town, knocked up his girlfriend, and then dumped the kid on our family and taken off again almost a year ago.

There wasn't a day that went by when my younger brother wasn't on my mind, though I couldn't deny that his vacant room in my mother's house was convenient for me now, but when I pictured walking into the room intended for Dixon and dumping my shit on the bed he should've been sleeping on, guilt pricked under my skin again.

I'd been gone from our home for twenty years. Dixon had only been gone two, but his absence was louder, and the fact that I'd spoken to him when the rest of our family remained clueless and worried about his wellbeing made the guilt burn in my gut like I'd swallowed liquid fire.

The house we'd grown up in sat half a mile away from the new house I'd built for my mother last year, crafted in a farmhouse style to match the old home. My brother Bax lived there now, with my soon-to-be sister-in-law Bea, my niece Athena and nephew Stuey, but instead of pale yellow, the new house was a deep blue color, the shutters crisp white.

"Thank you, Roxanne," I said, reaching for the door handle. "Or, excuse me, maybe I should call you Officer Fitts?"

"Roxanne's fine," she said, but she wasn't making eye contact. Was it just me, or was she blushing? "Or Roxi."

"Roxanne then," I said, noticing how her name slid from my tongue in a kind of purr.

You must be tired. Shut up now before you embarrass yourself.

"Good night. And thanks again." I opened my door and grabbed my stuff from her back seat.

She laid her hand on the seatback and looked over her shoulder. "My pleasure, sir."

The soft sound of her voice and the "sir" at the end of her sentence sent a flood of calm through me. It wasn't unusual for people to address me in that way. My money and the air of quiet expectation I seemed to give off could put even familiar people on edge. I hadn't anticipated it from Deputy Roxanne, but when her eyes finally met mine, my dick grew hard.

All it had taken was her kindness and her slightly argumentative nature, but her long legs and the unassuming way her eyes held mine didn't hurt either.

CHAPTER TWO

ROXANNE

IT WAS SO super fun when you showed up late to the function, and static sucked your sundress to the backs of your thighs, and then you realized that the seat your BFF saved for you was in the second freaking row of chairs in front of a really pretty wedding altar, but instead of everyone staring at the roses and wildflowers and the beautiful couple about to say their vows, they were all looking at you.

Ughhh.

"Hey." Leaning forward in the seat I'd just taken at the lakeside wedding she'd invited me to, I whispered to my boss, Deputy Sheriff Lee, or more precisely to the back of her head since she was the sister of the groom and was seated in the front row.

My best friend, Aubrey, couldn't have known about my connection to the man sitting next to my boss in front of us because I hadn't said a word about it to her, but she'd saved me the seat directly behind my boss's older brother, Brand— the guy I'd picked up on the side of the highway last week and drove to his mama's place not even a mile away from my current location.

"Sorry I'm late," I said to my bestie and boss both. "Accident out by Mr. B's tree farm. Everyone's okay. Light vehicle damage. Both parties insured."

Thank God Aubrey had saved me an aisle seat so I wouldn't have to listen to the groans and sighs of the person behind me when they couldn't see past my shoulders.

My boss threw me a thumbs up over her shoulder.

Aubrey pressed a finger to her lips. "Shh."

Brand Lee's head turned slightly, like maybe he wanted to say hello, but then, stiff as a board, he straightened.

I sat back, crossing my legs and smoothing the hem of the dress I'd changed into in the back seat of my truck. I tried not to turn my head, but I let my eyes wander the small gathering so I could scope out the attendees. My boss was the youngest of four siblings, and her oldest brother, Bax, and his girlfriend, Bea, were about to be hitched in a simple ceremony on the Lee family's property.

Lucky fuckers. I envied them.

Just then, Bea tossed her bouquet. It whizzed past my boss's head as she ducked and hit me in the face. I squeaked and sputtered and spit flowers from my mouth, then caught the bouquet before it fell to the ground. That was bad luck, right? I thought I'd heard that before, but maybe I was thinking of some other superstition.

"Everyone's lookin' at me," I whispered to Aubrey. "And isn't she s'posed to wait till *after* they say 'I do' to toss the flowers?"

Aubrey shrugged.

Seriously. Why was every person in attendance staring at me? Only one head still hadn't turned in my direction, and that was Brand Lee's. Like, the guy hadn't even twitched.

Whatever. I'd never caught a bouquet before. If anybody else wanted it, they could pry it from my cold, dead hands.

Everyone laughed at the irregular wedding etiquette. The bride shrugged and grinned, and said to her groom, "You knew I was weird before you asked me to marry you. Deal with it."

Maybe it was a little sappy of me, but I believed the old wives' tale, that if you caught a bouquet at a wedding, you'd be next to get married. So yeah, I was envious of Bax and Bea.

But not about the kid part, though. Bax's teenage daughter, Athena, was a great kid, and she looked so pretty in her purple and white dress, standing up next to Bax at the altar, but Bax and Bea were also raising his brother's little boy, Stuey.

Dixon Lee, the youngest of the Lee brothers, had disappeared after an unsuccessful stint in rehab a while back, and then a year ago, he reappeared, abandoned his surprise infant son with Bax and Bea, and disappeared again. No one knew where he was now, whether he was dead or alive.

Normally a hoot and a great boss, Abey had been pretty torn up about it. Her mom even more so. Abey might've been the youngest in her family, but she'd told me Dixon was her mama's baby. He'd never been responsible or a productive member of society. Bax, as the eldest Lee, carried the weight of the world on his shoulders, and when his first wife passed, that hadn't gotten better, but he'd found Bea and had been loosening up lately.

That left Brand Lee. The middle brother. The well-off owner of Lee Construction up in Sheridan who'd just moved home to be closer to family. He'd never been married that I knew of and didn't have kids. He was kind of mysterious, or at least it seemed that way to me since I knew all about his siblings and nothing about him.

Now, Brand watched his nephew Stuey wiggling in his

grandma's arms next to Abey, and a little smile curved the edge of his lip. Brand was clean-shaven, but I could see the hint of stubble filling back in.

Stuey was cute and all, with his waving brown hair and chubby, dimpled cheeks, but I could do without the sticky hands and wailing cries of babes in my life. Little Stuey stood on his granny's legs and peered over her shoulder. His baby blues landed on me, and he smiled and waved. Lifting my hand and scrunching my fingers discreetly, I wondered why I'd never really wanted kids. Did that mean there was something wrong with me?

I mean, not that I could do much about it now, single and in my forties. My five sisters all had kids. You'd think that'd make my mama and daddy happy, but they were back in Oklahoma, still praying for me to jump on the domestic-bliss chain gang.

Hope they brought kneepads to church.

Stuey flopped down onto his granny's lap, finally facing forward, and Aubrey bumped my elbow when she noticed me fidgeting and chewing on the cuticle around my thumbnail. I crossed my arms tightly across my chest to stop myself, and a memory of the old SNL skit filled my head, the one with the nerdy high school girl who was always sticking her hands in her armpits and then she sniffed them.

The preacher droned on, "Do you, Beatrice Baker, take Baxton Lee to be your…."

Hm. Brand has a really nice neck. Like, the guy's built. It's clear he works out, or maybe he stays fit because he runs a construction company. I thought he was just the suit in charge, but it looks like he gets pretty physical. His neck is smooth. The short, golden-brown hair there is sexy.

Biting my bottom lip hard enough to draw blood, I stared at the back of some guy's neck and found myself wanting to lick it. My leg started jumping, my finger tapped out a one-two-three against the side of my thigh, and my usual affirmation sounded in my mind: *You are enough. You are not too much.*

Aubrey elbowed me in the ribs this time.

Right. Pay attention, Roxi. It's not like every wedding isn't the same. I rolled my eyes. *You've been to 567 of them. By now you're practically ordained. Always the bridesmaid, never the bride? Five times had to be some kind of record. Isn't there a movie about that, a professional bridesmaid?*

The preacher wrapped things up. "By the authority vested in me by the state of Wyoming, I now pronounce you husband and wife. You may now seal your promise with a kiss."

Bax swept Bea up into his arms. She threw hers around his neck, balancing on the tips of her bare toes to press her lips to his. But then she reached down and hiked her long, lavender skirt up her legs, Bax lifted her, and she wrapped them around his waist. The flowing fabric bunched and draped itself over Bax's crisp Wranglers, and they attacked each other's mouths.

Cheers and whoops erupted from the crowd. Everybody stood, so I followed suit, trying to wiggle the underwear out of my butt crack without anyone noticing. Finally, the flexing and releasing of my ass cheeks did the trick, and I clapped in relief.

Leaning down closer to Aubrey, I whispered, "These pantyhose are makin' my butt itch." If I wasn't wrong, a little tear had escaped her eye. My comment made her laugh, which had been the point of me making it.

Aubrey and her boyfriend, Rye, had talked about marriage, but Aubs had been married before. It hadn't been a great experience to begin with, and then her husband went and got himself killed overseas when he was in the Army and left her with two teenagers to raise alone at the time. But Rye was nothing like Aubrey's former husband. Rye was kind and patient and all in for a life with Aubrey, even if she never said yes to his repeated proposals.

She would though. If I knew my best friend, and I did, she'd say yes soon. She just had to get over herself first.

Their love was the kind I'd longed for my whole life.

I hated to complain—actually, I kind of loved it—but growing taller than nearly every person I'd ever met by the time I hit seventh grade hadn't set me up for social success in high school. The only thing my height had been good for was guaranteeing me a healthy dose of insecurity and a place on the girls' basketball team.

Boys? Dating? Yeah, being six-feet tall wasn't the way to any boy's heart. Most teenage boys were insecure, too, and if they had to look up at their date, it kind of ruined the romantic vibes. I'd brought out the little-man syndrome in every guy I'd liked since I was thirteen. It was my curse in life and probably the root of all my self-doubt.

How the hell was I supposed to be swept off my feet when no man I'd ever dated had been able to lift me?

The party moved around the lake to where more chairs and tables had been set up. Big speakers surrounded a small beach and sandy area, and everyone was taking off their shoes and stowing them underneath their chairs.

Great. I hated my feet. They were big. Kind of cute though, but bigger than most men's. Just another reason to set me apart, to tell every guy in a five-mile radius that I was no petite, dainty lady, which was what it seemed every cowboy around here wanted, but whatever. It wasn't like I could dig my big feet into the sand and hide them, like a dang flamingo.

Aubrey claimed a table for us, we dumped our purses on

it, stuck our shoes beneath, and she hung Rye's jacket over a chair to save his seat since he'd been part of the ceremony and was currently having his picture taken.

If anyone wanted to go through our bags, the only important item in my purse was Honey Bee lip balm. I'd left my gun and wallet locked in my truck. I felt naked as a jay bird without the old Smith & Wesson 469 my uncle Al had given me when I enrolled in the police academy back home. But there were kids here, and people were about to get drunk. The bar table and keg had more bodies surrounding it than the buffet table did.

I sat while Aubs went to find her man, and I watched the guests all making their way up to congratulate Bax and Bea. There were many people in attendance I didn't know but most smiled or greeted me. I'd seen them around town on the job or at the local watering hole, Manny's Bar, but hadn't had occasion to get to know them. Aubrey and I had become best friends pretty much the minute I stepped foot in Wisper on my first day with the sheriff's department. I'd made friends through Aubrey and Abey, even joined a book club which had become like a family to me.

I missed my own family, but only one of my sisters still lived in Oklahoma near my parents. The rest had scattered farther around the US with their husbands and kids. The six of us kept a text thread going, and we sent memes and checked in with each other most days, but I hadn't seen any of my sisters in person in almost two years.

Aubrey returned with a beer from the keg for me, which I'd decided to pretend was an expensive Aperol spritz, and just as I brought the red, plastic cup to my mouth and took a deep whiff of the hoppy bitterness, my cell rang in my crossbody purse on the table. The dreaded *X-Files* theme-song ringtone told me it was my partner, Dan.

I ignored it. I was off duty, and he was probably calling to suggest again, like he had the one and only time I'd encountered him drunk, that since we were both single and lonely, we should hook up.

Yeah, never gonna happen.

He wasn't creepy about it. Just resigned to the inevitability, like a pact you make with your best friend in eighth grade that if you're not married by thirty-five, you'll marry each other. But I set down the beer, just in case Dan was calling to inform me of a bad accident in town, a reported crime, or maybe aliens had landed and were setting up shop at the top of Mount Bannon. *X-Files indeed.*

Abey approached with a petite redhead following at her side. The woman was all smiles and polished teeth.

"Hey, Roxi," Abey said. "This is Tabitha. She just moved here to work with Brand."

"Oh." *Huh.* Why did that grate my nerves? *One-two-three.* "Nice to meet you."

I extended my hand and Tabitha shook it, but the fact that she worked with Brand Lee rankled. She was perky and perfect. And short, or at least normal-woman-sized, which probably suited someone like Brand better than my telephone-pole height.

"Roxi works with me at the station," Abey said, but her attention drifted as we heard Stuey throwing a tantrum by the buffet table. The gargantuan, plastic bowl of grandma-style potato salad in the middle of the spread was calling my name, but I ignored the craving 'cause I didn't want to pig out and embarrass myself.

Abey's mama, affectionately known to her children as Merv, looked like she was at her wit's end as the kid stomped the ground, tugging on Merv's puce-colored skirt and pointing at the wedding cake. Stuey held his breath, and his little face turned the color of a beet.

"S'cuse me for a minute," Abey said, and she dashed over to assist and left me standing there, stranded and trying to make conversation with Miss Perky Everything.

If somebody started a conga line and I had to hold onto her hips while we hopped around the reception in a procession of stupidity, I was going straight back to my truck for my gun.

CHAPTER THREE

ROXANNE

"SO," Tabitha said. "You're a Wisper transplant too?"

"Huh?" I asked, watching as Abey got down on her hands and knees to distract Stuey away from the cake. She wasn't the kind to care about getting her outfit dirty.

Stuart Lee had recently decided he'd rather be a dog than a human, so sometimes the only way for the adults around him to "talk" to him was to pretend to be a dog too. If Abey were a dog, I figured she'd be a white shepherd, with her pale-blond hair and her noble stature. Stuey was definitely a yapping Chihuahua. Or maybe a corgi.

"Abey tells me you moved here from Oklahoma."

"Oh, right," I said, focusing on Tabitha's pretty face again, noticing her perfectly symmetrical features and the adorably nervous habit she seemed to have of sweeping her auburn hair over her shoulder with one perfectly polished finger.

Man, I really needed to stop comparing myself to her. I'd done it like six times already in my head, and I was starting to piss even myself off.

But, gah! She had gray eyes the color of sexy smoke,

which I imagined had the ability to lure men from all corners of the US with only a wink. Had she used her powers on her boss? That was what I really wanted to know. Desperately. But like, how was that fair? I'd only spent ten minutes with the man.

But he was just so sexy! God, just the sound of Brand's voice in my truck the other night...

Brand Lee had an air about him I didn't usually run into around here, like he *was* someone. Like he knew what he wanted and how to get it, and if anybody had plans to get in his way, they better watch out, and the thought of this Tabitha drooling all over him in his office made the insecurity inside me rage.

You're not good enough, rich enough, pretty enough, smart enough...

One-two-three.

It didn't matter. I'd get over it. I'd feel jealous and wistful for a few days, but then my daydreams would fade away and I'd resign myself to being alone again, like I always did. Maybe Dan's default-hookup pact had some merit.

For a while there, I'd gone on dates with every single man I could find in the tri-state area, but all that had gotten me was a lot of creepy first-date stories—one where I'd strongly considered using my Taser—no second-date stories, and many blocked cell phone numbers. When that got old and severely disappointing, I just tried to settle down. I spent time with my friends and focused on my job. I'd taken up crocheting and had gotten surprisingly good at it.

Ughhh. Now all I needed was ten cats, and I'd be set for life. Even my four-year-old nieces were sick of the crocheted bunnies and unicorns I kept sending them.

"Yeah," I answered Tabitha. "I've been here a couple years. Before I came to Wisper, I worked Yellowstone, but

I'm from the Oklahoma City area. Born and raised, actually. Where are you comin' from?"

"Joplin, Missouri. Do you know it?"

I shook my head. "Sounds familiar though."

"It's near the northeast corner of Oklahoma. Anyway, I've been in Sheridan now for about two years and at Lee Construction for almost a year. When Brand announced he was selling his contracts up north, he asked if I wanted to make the move down here to help him set up shop in his hometown. I love the mountains and the small-town feel, don't you?"

"Yeah," I said as my phone rang again. "Sure do. S'cuse me for a sec."

Grabbing my purse from the table behind me, I yanked my phone out. *Oh yeah,* I thought, *I just love the small town, where there's a sum total of one eligible guy, and this Tabitha, with her tiny hips and plump lips, is probably sleeping with him. Seriously, without some kind of liquid rubber filler injected into them, how did any woman have lips so perfect? Had she been born with those luscious sex pillows?*

"Yeah?" I clipped at Dan at the end of the line when I answered his annoying and repeated calls.

"All hands on deck," he said. "Lost hiker."

Aw, shit. "You call the boss? She didn't say anything."

"She didn't answer," Dan said. "You still at the party?"

"Yeah, I'll let her know."

"10–4."

I hung up and slipped my phone back in my purse, searching over the tops of the wedding goers' heads for Abey.

"Everything okay?" Tabitha asked.

"Uh, no, actually. I've gotta go. Do you see Abey anywhere?"

Tabitha pivoted on her feet, still in her cute, champagne-colored ballet flats, and I noticed her rack when she faced away from me. Dammit. Her double Ds made me officially hate her.

"There she is," she said, pointing across the party to where Abey stood talking to Tabitha's boss and, I realized, the hottest guy I'd probably ever laid eyes on. Brand stared back at us as Abey held Stuey, laughing as she tickled his ribs.

"Nice to meet you," I called over my shoulder as I rushed to Abey.

"Nice to meet you too. Maybe we'll see each other around…"

When I was standing in front of her and had startled her, Abey arched an eyebrow.

"Dan called. He says they just got a report of a missin' hiker. He tried to call you, but you didn't answer."

"Ah, dammit. Here." She pushed her nephew into Brand's hands, and Brand's eyebrows rose, too, but he was still staring at me. "Stay here," she said to me. "Let me go tell Bax and Bea I'm leavin'."

"Sure."

"Is the hiker injured?" Brand asked after Abey raced away, and Stuey tried to bite the side of his face.

"Dunno," I replied. "My partner didn't give any details, but a lost hiker is a priority around here. There's just too much wild to hope they'll find their way down the mountain on their own."

"Right." Brand pulled Stuey's mouth away from his face, where the kid had left a slobbery red mark. "Anything I can do to help?"

Besides give me orgasms? "Nah. If it gets to that point, we'll call for the public to help with search parties, but we don't have enough information yet."

Brand nodded, and suddenly ol' Tabby Cat appeared next to him. Their arms were almost touching, and then Stu laid his head on his uncle's shoulder. The three of them looked like the perfect family.

"Everything okay?" Tabitha asked.

How many times in a day could she ask the question? I'd just answered it not a minute ago. What, did she have some kind of quota to fill?

Roxi, your inner monologue is a bitch.

"There's a lost hiker," Brand told her as he looked down into her sultry eyes, which I now noticed had been perfectly lined with kohl liner. "Abey and Roxanne have to leave to help find them."

Ughhh. Why do my nipples turn to steel buttons when he says my name like that?

Brand's eyes slid from Tabitha's to mine, and then they slipped down my dress and followed the long lengths of my legs to my bare feet. *Shit. My shoes!*

"Um, right, well guess I should go find my shoes. Nice to see y'all."

Giving an awkward wave as I turned, I caught Lee Lake in my peripheral and hoped a tsunami would erupt from its depths and swallow me up. Or maybe a Kraken.

One-two-three.

"YOU LOOK REAL NICE," Dan said, taking in a sweeping eyeful of my dress, when Abey and I barreled into the station.

On the drive over from the wedding, Abey and I had learned that the missing hiker was a sixteen-year-old girl, but that was all we knew so far.

Still dressed in black tuxedo-style pants, with a white,

satin stripe down each leg, and a silky, white button-down tucked in, Abey tossed her bag on the front desk, and our receptionist scoffed at her, then grabbed the bag and hung it on the hook behind her.

Abey winced. "Sorry."

Shelley was the kind of woman you didn't want to find yourself on the bad side of. She was harmless, but it wouldn't have surprised me if she was the reason "passive-aggressive" appeared in the *Merriam-Webster Dictionary*.

Deputy Frank Sims was all business though, as usual. He'd already pulled out the maps and had scribbled all pertinent information onto the rolling whiteboard he'd set up in front of the shaded Main Street-facing windows.

"Thanks," I said to Dan, but I wasn't paying attention to him. My brain was already following trails in the Grand Teton National Park, which was where the hiker had gotten lost.

The girl had been picnicking with her family between Jenny Lake and Lake Solitude. The trails around Jenny Lake were moderate difficulty at most, but the same couldn't be said of the trail leading up to Lake Solitude, especially if the hiker had been injured somehow or was freaking out. In that case, moderate could escalate to difficult in a heartbeat. And if she'd veered off the trails, well then... Yikes.

Autumn was a beautiful time to explore the Tetons, but the temperature dropped quickly in the evenings, and nights could go well below freezing, depending on the altitude. The area could be blanketed in snow, even in September if conditions were right. And that was to say nothing about the wildlife.

I'd grown up outdoors. Although, Oklahoma wasn't exactly known for its mountains, and I'd lived in a pretty flat area east of Oklahoma City in Choctaw, but when I took the

Yellowstone job, I'd spent months hiking Wyoming on my days off. I wanted to get to know my new home, and I wanted to be able to help people on the job. Plus, being in the mountains, smelling the earth and communing with the trees and lakes and rivers had become a kind of religion for me. My mind and all the ways I'd never measured up went quiet out there.

I'd been alone a long time, but out there in the wilderness, somehow it didn't feel so lonely.

"How'd she get separated from her family?" I asked.

Frank sighed, probably putting himself in the missing girl's father's shoes. Frank had two kids and a wife, and they spent plenty of time hiking and camping.

"The mom and dad went chasing after the two younger kids," he said. "The older daughter got stuck packin' up the food, and they thought she was right behind them, but when they stopped, she'd disappeared."

"But *had* she been right behind them?" I asked. "Or did she disappear from the picnic site?"

A teenager could have all kinds of reasons for disobeying her parents. Maybe she was pissed they'd left her with the lunch mess, and she'd wandered off to try to find a cell signal to call her boyfriend or post her annoyance on TikTok.

"They reported she'd been behind them. The mom, Angie, said she spoke to her daughter ten minutes before they realized she wasn't behind them anymore. She said her daughter has a habit of wanderin'."

"Are they experienced hikers?" Abey asked as she studied a map of the area someone years ago had permanently tacked to the wall.

Frank shook his head. "The dad says yes, the mom says not so much."

"So no, then," I confirmed. "Who's workin' this so far?"

"Teton County Search and Rescue," Frank said. "Carey just got to Jenny Lake. He's ready to call in dogs, but it'll take a while for the handlers to get 'em there. They were loaned out to Idaho state the last few days for a homicide case. And then the Jenny Lake Ranger team has just clocked in."

"How long's she been missin'?" I asked.

"Four hours."

"Four hours?!" Abey shook her head in exasperation. "Why the hell'd they wait so long to call us in?"

"The dad went searchin' on his own, thought he could find her. Mom stayed put with the little ones, and then it took 'em a while to make it back to the ranger station on the other side of the lake. Cell service has been cuttin' in and out today."

"Damn," Dan said. "It'll be night soon. Not good."

"Okay," I offered, "then if they've got the search covered up there, what can we do down here?"

My job, the sheriff's station, my co-workers, these were all safe spaces for me. I was confident on the job. Helping people was what I'd been born to do, but the other parts of my life lacked the same assuredness. Maybe that was why I was still single.

Why couldn't life come with a set of instructions like a bookcase from Ikea? Of course, I didn't speak Swedish and wouldn't be able to read them, but at least they provided pictures: insert man here, part A goes into part B and repeat with remaining screws in holes.

"Carey wants us to investigate." Frank tapped the top of his computer screen sitting on his pristinely organized desk, indicating that he'd already done some preliminary searching. "The dad spent some time in jail before he had kids. It was a weed charge, so I don't expect anything to come of it. It's just a precaution. The guy hasn't had any run-ins with police in twenty years, but just to cover our bases." He looked right at Abey. "They're stayin' out at your family's place in one of the rental cabins."

"Wait. You said the mom's name is Angie?" She went totally still, a look of horror dawning on her face. "This is the Manning family? Natalie's the missin' hiker?"

Frank nodded.

"We had breakfast with them yesterday. Little Cody and Jamison helped us pick carrots from the garden after." Abey pulled out her phone. "I'm callin' Bax. Shit. They're still at the reception." She paused. "But maybe Devo or Brand will pick up. I can send them to the Mannings' cabin. Maybe Natalie caught a ride down the mountain and went back there." She punched her screen a few times, and as her call connected, she walked back to her office.

"Dan and I can scope out the cabin. Let me just get changed," I said, and I hurried to the locker room to get my back-up uniform.

When I was dressed and mostly professionally presentable, I walked back to the bullpen on bare feet with my boring, black flats dangling from my fingers. My socks and boots were in my truck parked out back. Dan's eyes zeroed in on my toes. Ew. Did he have some kind of foot fetish I hadn't been aware of the last two years we'd worked together?

"C'mon then," I said, trying not to gag. "Let's get goin'."

CHAPTER FOUR

BRAND

I ONLY MET the Mannings once, yesterday at breakfast.

My whole family had gathered for lemon and berry crêpes and bacon at the picnic tables outside Abey's house, since it was the closest residence to the cabin the Mannings had rented, and their twin eight-year-old boys helped harvest vegetables from Abey's and Devo's garden afterward. Little Stuey followed after them with sticky fingers, trying to be a big boy too, and so many memories of his dad rushed through my head.

Stuey was just like Dixon had been when he was a little boy, inquisitive and enigmatic, and the sadness I felt when I thought about how that had all been stripped away from him when he was older made me sick to my stomach.

None of my family could understand why Dixon had given Stuey to Bax and Bea, but I did. Just like me, Dixon was trying hard as hell not to turn out like our father. He was trying to protect Stu from his failures and bad habits.

The missing girl, the Mannings' daughter, Natalie, had taken the opportunity to utilize the strong Wi-Fi signal at breakfast and had spent the entire meal on her phone.

They seemed like a nice family. The dad, Xavier, was a warehouse supervisor for a beer distribution company out of Nebraska, and the mom, Angie, if I remembered correctly, was a dental hygienist. The kids had a long weekend off from school. It was fall break, so Xavier and Angie had dragged them to the Tetons for some family bonding, fishing and hiking.

But now, that bright, happy breakfast filled with laughter and smiles seemed tainted in my memory as Tabitha and I met Deputy Roxanne and her partner at cabin five, also known as Cowboy Court. Athena had insisted on naming each cabin with ridiculous monikers like Wilder West, Mini-Moose Lodge, and my favorite, Teton Taj. Cabin five, Cowboy Court, was a mid-sized rental, bigger than cabin one but much smaller and half the square footage of cabin ten, Teton Taj.

"Hello again," I said, trying not to notice the tight fit of Roxanne's uniform as she stepped from her truck. She looked pretty amazing in her dress at the wedding earlier, long legs flowing from the thigh-length skirt. But damn, the way her uniform hugged those thighs had me imagining slipping my hand between them.

Shit.

"So, no one's heard from Natalie?" I asked, trying to steer my brain back to rational thoughts while a shorter, fit man exited the passenger side of Roxanne's truck and anchored his hands over his hips.

Along with his uniform, he wore a Teton County ball cap, and a pair of Ray-Bans hung from his vest pocket. All the usual law enforcement tools had been clipped to his belt: small flashlight, pepper spray, Taser, and handcuffs, and his nametag was clearly displayed above his right vest pocket. A holstered black handgun had been strapped around his thigh, and a metal sheriff's department star shone over his left pocket.

Roxanne was dressed similarly, and the difference in the deputies' heights was almost comical, but in my view only made Roxanne that much more stunning. I'd met her three times now, and each time, she was more beautiful than the time before.

Something about seeing her decked out in all her weapons again made adrenaline zing through my bloodstream like a very bad idea.

"No, sir," the man answered. Roxanne's partner extended his hand and we shook. "Deputy Dan Draven."

"Brand Lee." I motioned to Tab. "This is my office manager, Tabitha Ketterman."

"Ma'am," Deputy Dan said in a stiff greeting.

"Nice to meet you," Tab said. "Wish it were under better circumstances."

Dan nodded.

I addressed Roxanne and handed her a key. "That's the master key for cabin five. We asked around at the reception. No one has seen Natalie this afternoon. Abey texted a picture she took yesterday to show the guests, but no one recognized her. We did a quick search of the empty cabins, and I knocked on the occupied cabins' doors, too, and asked anyone available, but no luck."

"Thank you," Roxanne said, and she took the key from my hand. She smiled but there was a determination etched in her eyes, different than I'd seen from her before. She was taking Natalie's disappearance very seriously. "Have you been inside?"

"No. We looked in the windows, but we didn't touch anything, and we didn't see anybody inside. If this turns out to be somethin' more than a kid who got lost in the mountains, my sister will have my head if I mess up her crime scene."

"Stand back, please," Dan said as Roxanne slipped on a pair of thin, black gloves she'd had in her pants pocket and inserted the key in the front door's lock. Her right hand went to rest on the gun at her hip. She flipped the catch on her holster with her thumb so the weapon would be accessible if she needed it.

"Whoa. It's really that serious?" Tab whispered to me, leaning closer, but Dan heard her and answered.

"We don't know the circumstances, ma'am, so until we do, it is that serious. Yes."

Tab slipped her arm through mine and leaned against me, watching the deputies, and a little hum sounded in her throat. Seriously? She was into this short, brusque deputy, Dan? But I supposed I couldn't talk. The uniform on Roxanne was doing things to me too.

But we were here for way more important reasons, so we waited like that, listening to the deputies clear the cabin's rooms, until a couple minutes later, they exited and stood on the porch.

"Empty," Roxanne said.

"That's not good, right?" I asked.

"It's not bad," she answered. "We were just hopin' Natalie had caught a ride with someone and maybe they'd dropped her off here. It sure would be nice to be able to call her parents and tell 'em we found her safe and sound."

Tab let out a little whimper. "What can we do?"

"Just be on the lookout, ma'am," Dan said. "If you see the girl, call us immediately."

Roxanne's eyes darted from my face to Tab's, then they brushed quickly over Tab's arm still holding onto mine.

It wasn't normal for my employee to be so informal, but

technically, she was my plus-one at my brother's wedding, and we'd kind of been thrown into uncharted territory with the move and the changing business, but there were zero romantic feelings between the two of us. Tab was more like a little sister to me.

"Do you have a card or somethin' with your number?" I asked Roxanne.

Roxanne shook her head, but Dan nodded and slipped Tab a card from his pocket with the local sheriff's logo printed on it. "Both our numbers are on there. We'll let you know if there's anything further," he said.

"Sure. Thanks." I smiled at Roxanne, and she gave a curt nod and one more glance at Tab's hand on my arm, then they left.

"You got a thing for Deputy Dan?" I asked my friend as we watched them drive away.

"What!" Tab said, astounded I'd put her on the spot like that. She smacked my forearm playfully. "Are we talking about boys and girls now? And for your information, I was just admiring his professionalism."

That earned my office manager a snort from me as we headed past the cabins to the trail that would lead us back to the party by the lake. But she was right that since she'd come to work at Lee Construction, we hadn't been the kind of coworkers or friends that talked about our dates or love interests. Like I'd said, things were changing, and I didn't hate it.

"Is that okay?" I asked. "If you're not comfortable, please let me know."

Tab laughed. "Boss, we're friends, aren't we? Isn't that what friends do? So tell me." She squeezed my forearm. "What about you? Could you be any more obvious you were into Officer Fitts?"

"I was just admirin' her work attire." It felt nice to relate to my friend and poke fun at each other. Why had it taken me moving back home to relax enough to joke with her?

Tab giggled. "Or more like how she fits into it."

"The woman is fine."

"You really are old, you know that?"

"What? The kids don't say 'fine' anymore?"

"No, old man, they don't. Speaking of, I hope they find Natalie. I'm so worried she's hurt. What if they can't get an ambulance up there when they find her?"

"Depends on where she wandered off to, but they have helicopters. They use them when people get stuck in avalanches during ski season."

She lifted her hand to her chest. "Oh my."

"Ha! Who's old now?"

"IT FEELS RIGHT for Bax to be married again," Merv said later that night as she relaxed into her recliner and grabbed her TV remote.

It still felt weird seeing her lounging on brand-new furniture. My mother had owned one couch for the last twenty years until I built this house for her and bought her all new furniture. She cried when she opened the high-end set of ceramic pots and pans I'd picked up for her after I saw her eyeing them at the home goods store the last time I'd come home.

"They seem happy," I agreed, leaning against the counter in her kitchen, sipping a beer and admiring my crews' handiwork. I couldn't remember the last time I'd enjoyed a beer. Not at a work dinner or a fundraiser, but just because I wanted one and had the time to drink it and taste it.

The three houses we'd built last year for Merv, Abey and

Devo, and Rye had turned out really well. Merv seemed happy to be in a house again, as opposed to the beat-up trailer she'd sequestered herself to after my father died. She also loved the picture I'd shown her of the SUV I'd bought for her, and hopefully she'd get to drive the damn thing when the dealership delivered it. The engine had some defect that had triggered a recall, but my standing and name had earned me a brand-new vehicle. I didn't have to wait for an appointment with the Ford service guys, and someone would register the new truck at the DMV for Merv and deliver it personally, free of charge.

Thankfully, Tab had agreed to drive my truck down when she moved to Wisper so she could use the bed to haul some of her belongings to her new rental cottage in town. She had been planning to go back for the rest of her things, but I'd convinced her to let me hire a moving company to bring down her furniture, bed, and her car. She'd stayed in Abey's and Devo's guest room while she waited for it to arrive.

Thinking about her getting stuck in the dark on the side of the road like I had, my thoughts drifted back to Natalie.

Merv mumbled, "Wish I could see you and Dixon married before I die."

"You alright here, Mama?" I asked, completely ignoring that comment. "I think I'm gonna go out and have another look around for Natalie."

"You can't go out there!" she yelped, swiveling in her chair to look at me. "There's a serial killer on the loose."

"What? Who said that?"

"Nobody, but it could be. That poor girl."

"She's not dead, Mama. She's just lost."

Leave it to Merv to draw the most dire conclusion. "You don't know that."

"Okay, well if there really were a killer on the loose,

wouldn't you rather it be me who goes up against him and not you or Athena?"

"Don't even say that."

"I'm right though. Admit it."

"Just be careful," she said. "And don't forget your bear spray."

"Yes, ma'am."

I grabbed my lined flannel from her front closet, swiped the bear spray, a flashlight, and a blue Lee Construction ball cap from the closet shelf, and I left as she clicked on her TV. I'd bought her a new satellite and a sixty-inch flat screen that I mounted on the wall, and you would've thought she was thirteen and the TV was a pony. I'd never seen her so damn happy. But what good was money if all it did was sit in a bank? Although, it occurred to me that maybe I had used my good fortune to try to make up for being gone from my family's lives for so long.

It wasn't my intention, but they'd never asked me for anything, so outfitting Merv's new house with nice things and setting up a college fund for Athena and Stu was the least I could do. To know that if Bax needed the money, it would be there for him and the kids filled me with pride. I knew how hard it was to work full time while trying to go to school, and if a small portion of the ridiculous amount I had in my savings would afford my niece and nephew peace of mind, I had no problem parting with it.

My money was also there to support Bax in our new businesses. Farming could be a crapshoot these days. If the ranch business failed or took too long to bring in a profit, I could help. Bax and Rye seemed to have things under control, so it most likely wouldn't be necessary, but if it ever were, my brother would never have a problem feeding his family.

There'd be no fucking bologna and cheese sandwiches for them.

Technically, I'd be helping myself, too, since I was part-owner of both the cabin business and the ranch, but I was more of a silent partner. Lee Construction had always been my main focus and I wasn't sure that would ever change.

Moonlight illuminated my foot path to the cabins. I could've taken one of Bax's ATVs to look again for Natalie, but it probably would've woken Stuey up at the main house, and at eight in the evening, I knew he'd already be asleep. Abey was busy with the search, but she and Devo had offered to stay with Stu and Athena while Bax and Bea sneaked off to a nice hotel in Bozeman for a short honeymoon. Devo was on her own tonight, but she was the "fun aunt," so no doubt the kids were having a good time. But neither of the newlyweds wanted to be away from them too long, so they only meant to stay in Montana overnight. They were planning to take Athena and Stu to Universal Studios and the Florida Keys in the spring to celebrate as a family.

I'd missed their departure when Tab and I met Roxanne and Dan at the Mannings' cabin, but I hoped Bax and Bea could put the missing girl out of their minds enough to enjoy their wedding night. My brother deserved happiness, and so did Bea. They'd both been through enough heartache.

The night was crisp and quiet, and as I walked, listening to a light wind rush through aspens and twist through pines, the unfamiliar feeling of peace washed over me. It occurred to me I hadn't felt anything other than discontent on this land in probably twenty-five years or more. My father's memory used to be a stain on the dirt beneath my feet and a stench in the air.

I'd loved him. Who doesn't love their dad when they're a

little boy? But before I'd even hit my teens, that love had become inextricably complicated.

The farm became his focus in life, but Lee Family Fleece had never thrived or become a high-earning venture like my father had been sure it would. Our family survived, but we'd never prospered. The constant financial desperation was probably where my drive to operate a successful business had come from. And after I left home, taking classes at night while I worked on a crew during the day hadn't felt like a sacrifice to me. I'd been hungry for it. And once I'd had a small taste of success, it drove me harder.

As a kid, I watched as my father worked day in and day out, making less money each year and taking his frustration out on the people around him, the people who loved him the most. Emotionally, his affection had been tied to his children's ability to work and produce for him. And when that didn't happen, his love disappeared.

I'd turned inward. Became quiet as I watched all the things he did wrong, marking them down mentally and saving the knowledge for later.

As I walked, I kicked a rock in my path, chased it with my flashlight, and watched it skitter down the dirt lane, and I let the truth sink into the moment. The truth was that I owed my father. I hated to admit it to myself, but if he hadn't failed so epically, I wouldn't have learned how to be a good businessman.

The family shit that came later with my little sister, when she realized she was gay and how it turned our father into a raging, intolerant asshole, only made me more determined to prove him wrong in all the ways of the world.

It felt now like I'd been successful. I'd just sold part of my business for millions more than my father had ever seen in his life. My debts were paid, plans were in place to build on my success, but my heart felt heavy.

I felt empty.

Whatever it was I'd been missing, I didn't want it to fester.

I didn't want it to turn me into my father.

It made no sense to me. My family had come back together, minus Dixon, but the rest of us had made it back to our land and were working together, free from the constant berating we'd grown up with. Athena and Stuey and even Merv filled the days with laughter and warmth, but something was still lacking in my life.

I'd had no clue what the missing puzzle piece was until today. Until I watched Bax marry Bea and saw the way they looked at each other and the way they were always touching. I didn't think they even realized it sometimes, but it was like their bodies and hearts had been magnetized toward the other person at a soul level. When one moved, the other reacted.

Their connection was tight and seemed unbreakable, and unlike my parents, Bax and Bea communicated. They discussed everything, made decisions and plans together. Each had their strengths, sure, but they only served to make the couple stronger together.

It was admirable. Something to aspire to, but I hadn't aspired to anything other than distance from my father's subjugation and professional success since I was seventeen years old.

Thinking about that, about what it would mean for me to let someone into my life in an intimate way, led me back to thoughts of Deputy Roxanne.

The cabins stood ahead of me. My eyes scanned the darkness for Natalie, but I kicked more rocks like I was trying to kick thoughts of the beautiful deputy away. I bent to tear tall grass from the side of the path for no reason, like I was seven years old again, and when I straightened, suddenly she was there.

Roxanne.

I shined my flashlight near her body. "Deputy? I didn't know you'd come back." Had she caught my juvenile display of longing and dissatisfaction? "You startled me."

"Sorry 'bout that," she said.

"Is there news? Did they find Natalie?"

"No. Not yet." Slipping her hands in her pants pockets, she sighed and twisted her lips, but again I noticed her fingers tapping the side of her thigh three times beneath the fabric.

I nodded to her uniform. "Still on duty?"

"No. I'm off the clock, but I'm gonna head up to the search area, lend a hand. I wanted to check here one last time, though, just in case, but there's no one in the cabin."

"Me too. I mean, that's why I'm here too."

She nodded and held the key out to me that I'd given her earlier in the day. "Sorry," she said. "I meant to give that back to you this afternoon."

"Thank you, but no apology necessary. I would've gotten it back one way or another. If you're headed up to search, may I accompany you? Since you're off duty, is that permitted?"

"Um, okay. I guess it couldn't hurt to have another set of eyes. Are you sure though? We might get into some deep backcountry up there."

Realizing it was still true, I pulled the brim of my cap down low and said, "I may look like a city boy, but darlin', I'm all country. Let's go."

CHAPTER FIVE

ROXANNE

WHY DID the presence of this man in my truck make me a bad driver? And when he'd declared himself "all country"?

Could vaginas twitch? I was pretty sure mine had.

Twice, I'd almost veered off the side of the road leading away from Brand's family's houses on our way out to Old Fish Creek Road when he did nothing more than clear his throat and turn his body toward mine in the passenger seat. I kept looking over at him, which was why I almost missed the glare of headlights headed straight for us.

Dang him and his baseball hat. Brand Lee made me more nervous than I could remember being in a long time.

By his sister's account, the sexy, quiet man sitting next to me, with his sinful lips, dark stubble covering a jaw cut from glass, and eyes the color of a summer sky, was loaded. Not like me. If I had more than twenty bucks in my bank account and a pot to piss in on any given day, it felt like God was raining fortune down on me.

The skinny gravel lane didn't allow two big trucks at the same time, so I pulled over and put mine in Park, and confusion crossed Brand's face when he recognized the other vehicle stopping next to us. I rolled down my window and nodded hello at Bax and Bea.

"What are you doin' here?" Brand asked. "Shouldn't you two be holed up, naked in a hotel somewhere?"

I couldn't stop the flush that traveled up from my navel to my face or the elicit images in my head the man sitting next to me had just conjured. It felt like the heat would scorch me from the inside out as I pictured myself and Brand, lying clothing-less and spent in a pile of messed-up bedsheets, bodies slick with sweat after fucking like bunnies.

Not that that was even a remote possibility. No, Brand would probably rather be doing it with someone like Tabitha, pretty and perfect. Maybe he already had. She looked like a vixen of a woman. I'd bet she was like a little mewling bomb in his bed.

One-two-three.

But dammit. Book club had turned me into a shameless slut, because after reading all the romance our librarian, Sam, could fit on the shelves, all I could imagine was the authoritative sound of Brand's voice when he told me to get on my knees to suck his dick and his hand tangled in my hair, pulling and guiding my mouth on him.

"We got halfway to our hotel," Bax said, "and realized there was no way we'd enjoy ourselves with Natalie missin'."

"Is that where you're headed?" Bea asked, leaning over Bax's center console. She held her husband's hand, and seeing the simple display of affection between them made something clench in the pit of my stomach. "Can we join you?"

"It's your special night," I said. "You don't have to do that. There's a mass of search and rescue people up there already."

"We want to," Bea said with a gentle smile. "Bax here's

good with his hands. He can thwack at some brush with a machete, and I can holler with the best of them. If Natalie doesn't hear my voice, she ain't on that mountain."

I intended to let out a sexy little laugh, but it came out more as a guffaw. Could I be any more embarrassing? But I said, "Follow us up then?"

"You got it." Bax rolled up his window and they made a U-turn on Bear Lane, the dirt road that led to the cabins, and then they followed my truck out to Old Fish Creek Road and further onto the highway.

Brand was quiet for a while. It seemed to be his way, but finally he spoke, and the sound of his deep voice I'd just been imagining set sparks to bursting in my belly.

"Is this common? A missing hiker?" he asked. "I remember one or two from my childhood, but I haven't lived here in almost twenty years now."

"It happens. But there hasn't been a missin' kid in a while. It gets everybody in a twist, imaginin' their own kids lost in the night."

"Do you have kids? I don't remember if my sister ever mentioned if you were mar—"

I shook my head. "No kids. Never been married. You?"

"No. Same. I'm better as an uncle."

"Same." I laughed. "I'm Auntie Roxi to fifteen nieces and nephews."

"*Fifteen*?"

"I have five sisters."

"Ah."

"One of my sisters only has one kid, but the others made up for that with three or more. Put my parents over the moon."

"And did you not want children or—" He cursed under his breath. "I'm sorry. That was insensitive."

"No." I shook my head. "It was just a question. And to answer it, no, I've never wanted kids. I thought when I got older and more settled in my career, I might, but that time came and went and I'm happy with my decision." I shrugged. "Why do you think it's insensitive?"

"You could've been unable to have children or maybe were in a bad relationship or somethin'. I don't know your story."

"Ain't much of one to tell," I said as I turned onto Highway 191 in Jackson.

We could've taken Moose Road, but it would've been a lot slower with all the mountain switchbacks. The highway to Teton Park Road was quicker, and I could use my lights if I needed to. Neither route was direct. Direct routes didn't really exist in Jackson Hole.

"Grew up in Okie and moved to Wyo after the academy. Worked as a beat cop for a couple years in the eastern part of the state and then moved over to Yellowstone. That's where I met Sheriff Michaels. He offered me the position in Wisper, and I've been here ever since."

And probably would be until the day I died. Wisper, Wyoming had become my home. Oklahoma would always be my beginning and my touchstone, but the autonomy of living somewhere my sisters and mama didn't had become more important to me than the desire to be close to Choctaw.

I peeked at Brand out of the corner of my eye. "What about you?"

"Me?"

"How'd you end up in Sheridan?"

"Oh." He laughed softly. "Well, I graduated high school and then got the hell out of Dodge. Our father wasn't the easiest guy to live with or work for and I wanted out. I started on a house crew at eighteen, saved every penny I could, went to school at night, and worked my way up from there."

"That's impressive. Your sister said those contracts you sold up north went for a nice price."

Ah, crap. I felt like a heel bringing up money. I hadn't meant to, but it didn't seem to bother him. He just kept staring out his window at the fields whizzing by and the moonlit mountains in the distance, nodding silently.

"Aren't you happy about that?"

"Of course I am. I'm fortunate. I've made some good decisions and had some good luck. We just passed the billion-dollar mark in revenue." He looked at me. "I've never told anyone that. I'm sure you know, in certain areas in Wyoming, house prices are insane. That worked in my favor, and we don't only build houses. We've worked on some pretty big commercial projects too."

Jesus. How much even was a billion dollars? I couldn't count that high on my fingers, that was for sure.

"But it's just—"

"What?" I asked, daring to look away from the road now to see the discontent in his eyes. "It's just what?"

He turned to face me. "Bein' back home, it feels different than I thought it would. You know?"

"I don't," I said, "but I can imagine. If I had to move back to Choctaw, Oklahoma, I'd go out of my mind."

"No, it's not like that. I'm happy to be home. I've missed it. I've missed my brother and sister. My niece and nephew. Even Merv. But I feel different inside now, and it's almost like I don't fit anymore. Does that make sense?"

God, does it ever.

Turning left onto the road leading up to Jenny Lake, I said, "It makes perfect sense. To be honest, I've never felt like I fit in with my family. Too many expectations I've never been able to meet, but maybe I'm projectin'.'"

Evergreens blurred outside his window now while he thought about what he wanted to say. It was dead quiet between us, and night surrounded us on all sides. It wrapped around my truck and flowed beneath my tires, and it felt like we were the only two people in the world. A tentative familiarity with him eased my nervousness, and I breathed a little easier. I hadn't expected to have anything in common with Brand Lee.

"It's ridiculous for me to feel this way, but I guess up in Sheridan I was always so busy that I never really had to face the fact that somethin' was missin' from my life, but now I'm home, I feel it everywhere I go."

Whoa. I'd never met a man so honest with his feelings. Had I entered some kind of twilight zone?

"It's not ridiculous," I assured him. "It's honest."

"We're here," he said, pointing to a wooden Jenny Lake sign on the left-hand side of the road.

He didn't reply, and we drove a bit further, until we saw trucks and cruisers parked in the lot that led to the Jenny Lake boathouse, a sea of lights flashing in front of us.

Pulling up behind Abey's truck, I parked next to the county sheriff's, and we stepped out into the chilly air. Bax and Bea parked behind me, and when they climbed from Bax's rig, I noticed they were prepared and dressed in jeans and hiking boots. Either that was what they'd worn for their drive up to Montana, or they kept hiking boots in their vehicle. Either way, they were my people. Nothing fancy about them, or me, and they made me feel a little more at home in a place that wasn't my actual home.

As a group, we set off to find my bosses.

"Roxi?" Abey saw us approaching from where she stood

next to the sheriff. Her blond hair looked like a rat had taken up residence underneath her hat, all tangled and tied hastily in a low bun. She was worried. "Did you find somethin' at the Mannings' cabin?"

"No. We just came up to see if we could help."

"Thanks." She frowned at her recently married brother. "Bax, Bea, shouldn't you be in Montana by now?"

"We couldn't sit around waitin' for news," Bea said, and Abey smiled and nodded.

"Actually, it's great you're here," Sheriff Michaels said, standing tall and stoic next to Abey. He tipped his hat up off his forehead, his rusty red hair sweaty and disheveled beneath. "We could actually use a few more bodies on the trails around Jenny Lake. The rangers are focused on the Lake Solitude trail since it's further and more remote, but we've still got the paths around here we need to search. Just make sure you sign in." He pointed to a woman holding a clipboard standing next to a volunteer ranger in a yellow jacket by the trailhead that led south around the lake. "And make sure you have water and warmth. And Roxi, I know you're not technically on duty, but consider yourself clocked in. Keep your radio on."

"Yes, sir."

"You're in charge of these hooligans." He smirked at Bax and Brand. "Their mama will sue my ass if anything happens to her precious baby boys."

The guys laughed, and Bax delivered a playful but powerful punch to the sheriff of Teton County's midsection. Carey grunted and knocked Bax's cowboy hat off his head.

Bax retrieved it from the dirt with the swipe of one hand, stuck it back on his head, and introduced his new bride. "Carey, this is my wife, Bea. We just got hitched this after-noon." A big smile showed his teeth, and they gleamed under all the lights that had been set up to illuminate the parking area. "Bea, this man here is the big bad county sheriff, Carey Michaels. You've eaten his wife's donuts. It's that place in town Athena loves to stop off at after school."

"Frannie Goes French? Your wife is Frannie? Grace and Gabby are your daughters?"

Carey nodded proudly.

"Please tell Frannie that Athena and I are big fans. Also, tell her I have a bone to pick with her 'cause I've gained ten pounds since Athena got me hooked on her mousse au chocolat and éclairs." She winked. "Athena adores Grace, and little Gabby is cute as a button."

"You're preachin' to the choir." Carey chuckled and patted his stomach. "Thank you. Will do, and congratulations. It's nice to meet you."

"You too. I wish it wasn't because of Natalie."

Everybody grumbled agreement.

"Alright, y'all," Carey said. "Get to work. Radio in anything you find, even if it's just an empty water bottle."

"Have you brought in the dogs yet, boss?" I asked.

Carey shook his head, and Abey answered. "They should be here in an hour or two."

"Good." That made me feel better. The SAR dogs could find Natalie faster than any human. The trick was keeping up with them. "Is there any sign of foul play?"

"No," Carey said, "not so far. Natalie's parents and brothers are at the ranger station. They're worried sick."

"We'll get started."

Abey motioned again to the lady with the sign-in sheet. "When you sign in, she'll give you maps and point you in the right direction. She has flashlights with new batteries."

Brand asked, "What was Natalie wearin'?"

I should have asked that. He had good instincts and clearly seemed to care about finding the girl.

"Jeans," Abey answered her older brother, "and a gray Nebraska Cornhuskers hooded sweatshirt with a big red 'N'. Purple sneakers."

As we walked toward the woman with the clipboard, I noticed Brand surveying all the law enforcement officers poring over trail maps spread over the hoods of their vehicles.

"I feel a bit underdressed," he said, smirking at me. He nudged his arm against mine. Was he flirting with me? In the middle of a missing persons case?

And people thought *I* was weird?

But I nudged him back.

"You got the right shoes for a midnight hike," I said, looking down at his worn, tan work boots. I imagined him wearing them with a pair of roughed-in jeans and a dirty white T-shirt on a construction site somewhere, sweat running down his neck as he lifted raw lumber, and a tingle sparked between my legs.

And when he turned his ball cap backwards and nodded, I practically groaned out loud. "Just keep your ankles loose, and if you get scared in the dark, you can hold my hand."

CHAPTER SIX

BRAND

FOLLOWING BEHIND ROXANNE, watching her long, limber legs eat up the trail was some kind of punishment.

I had no clue what I'd done to piss off the fates or God or whoever was in charge of my destiny, but it seemed I'd ticked somebody off well and good because I couldn't seem to focus on anything else besides getting my hands on them and possibly my mouth.

Roxanne Fitts was utterly distracting.

But the statuesque beauty was nothing but business now as she charged forward, occasionally looking over her shoulder to make sure her followers stayed in tow, but she never stopped moving. Up until this very moment, I had considered myself in extremely good shape, but Roxanne was proving me wrong with each sure step she took while I stumbled to keep up.

Time to focus.

The beams of our flashlights crisscrossed each other, searching the woods and ground for any sign of Natalie Manning. Occasionally, we stopped to drink water and catch our breath, but the mood between the four of us was serious. The darker the night became and the lower the temperature dropped, the more intense it got. If we hadn't been moving and working up a sweat, we would've been freezing.

Rocks and tree roots tried to trip me, but I'd taken Roxanne's advice to heart and kept my body loose as best as I could. The way utter blackness clung to the tree trunks and how even the moon seemed to hide from it above the tops of their boughs was worrying. Outside the glow from our torches, there was so much country we couldn't see, but we called for Natalie over and over, hoping that if she was close, she'd hear us.

When we began, we'd heard the sloshing of the water against the shore and occasionally caught glimpses of Jenny Lake. We'd seen other searchers' flashlights. From far away, they looked almost like faint Christmas lights or glowbugs flitting through the trees, but we'd been searching for a while and were further away from the lake now, almost to where the Jenny Lake Trail connected to the Cascade Creek Trail.

Memories of hiking these trails with my brothers and sister when we were teenagers swarmed me as we walked, and a little bit of the belonging I used to feel to my home grew inside me. Maybe I'd just been away too long. Maybe now that I'd come home, the feeling of knowing I was right where I needed to be would find me. And it wasn't lost on me that the circumstance entangling my hometown and what a month ago I would've referred to as drama, had cleared my mind of business.

Nothing mattered more than finding the lost girl.

I had no signal, but according to my phone, we'd been at it for more than two hours with nothing to show for it when Roxanne halted in front of me. I almost ran right into her, but we stopped, and she shushed me when I tried to ask what was wrong. She closed her eyes, trying to hear something in the night.

Tipping her head the slightest bit to her left, she let out some kind of high-pitched, two-syllable whistle, and a responding "Hey-oh" floated back to us from deep in the trees.

Roxanne shined her light in the same direction. She veered off our trail, and Bax, Bea, and I followed closely. Soon we came upon a man and woman dressed in Search and Rescue gear, their yellow jackets glaring under the moon's elusive glow, and I immediately recognized the man crouching and studying something near the ground.

"Evan? Evan Moran?"

Evan turned his head and looked up at me, squinting. It had been years, but he still looked like the same cowboy I'd known in high school, except instead of a cowboy hat, tonight he'd swapped it for a Teton County SAR beanie. "Yeah? Who's that?"

"Brand Lee, man. Long time no see."

He stood, trying to see me in the dark without flashing his light in my face. "Brand Lee? Shit, ain't you a blast from the past. How you been?"

"Good—"

"I'm sorry for interruptin' this heartfelt reunion," Roxanne said, exasperated with us both, "but Evan, why were you down in the dirt? Did you find somethin'?"

The woman with Evan hadn't yet spoken, but she shined her light on a low bush and I saw a flash of purple—a shoelace.

"The girl's been here," Evan said, "or near enough."

Bax and Bea rushed forward to look, and my heart kicked into overdrive.

Evan and Bax shook hands, nodding familiarity toward one another, and Roxanne crouched to get a closer look. "Did you radio it in?"

"Yeah," the woman said. "They're bringin' the dogs this way. Should be here soon."

"While we wait," Roxanne said as she stood, the sound of her voice tight but hopeful, "fan out. We'll go in pairs but call out every few minutes so we can hear each other. Evan and —" She waited for the woman to provide her name.

"Misty. Misty Summers."

Roxanne smiled at Misty. "I'm Roxi and this is Brand, Bax, and Bea." She motioned toward me, my brother, and Bea. "Okay, so Evan and Misty, you stay here, and we'll work our way around your position, see if we can find anything else."

"Good plan," Evan said. "If y'all find somethin'"—he looked at Bax, Bea, and me one at a time—"don't touch *anything*. Just stay with the evidence and call it out to us."

Bax and Bea took off, and Roxanne and I followed, staying several yards behind and to the right of their path. After about twenty minutes of traversing around trees, knocking low branches out of our faces, getting scratched and dirty, and trying not to get tangled up in bushes, we couldn't see Bax and Bea anymore and could barely hear them.

I moved closer to Roxanne. "How are you holdin' up?" She'd been eerily silent, and I felt the need to hear her voice again.

"I'm okay," she said. "I just really hope we f—" She stopped fast, and this time I did smack into her back, and my breath punched out and whispered over her neck.

"What is it?" I asked quietly, my hands on Roxanne's hips to steady her, but I realized I needed the connection just as much.

"A wolf."

She shined her light ahead of us, and I peered over her shoulder toward the huge bases of two trees standing next to each other. The roots of one tree had grown over the other's, like the tentacles of a hungry octopus, and they'd created a basin between the tree trunks. Low to the ground at the end of our flashlights' glare, two unblinking eyes glowed in the dark, and we heard the hair-raising warning growl of the animal. Tucked behind it, a person lay curled into a ball in the basin.

The wolf was guarding Natalie.

"Shit," Roxanne breathed. "I really don't wanna have to shoot that animal."

"Here," I said, and I pulled the bear spray still tucked inside my jacket pocket. She probably had some strapped to her belt or her vest, but mine was readily available.

I handed the canister to her slowly, and she flipped the safety up with her thumb easily, obviously practiced with bear spray. The natural capsaicin wouldn't hurt the wolf, but it would annoy the shit out of its sensitive olfactory receptors.

"Oh God." Roxanne looked up to the sky for a second, like she was pleading with it. "*Please* don't let this girl be dead."

But before she could disperse the spray, the wolf rose carefully from the dirt. Not taking its eyes off us, it shifted closer to Natalie still lying motionless behind it and moved its head in her direction, scenting the air. It let out another low growl and then loped off suddenly and disappeared into the trees.

We rushed to Natalie, and Roxanne searched her body for any signs of injury or bloody wolf bites, and she checked her pulse with two fingers on the girl's wrist.

"Thank God," she whispered. "She's alive."

Roxanne pulled the radio transmitter from her shoulder and called in that we'd found Natalie and that the medics should get the exact coordinates from Evan.

"Natalie," she urged, caressing the girl's dark, tangled hair out of her face. Leaves and twigs had been embedded in it, and she was covered in smudges of dirt. Her sweatshirt and jeans had been ripped and torn, like maybe she'd fallen at some point and got caught on trees or rocks, and one of her tennis shoes was missing. "Can you hear me?"

I stood guard in case the wolf came back, but I had a feeling it had run away from us pesky humans as fast as it could.

Natalie moaned when Roxanne said her name again. "C-cold," she stammered. "Fell. My ankle. Couldn't go further. S-so tired."

"I'm Deputy Roxanne Fitts with the Teton County Sheriff's Department. A lot of people have been lookin' for you."

"Where's m-my mom and dad?" Natalie asked meekly, her teeth chattering. "They're gonna be so mad at me." She barely looked like the same girl I'd met and eaten breakfast with yesterday. Her face was flushed from the cold but looked a little gaunt, and she had dark circles under her eyes and a long, angry scrape across the side of her face.

"They're waitin' for you," Roxanne assured her, "and they're gonna be ecstatic that we found you. We'll get you back to your family soon, but try to stay still, okay? The paramedics are on their way."

Natalie began to sob, her whole body shaking with the force of her relief, and if I wasn't wrong, Roxanne was trying to blink back tears, too, but I didn't think she'd let them fall.

I had learned quickly that Deputy Roxanne Fitts took pride in her job. She would always do it to the best of her ability, and she didn't joke around when it came to public safety.

I removed my jacket and handed it to her, and she draped it over Natalie, and then she pulled a plastic packet from an inside pocket lining her own jacket. She ripped the packet open with her teeth and pulled out a square that looked like folded aluminum foil, unfolded it, and tucked the mylar blanket around Natalie to keep her body heat in.

Just then, we heard the rush of barking search dogs in the distance, and within twenty minutes, the area was crawling with SAR volunteers and law enforcement. Medics assessed Natalie, and they loaded her onto a stretcher. She screamed when they stabilized her broken ankle, but they had to before they attempted to carry her from the woods.

Her parents were notified that Natalie had been found alive, and we heard her mother over the sheriff's radio, sobbing as relief washed through her.

As the teams headed off to reunite Natalie with her family and get her to the hospital in Jackson, Roxanne and I stood motionless, staring at each other.

"That wolf," I whispered.

"That was…"

"Crazy," we said at the same time.

"It was probably Edwina," Evan said as he, Misty, Bax, and Bea joined us. "She's an old, deaf wolf people have reported seein' around here this fall. The older she gets, the more often she strays from her pack."

"She's deaf?" Roxanne said. "That's why she didn't run until she saw us. She didn't hear us."

I shook my head in disbelief. "I've never seen anything like that. She was protectin' that girl."

"It's unusual," Evan said, shrugging, "but not unheard of.

The animal could sense that Natalie was injured and weak. Edwina could relate."

"C'mon, ya'll," Misty said, swinging her arm behind her when she turned. "You're gonna have to relay that story fifty more times tonight. We better get back so you can get started."

CHAPTER SEVEN

ROXANNE

THE HIKE BACK to the parking area took for-freaking-ever.

It was well after midnight, and I wanted to curl into a ball in the dirt myself and take a nap. The mountain and the feeling of success buzzing through my body had melted my anxiety away, and the lazy lapping of the water against the lakeshore could've lulled me right to sleep. Above the trees, stars dotted the night sky, twinkling like little congratulatory sparks of light.

Bax and Bea had hurried ahead of our group with a quick wave goodbye, probably excited to get to the consummating part of their wedding night now that Natalie had been found safe. Evan and Misty had gone on ahead too. Brand and I were the weary stragglers, but he let me lead us back.

"How do you know Evan Moran?" I asked as we walked.

"Went to school with him. He lived up in the woods outside the park, but he got bussed down to Wisper for high school. He's younger than me, but he used to rodeo, and my brothers and I would go out to watch him sometimes. Kid was damn good with a rope."

"Huh. I've met him several times on search and rescue

cases. He volunteers. He knows the GTNP like the back of his hand, but I never knew he rodeoed."

A few minutes passed in silence except for our breath as we hiked up and down the small hills along the trail.

"Do you have to work tomorrow?" Brand asked.

"S'posed to, but Dan will probably take my shift. The Wisper sheriff's station is a small outpost, so when there isn't a big case goin' on, we work solo for traffic stuff and non-emergency calls. I'll shoot him a text when we get back to my truck and can get a better signal."

"It's nice you can rely on and help each other."

"Yeah."

His footsteps on the dirt trail behind me were nearly silent. "You and Dan ever…"

I snorted and looked over my shoulder while Brand caught up to me. "Uh, that's a hard no, sir. I have never hooked up with Dan Draven. Ew."

He smiled at my answer. "So no, then. Got it."

We continued walking. "No, he's a nice guy, extremely dedicated to the job, but he's not my type. Plus, we started the same day at the Wisper station, and I made the decision to loathe him pretty much from the first minute we met."

"Loathe is a strong word."

"I'm jokin'. I don't hate him. He and I just get under each other's skin sometimes. He's like my shorter, older brother who I'd like to poke in the face with a stick."

Brand laughed, and I practically swooned right there in the middle of the Grand Teton National Forest, his low, rumbling voice like a little generator instantly revving my body into overdrive.

Tired? Who's tired?

"He's too short for me anyway. Can you imagine us tryin' to get it on in the shower?"

I stopped short, clapping my hand over my mouth. I couldn't believe I'd just said that.

"Scratch that. Please don't imagine that." *Oh my God, Roxi, the shit that comes out of your mouth sometimes is enough to mortify you to death!* "I'm sorry. I'm tired. I'm not makin' sense."

"Oh no? Makes perfect sense to me."

Brand moved in front of me. He didn't laugh this time, and gently, he removed my hand from my mouth and lowered it to my side. The hooded look in his eyes sent shivers down my spine and sparks to my special girl cave.

When he spoke again, I nearly melted and it was still only thirty degrees outside. "Thank God you're not into him because I can't imagine it. I don't want to. What I *want* to imagine is you in that shower, naked and waitin' for *me*, the water running over your body, slipping between your thighs." When he said it, he looked down at mine, and suddenly, my whole body flushed. I felt like a juicy piece of chicken. All he needed was a bottle of barbeque sauce, and he could slather me up and take a bite.

Breath punched out of my lungs in a rush. "You do?"

"Yes."

Had I lost my mind, or had his breathing rate sped up too? He looked over my shoulder and turned to make sure there weren't any other cops or volunteers nearby. There weren't.

We were completely secluded in the forest.

"Am I alone in this fantasy?" he murmured, the dark surrounding us making his eyes seem even more mysterious than I had already determined them to be, but they sparkled like aquamarine as they searched my face.

"N-no." The nerdy, tall, basketball-dunking Roxi couldn't believe what he was saying, but adult Roxi was about to throw down in the dirt with this man. And the fact that he had to tilt his head down to make eye contact with me didn't hurt one little bit. "I can imagine you too."

Looking in his eyes was too much. When I did, I thought my heart might beat right out of my chest, so instead, my slow gaze traveled down the cords of his neck to his T-shirt covering his chest beneath the open, red and black fleece-lined flannel jacket the paramedics had returned to him. And when my appreciative study landed on the front of his jeans, nerdy Roxi was quite sure she could detect a bulge thickening beneath them. He still wore his hat backwards, and little flips of soft brown hair licked around its sides.

"Good. Now," he said, "imagine that same scenario with me. How tall are you? Six-foot? I'm six-two. A perfect fit."

I whimpered. What else could I do, because the tinge of bossiness in his tone was hot as sin, and I was already picturing it: Brand pressing me to my shower wall, his chest stuck to my back, warm water fusing our bodies together and my hands planted flat on the ceramic tiles, his strong fingers gripping my naked hips, his knees bent just a little as he pounded into me from behind.

Oh God. The ladies at book club would get a kick out of that little daydream. I was sure I'd read a close representation of the same scenario in a romance book at some point.

But when I imagined myself replacing the heroine of some epic story and pictured Brand as the hero, my eyes fluttered closed, and I whispered, "Perfect."

He hummed quietly. "Yes, you are."

Some kind of boldness took over my body like an alien invasion, and without bothering to look behind me, I grabbed him by his belt and backed up, dragging him with me and hoping we wouldn't stumble over a tree root and fall on our asses, but I knew there were trees behind me somewhere. Eventually, I'd bump into one.

Finally, my back hit bark, and Brand followed willingly. He stalked me to my tree and placed his hand over my stomach above my jacket, and then he unzipped it. Cold air rushed over my chest, and my nipples hardened beneath my uniform and undershirt.

My mouth popped open, but I swallowed down the moan that wanted to slip out, and then his tongue was inside me as he kissed me. He held nothing back, and it felt like all the heightened emotion from our search for Natalie had taken over.

Heat ruled the moment. He slipped his hand between my legs, the moan crawled right back up and rushed past my lips, and the little tingle I'd felt earlier turned into exploding bottle rockets in my belly.

He breathed, "Tonight was insane, right?"

I nodded, my head knocking the tree trunk behind me. My hat had fallen off at some point, but I had no clue where it was. "It's understandable we'd be amped up."

Against my lips, he mumbled, "Maybe, but that isn't all this is." He moaned this time and kissed me harder, one hand planted above my head on the tree and the other searched beneath the waistband of my ugly, polyester work pants.

"Huh?" I couldn't concentrate with his fingers so close to such sensitive areas. I imagined them sliding inside me, pumping…

"I've wanted you since you rescued me from the side of the highway the night I came home."

"Y-you have?"

Yes! Thank the sweet baby Jesus, Mother Mary, and Joseph too!

"Yes," he breathed, and he gave up trying to find his opening between the bottom of my tucked-in shirt and the waist of my pants. He popped open the button and unzipped them, and then his hand found hot flesh, and he caressed my skin, moving lower, his fingers toying with the elastic band at the top of my boyshort briefs.

"Brand, wait." *Oh God. Somebody shut me up.* "I-I can't do this."

He stilled, his hand and those obscenely long fingers hovering an inch away from where I really, *really* needed them. I couldn't even remember the last time I'd had sex, I mean, besides with myself and my handy little silicone helper.

"I'm armed. I can't do this with a gun strapped to my thigh."

"I know," he murmured, and he licked and pinched my bottom lip between his teeth softly. "It's really turnin' me on."

This could not be happening to me. I'd finally found a man who wanted me, who I wanted right back, and who might want to rip off my clothes and ravish my overly tall body, but I couldn't let him.

But damn, he was so hot, I was afraid to touch his skin for fear of my fingerprints burning off. When the SAR dogs found the wrecked, spent—and utterly satisfied—carcass of my body, nobody would know it was me. They'd have to pull some DNA for that shit.

Tearing his mouth from my lips, he moved to my neck and reached up to pull my hair out of the low pony I'd gathered it into before our hike. It billowed down to my shoulders, fluttering against the side of his face, and he inhaled deeply against my skin and groaned.

"God, you smell so good. What is that?"

I was sliding down the tree now, inch by inch, my body trying so hard to make me give in. It was like he'd shoved a goddamn tuning fork inside me, and it rang like a bell and buzzed for him. "Sh-shampoo. Honeysuckle and roses."

He moaned, but somehow, I found the will to correct the mistake I was currently in the middle of making.

"Stop."

He did, and he looked up at me. His cheeks were flushed from the heat between us and the need for sexual release, and I almost said, "fuck it," but anybody could've come traipsing back down the trail. We'd signed our names on that form. Someone would try to account for us at some point, and then they'd come looking.

And then I'd get fired.

"Nearest hotel?" he asked, his hand sliding over my hip under my pants, and he grabbed my ass.

"Um," I said, breathless. I had to think about it. "There's a couple inns back down the highway. Not too far."

"You drive. I'll get us a room. Let's go."

Once he'd rezipped and buttoned my pants, he bent to fetch my hat out of the dirt at our feet, and then the speed with which he dragged me back to my truck by my hand was impressive.

When we exited the trail and found a few officers and rangers still lingering in the parking area, I pulled my hand from his. We checked in with the volunteer so she could tick our names off her list, and we did have to retell our wolf story a couple times, but then we were both feigning utter exhaustion.

But the last thing on my mind was sleep.

Yawning dramatically one more time for optimal effect and waving awkwardly to the men as Brand backed toward my truck and tugged at the back of my jacket, I turned and we picked up our pace. But ever the dork, I called over my shoulder, "Congrats on a successful mission, lads!"

Brand snorted, and when we were out of sight, he slid his hand over mine again, his fingers grasping mine tightly.

He held my door open for me, and once I was in my truck, I started the engine, then unhooked my gun holster and began to discard Tasers and flashlights and the rest of the tools attached to my body. I stowed them in my center console and locked it, but I didn't miss the way he eyed my handcuffs as he clipped his seatbelt into place.

I asked, "Are you sure you want to—"

"Yes. Drive."

"Okeydokey then."

Oh my God, Roxi, SHUT. UP.

CHAPTER EIGHT

BRAND

THE MOTEL ROOM appeared to be nothing special, at least from what I could decipher in the dark, except for the fact that Roxanne was inside it and about to shed her uniform in front of me.

My dick had hardened somewhere on the trail and stayed that way the whole drive down the mountain. I'd barely been able to chase after her when I came out of the motel office and handed Roxanne the keycard and she'd dashed from her truck to room 107. But I managed.

When the door thudded shut behind us, she didn't bother to turn on the overhead light. She whipped in a circle to face me, threw her arms around my shoulders, and we became a tangle of twisting tongues, heavy, panting breaths, and loud moans. My hands found her ass, hers slid down my chest, and she pushed my jacket off and to the floor.

Gripping my waist, she slammed the front of my body to hers, pressing me against her and holding me there, as if she'd never let me escape.

I didn't want her to let go.

My body sought hers with an intensity I hadn't experienced in a very long time.

I'd had sex, dated a few women over the years. None of them had been anything like Roxanne. She wasn't my type, or at least the type I'd thought all those years was mine. The women I'd dated had been the definition of feminine, had worn high heels and a lot of makeup. They'd all felt small standing next to me, and most of them had long hair. Roxanne's was barely shoulder length, and the only makeup I'd noticed was ChapStick or lip gloss and maybe a little mascara.

She needn't have bothered with any of it, though, because her skin was bright and beautiful, her eyes warm and inviting. The look in them always made me think of home.

She was kind of a tomboy, a little rough around her tall edges, but I couldn't remember wanting any of those women the way I wanted Roxanne.

Why was that? I hardly knew her.

Rubbing myself against her, I bent my knees and notched my hard cock between her long legs over our clothes, eliciting a gasp from her mouth, and she began to back us toward the king bed.

When we got there, I pulled her hands away from my ass cheeks, where her short fingernails had been trying to pierce my skin through my jeans, and I pushed her gently.

She fell back on the mattress, instantly messing up the sheets and blanket, and the moon's glow from a gap in the curtains outlined her body in perfect detail. Her hair lay in a pool of sandy brown silk that formed a halo around her head, and she moaned as I looked at her. I tugged at her boots. They came off first, and then her socks, and she scrunched her bare toes.

Every part of her was long and sexy—her legs, her

fingers, her neck. I wanted to take my time, wanted to undress her slowly and look at all of her, but the need inside me to *feel* her urged me to move.

I unbuttoned her pants again, unzipped them, and slid my hand over the soft skin below her navel. But as I looked down, I realized I was filthy from our search for Natalie. Dirt covered my hands and had worked its way beneath my fingernails.

"Hold that thought. I need to wash my hands."

"What?" She whimpered again, rubbing her thighs together. "Hurry up!"

I rushed to the bathroom, flipped on the light, and twisted the knob for the hot water, wishing I had a fingernail brush. I didn't want to touch her beautiful body with anything less than perfectly clean hands, but before the water had even heated up, she was behind me, silently lifting my T-shirt over my head and watching my face in the big bathroom mirror.

My hat fell with my shirt, and she scratched her nails in the short hair at the back of my neck, then kissed a slow trail down my spine. Every cell inside my body came to attention at the touch of her lips on my skin.

As she slid her hands over mine and led them under the now warm water, she said softly, "I want you just like you said back on the mountain—in the shower."

She took a moment to unwrap the tiny, complimentary bar of hand soap and lathered it between her palms, then caressed her fingers over mine, working the soap between them and over the tips.

It was such a personal, intimate way to touch someone she barely knew, and something about her touching me like that made me want to possess her. To mark her somehow, make her mine. I couldn't remember the last time a woman had cared for me like that. Maybe no one ever had.

My eyes never left her reflection in the mirror, and she rested her chin on my shoulder, but again, eye contact didn't seem to be easy for her.

Her skin was hot against mine, and her wet hands moved to my fly. She popped it open and unzipped my jeans, and then her hand slid beneath my boxers and gripped my hard-on tightly. She pumped, and my eyes rolled closed, my hips thrusting and trying to chase the motion. When she pumped again, breath rushed from my mouth in a low groan.

Something snapped inside me then. My eyes flew open and finally held hers in the mirror, silently asking her consent to go at her hard. She seemed to understand. She lifted one sexy eyebrow, but then she nodded. Just once, but it was all I needed.

Spinning to face her, I almost ripped the plain, white T-shirt she'd been wearing beneath her uniform over her head, pushed her pants and what looked like a sexy, feminine version of a pair of men's white boxer briefs down her legs. Her white bra clasped in the front, and I flicked it open and watched it fall to the floor, watched how her nipples tightened and beaded into peaks for me.

I knelt at her feet on the hard tile, and her hands clamped down on my shoulders as I looked up at her and slipped two fingers inside her pussy, watching as her eyes rolled closed and any lingering tension eased out of her body.

Her shaking exhale and rasping moan were the only sounds in the whole state of Wyoming, or it felt that way. The sounds caressed the air around us and whispered over my head, and she swayed but reached for the wall with one hand to steady herself.

She was ready and waiting for me, wet like water, and I smashed my face to her body, spreading her open with two fingers and seeking her clit with my tongue.

When I found it and lapped at it with the flat of the muscle, she laughed softly and breathed, "Yes. *Oh yes, please*."

It didn't take long to make her come. She rode my hand hard. She wasn't shy or bashful about it, and I worked at her clit while my fingers pumped furiously, until she exploded around them, her hands buried in my hair, her head tipped to the ceiling.

I said nothing, but I untangled her hands and placed them at her sides, and then I rose slowly and stood.

We weren't making it into the shower. There was no time for that.

I needed her now. Needed to be buried inside her, needed to watch her breasts bouncing for me while I fucked her.

Moving behind her, feeling her soft, full ass cheeks pressing against the hardest part of me, I pushed her against the vanity. She planted her hands on top, her fingers clutching the sides, and I gripped her hips.

I still had on my jeans, but I lowered them just enough, freeing my aching cock, and I wrapped my hands around her hips again, watching her in the mirror.

Her lips parted.

"Tell me yes," I begged.

Her eyes lifted to mine, and she blinked once. "Yes."

My dick was as stiff as cured concrete, and it sought the ecstasy I knew in the moment only Roxanne could give me. Bending my knees and sliding through pubic hair dripping with her cum and soft, swollen lips, I took her in one hard, possessing thrust.

She bit her lower lip, and her head fell forward, her hair whispering over her shoulders and cutting off my view of her eyes. I closed my fist around a handful of the soft strands and lifted her head.

Oh, she liked that. Defiance shone in her eyes now, but they glittered like sunlit amber in the mirror, and the side of her mouth tipped up just a little, her tongue peeking out between her lips, and she bit the tip between her teeth.

"I need to fuck you hard now," I whispered against her neck. "Be a good deputy and spread your legs for me."

Her eyes narrowed a bit, but she did what I'd commanded. She stepped wide, and I punched my cock deep inside her, watching the way my body made hers quiver. Her small breasts bounced from the force of my fucking, just like I'd imagined, her nipples puckered and tight and pointing at me in the mirror.

I pulled almost all the way out of her body and pounded back in, loving the way her hot core tried to hold me inside, and she moaned and her heavy eyelids lowered, eyelashes dusting the high planes of her cheeks.

"Eyes on me, Roxanne," I said roughly. God, how I wanted to watch her come again.

That earned me a soft growl, but I didn't relent. Instead, I anchored one hand at the base of her throat so she couldn't look away from me, and the other slid down her soft hip and belly. I rubbed her clit with my middle finger, and her whole body shuddered in my arms.

She widened her legs a bit more, her smooth stomach tightening as she took me, showing strength beneath her skin, and then the chase for release took over.

I rubbed and fucked, never releasing her gaze in the mirror. My ass cheeks tightened with each thrust, and a primal grunting sounded around us. It bounced off the bathroom walls, and I couldn't figure out where the noise was coming from, until I realized it had come from me.

I liked that. I'd been quiet for so long, my head down, working and building my business. But I realized I had always been that way. I'd always kept my mouth shut, kept my opinions to myself when my father was still around. Now, maybe I wanted to be heard.

Roxanne heard me. A hungry smile grew in her eyes and on her rose lips, and suddenly, I needed to claim them.

"Give me your mouth."

She turned her head, and I rubbed her clit round and round, my fingers sliding in her cum, but when her mouth found mine and she slipped her tongue inside, I stilled.

She cried out softly, her heartbeat quickening beneath my hand still on her throat in anticipation, and her breath washed over me.

My entire body was wrecked and rock hard. I needed release, too, maybe more than I ever had before. Pounding inside her one more time, I felt her orgasm cresting and gripping my cock, and I came with a shout.

She swallowed it and sighed into my mouth, shivering as she came again, and any leftover anxiety about the missing kid or the fact that we were practically strangers engaging in the most intimate act leaked out and bled from the both of us.

CHAPTER NINE

ROXANNE

THICK STEAM FILLED THE BATHROOM, and hot water rained down over my body from the showerhead.

I tipped my head back to feel the warmth on my face while Brand rubbed a soapy hand between my legs. He licked at my breasts, sucking the water sliding over them and teasing my nipples with his teeth.

He'd taken me into the shower for a little aftercare, but I was so turned on again that I couldn't even find it within me to feel awkward or be silly, to make jokes.

All I could do was *feel*.

Pressing my shoulders to the shower wall with his big hand at the base of my throat again, he continued his oral assault on my breasts, moving from one to the other and back almost frantically, as if he couldn't get enough of them, his other hand still soothing and slipping between my thighs.

My body danced around another orgasm just slightly out of reach, but when he stilled and raised his head, the intense look in his eyes told me to prepare myself. He had grown hard again; his rigid heat pulsed against my belly.

"Let's go to bed," he rasped, and I shivered.

He offered his hand as I stepped from the shower, blatantly admiring his body and all its muscled edges, and then he wrapped me in a towel and picked me up like I weighed nothing.

No one, and I mean *no one*, had ever tried to lift me, and especially not while I was wet and slippery, but Brand accomplished it easily, and then, licking his lips like a hungry tiger, he carried me to the bed and placed me gently on the messed-up sheets, fulfilling the fantasies I'd been having all day.

I hoped I'd done a good job of washing my mascara off in the shower, 'cause if not, raccoon eyes were a definite possibility. He didn't seem bothered though.

Carefully, he lay me down and tugged the towel away, and then careful went right out the window when he gripped the backs of my thighs and dragged my ass to the bed's edge.

His mouth teased and his breath heated my inner thigh. It felt like he was searching for just the right spot, and when he found it, his teeth sank into my skin. Not enough to break through, but enough to leave a mark no one but him would ever see.

I gasped at the pinch and moaned, and he dropped to his knees on the floor and ate at my wet pussy like he was starved for me.

"Brand!" I cried out, trying to close my legs because the pleasure was too much. His tongue on my clit, flicking and fluttering, was almost ticklish now after two intense orgasms and nearly another, but he didn't stop. He cupped his hands over my boobs and moved my body to the rhythm of his mouth. "Oh my God."

And when he closed his teeth around the extremely sensitive, swollen nub, cum rushed from my body.

I screamed as I came, but he reached up to cover my mouth with his hand while his other moved inside me, fingers curling and coaxing my orgasm to heights I'd never reached before. Liquid literally squirted out of me. *That* had never happened before.

I'd read about it in book club, but damn! It was a strange sensation, but it was so hot, and the way he sucked it all down his throat, moaning and chanting, "Fuck yes," was the sexiest thing I'd ever experienced.

I didn't even have time to breathe before he was kneeling between my thighs, hooking my legs over his shoulders, and looking between us to watch himself enter and fuck me like I'd never, *ever* been fucked before.

I looked, too, and was shocked at the sight of his wide, reddened cock breaking me open at my core, like a fucking earthquake cracking gaping chasms into roads and earth.

My gaze latched onto his tightened abs as he rocked my whole body with his thrusts, and it moved lazily over his chest, smattered with coarse brown hair. His arms and shoulders were steel anchors over strong hands grasping the bedsheets beneath me, and still he pumped and rammed his cock inside me relentlessly.

The sound of his urgent, panting breath turned me on like nothing I'd ever heard before.

"Roxanne," he whispered, lowering his head to rest in the hollow below my throat, his hips pistoning his cock in and out of me now in the most perfect rhythm. He'd practically folded me in half. I had no clue I was that flexible, but I'd never been happier to learn something new about myself.

Breathing in the scent of his sweat and shampoo from our shower, I wondered how much more my body could take. I wasn't sure, but I was more than willing to find out. He could break me if he wanted to. At this point, I'd probably thank him.

Gripping the backs of my thighs in his hands, he pushed them closer to my chest and—

Oh!

Now I was chanting, "Yes! Oh yes, yes, yes. Harder!"

The angle and the force with which his cock pounded at my cervix or whatever the fuck that slippery, fat, delicious appendage kept sliding into was utter divinity.

My eyes rolled to the back of my head, and my whole body froze and locked in place like I'd been suspended in thin air.

My fingernails embedded themselves into his ripped back, and Brand cursed against my sweaty neck when he came and my body devoured his cum like fucking Cookie Monster, chomping down chocolate chip cookies right there in the middle of Sesame Street!

MY MEMORY of what happened after the mind-altering sex was hazy at best the next morning.

The embarrassment I felt when I'd caught a glimpse of the bird's nest my hair had become in the bathroom mirror made me want to run screaming from the room. I used my fingers and water from the sink to calm it down as best as I could, thinking Brand probably wasn't used to waking up next to a yeti after a one-night stand.

All I could recall from last night after the sexcapades was Brand lifting me from the bed, readjusting my legs beneath the covers, and then his big, taller-than-me body slipping under the sheets next to me. I think I might have nuzzled back against him, and he might've wrapped his arms and legs around me as we fell into deep sleep.

I was only guessing though.

He panicked for a second 'cause we hadn't used protection. How many times had he come inside me and no condom?

But I remembered mumbling something about birth control shots, and I'm pretty sure I made a joke about the side effects turning me into a nauseated, rabid bitch every three months.

At least, I *thought* I said all that. Had I? Because Brand had screwed me into near unconsciousness so thoroughly that now I wasn't sure the conversation had been real.

But as it happened, I was due for my next shot in a few weeks, so I would just schedule an exam too and freshen up my STI tests. Not that I'd thought Brand had lied when he'd said it had been a year since he'd gotten laid and had used condoms then, but a woman could never be too careful. And again, I couldn't be completely sure I hadn't dreamt those words.

A return text from Dan, complaining but agreeing to work my shift, had woken me way too early, and now I watched, sipping a cardboard cup of terrible coffee from the communal pot down in the motel office, while Brand rustled into his dirty, wrinkled clothing.

The only thing he said to me before we left to drive back to Wisper was, "Wanna go again?" as he swiped his baseball hat from the floor and tugged the brim down low over his eyes.

Snorting into my cup, I chewed on the edge as I watched his blue eyes twinkle.

"We can't. You and I need to stop by the station to give

our statements about findin' Natalie last night. And then I need more sleep. I think we only got, like, three hours."

The three most blissful hours of sleep I've ever had.

He shrugged. "*Your loss,*" his smirk seemed to say, and dammit, didn't I know it!

I could already feel that loss throbbing between my legs.

In my truck, I passed him the cup of coffee I'd filled for him when I filled my own. He drank it but made a sour face. He didn't comment, though, which told me either he didn't like coffee and was only drinking it because he was polite, or he did like coffee and maybe he had some taste, or he liked frou-frou coffee like Abey and her skinny white-mocha lattes with extra whipped cream and chocolate sprinkles on top.

Whatever the reason for his scrunched-up nose, I decided it was cute. It was the only cute thing about him, though, because every other nuance of the man radiated utter sexiness.

After driving back to town in silence through the misty, overcast morning with my truck's heater on high blast because it was colder than a witch's tit outside, twenty degrees colder than it should've been in late September, we pulled up to the Wisper station in the middle of downtown as streaks of pale sunlight began to peek through the low clouds.

I'd been quiet because I was reliving last night in my head and trying not to moan, but I had no clue what was going through his mind.

I parked in front of the building on Main Street, and he reached for his door handle, but before he opened it, he paused and turned back toward me.

"Why do we need to give statements if there was no crime?"

"Well, for one thing, the amount of hours worked needs to be accounted for, and also, Natalie's a minor. If God forbid anything were ever to happen to her again, anything that might need to be investigated, this incident will show when someone looks up her name." Brand watched my mouth as I spoke. I shrugged. "You never know what kind of information could be useful to a case. A lot of times, it's the simplest, most innocuous things that will break an investigation wide open."

"Hm." He nodded, still staring at me. "That makes sense."

"What? Why are you lookin' at me like that?"

A little fire lit behind his eyes as they lifted to mine. "I find you extremely sexy this mornin'."

I blushed hardcore, looking away out my windshield and patting at my messy ponytail, but that reminded me… "Um, so, your sister."

"What about her? I don't find her the least bit sexy."

I laughed. "I hope you don't, but she's kinda my boss. We're pretty laid back around here, but I don't know how she'd feel about this. About you… and me."

"I wouldn't worry about Abey. She'd probably be pleased as punch to know I'd—"

He paused in the middle of his sentence for the same reason I was a little bit anxious to walk into my place of work, arm in arm with my boss's brother. Abey and Brand's brother Bax got together with Brand's employee last year, and now they were married. Brand hadn't cared, but that didn't mean Abey would feel the same.

And we had no good excuse to explain what had happened between us. Not that we needed a reason other than insane physical attraction and heightened adrenaline levels after the whole "finding a missing girl/wolf encounter." We were both consenting adults, but still.

Technically, Abey couldn't fire me, not without Sheriff Michaels's approval, but she was my superior and my friend, and I respected her a lot. Unfortunately, last night, I couldn't have remembered her name if someone had asked while her big brother's mouth had been on my body or his cock inside it.

Brand couldn't even finish his sentence, so he had no idea what had happened between us either. It probably wouldn't happen again. I mean, I felt pretty certain I wasn't his usual type. In fact—

I peeked over at him. "What about your friend?"

"Friend?" he asked, his eyebrows dipping with confusion.

"Tabitha?" It felt like a rock had dropped into the pit of my stomach when I said her name. I should've asked Brand about her last night, *before* he ravaged my body countless times. But again, who, what, where, huh? But I didn't want to be *that* woman. I was no homewrecker.

"My office manager?"

"Yeah," I said. "Have you two— I mean, are you and Tabitha… you know, knockin' boots?"

"God, no! Why would you think that? She's my employee, and that's a line I will never and have never crossed."

The relief filling my body whooshed out of my mouth with my next breath, but I tried to disguise it by saying, "And now you see the predicament I'm in with your sister."

"I get your point. If you want to keep what happened between us, I'll support that."

"Thank you."

"Sure." But there was some kind of ambiguity in his eyes when he said it.

Although, now I felt like a harlot for keeping it from Abey. I'd tell her eventually, but before that happened, I needed to wrap my head around the last twelve hours.

It still all felt like a horny dream.

"Full disclosure, though. I am gonna tell my best friend," I added right before he opened his door. "I should probably be up front about that. I can't not tell her. But she won't say a word to anyone."

If she does, I'll be forced to tattle to Rye about how she tells me he likes to tittie fuck her in the back of the bookstore.

There are no secrets between besties.

CHAPTER TEN

BRAND

WE WROTE out our statements at the sheriff's station, and Roxanne dropped me back at Merv's place.

No one besides Deputy Sims had been in the office. That guy was so burly and tight-lipped that I didn't think we had to worry about him gossiping. I'd only met him a few times because he'd worked with my sister for years, but Frank Sims seemed more like the kind of guy who'd arrest someone for spreading gossip than the kind of person to offer it, though he did let us know that Natalie was okay and resting comfortably at the hospital.

I hadn't been sure at first how I felt about Roxanne wanting to keep what happened between us a secret, but I supposed she probably had a point. Small-town Wisper could whip up a frenzy with information like that.

Besides, I wasn't under any false assumptions that Roxanne was my forever person. Yeah, I was searching for something, or someone—someone who understood me—but what were the chances I'd found that person the very second my tires had crossed into the Wisper town limits?

Zero to none.

But that didn't mean it had been wrong for us to enjoy each other.

Damn, that woman.

Last night was the hottest sex I'd ever had. Roxanne had been completely unexpected and surprising in the best way. The urge to bite and possess and command wasn't new to me. I'd been wanting it since I could remember, but no one I'd ever been with had been into it.

Roxanne was more than into it. I couldn't get the image of my red teeth marks on her supple thigh out of my head. And no woman had ever been so beautiful when she'd come.

And this morning when she dropped me home, the way she'd blushed when I walked around her truck and motioned for her to roll down her window and then leaned in without a word and left a lingering kiss on her cheek and my business card and cell number beneath the strap of her bra? She was even more beautiful then, and her unassuming demeanor was endearing.

It seemed I'd gotten used to women who expected to be pampered and given expensive jewelry every weekend. Besides her dainty, gold cross, which I could still feel digging into the palm of my hand, Roxanne hadn't worn jewelry. Maybe that was because she'd been in her uniform, but she wasn't flashy at all.

She seemed like the kind of woman who'd be willing to sit next to me by the lake while I fished. In fact, she'd probably fish with me, and that was kind of refreshing.

Sitting at the desk in my bedroom at Merv's house, nursing a second, more palatable cup of coffee, I was getting hard again just remembering Roxanne's eyes on mine in the mirror, her lush body, and to be honest, the gun strapped around her thigh back on the trail. That last particular fantasy drummed up sultry images of her in strappy, black lingerie, her long, strong legs straddling me and my hands digging into her skin, leaving more marks that I'd kiss and soothe later.

Shit. At this rate, I'd never get any work done.

My hair was still wet from a shower as I stared at my computer, at the list of names Tab had sent me to look over before she started making phone calls on my behalf to try and get a permanent home crew together. I had my project leads all lined up, Bea, Clay Marveaux, and Tweety, who would be making the move with me from Sheridan, but I still needed the majority of the positions filled before I could start bidding on new jobs.

The letters on my laptop screen blurred together, and I leaned back in the uncomfortable desk chair from Dixon's childhood bedroom, replaying more memories of last night in my mind: Roxanne naked in the motel shower, her wet body glistening under the spray of the water. One of my hands gripped her throat and held her still, and the other moved between her legs while my tongue searched her mouth. And the sounds she'd made while I'd given her plea-sure over and over, pleasure I hadn't been able to stop myself from giving.

I wanted more moans and raspy laughs, more begging.

I'd demanded things from her. I'd never done that before with a woman. But something told me—maybe it was the defiance I'd seen in her eyes—that Roxanne might've been just as comfortable serving the demands as she was obeying them. She *definitely* liked me giving them, though.

I didn't think my dick could get any harder, but then I almost dumped my coffee on my keyboard when, behind me, Merv said, "You coulda called to tell me you weren't comin' home last night."

She stood in the doorway in her bathrobe and pajamas, cradling her own coffee in her hands, and if the sound of my mother's voice wasn't a boner deflator, I had no clue what would be.

"Jesus, Merv!" The coffee splashed and swirled around my mug's rim, but I managed to keep it inside the ceramic. One drop sloshed onto my Enter key, but I wiped it away with my finger.

She didn't chastise me for cursing or calling her Merv. It would take a lot more than that for her to scold a man, even one of her children, especially me because I'd kept myself apart from my siblings all these years.

"Sorry, son. Did I startle you? It's just nice to have you home again. You stayed away too long, so I don't think you can blame me for takin' the opportunity to catch up with you in the mornin' like we used to. I feel like I barely know you anymore."

Guilt clenched in my gut, but then the absurdity of the situation dawned on me fully: me living with my mother again at the age of thirty-seven and concocting X-rated images of the woman I'd hooked up with, thinking about hiding in the bathroom to jack off like I was fifteen, while Merv lurked behind me, demanding to know why I'd stayed out past curfew.

I didn't respond to address the angry elephant in the room, so Merv moved on. "Abey texted to tell me you and her deputy found that girl. If it wasn't for your little sister, I would've thought you were dead."

"Well, I'm not," I said, turning in the chair to face her now that there was no danger of her seeing the bulge in my pants that had quickly fled from the house in horror. Thank God. "And yes, Deputy Roxanne and I did find Natalie. A group of us did."

"She okay? She hadn't been murdered or killed by a grizzly?"

I shook my head, although the possibility of the grizzly wasn't that far-fetched. "No. She was pretty banged up and scared. Did Abey tell you about the wolf?"

Merv shook her head so I retold the tale. "It was a pretty extraordinary thing to see, but Natalie was okay. She has a broken ankle and was probably dehydrated, but the paramedics thought she'd be fine once they got her to the hospital. I was thinkin' about sendin' flowers from the family. You wanna pick some out for us?"

Merv's face brightened. "That's real kind of you, son. I'd love to."

It was enough to distract her from the hunt she'd been about to go on to find out where I'd stayed last night, or who I stayed with, which was exactly the redirect I had intended.

SLEEP ELUDED ME.

I needed more than three hours, but I hadn't taken a nap since I was probably twelve years old, so I worked as long as I could, made several phone calls, and finished some paperwork, but when my eyes blurred and the only thing between my ears was static, I stood and stretched.

I wanted to check on the slow progress of Lee's Spitfire Inn. We wouldn't open to the public until next summer at the earliest, but a lot of the groundwork had recently been laid. Bea was running the project for me, but it would be good to check in.

Brisk afternoon air and warm autumn sun jolted some life back into me when I stepped onto the porch, so I walked again.

Late September was maybe the best time to be in the Tetons. The days were all bright blue skies and mild temperatures, but nights were cold, perfect for sitting by a fire or an evening walk through town. As I had the thought, I snorted to myself when it occurred to me that Tab was right—I really was turning into an old man.

Far-off trees rustled, but I could see and hear the glowing yellow leaves of ancient Quaking Aspens in the soft wind. Mountains stood proud and tall around my family's land, their dark crags and valleys like rocky shoehorns from my childhood trying to make me fit and belong here again as memories came at me like automatic gunfire, one right after another.

Working with my old man had been a misery I wanted to continue to forget, but it wasn't those memories bombarding me now. Instead, I remembered the first time my sister had driven an ATV and the joy showing on her face that day when she only flipped it once. I remembered the first time Bax and I had shorn a sheep by ourselves and the pride we'd felt. Birthdays and Christmases came back to me in vivid detail.

Dixon's buck-toothed smile when he'd learned to swim in Lee Lake was a memory seared into my brain because Bax and I had been the ones to teach him.

But as I walked, the happy memories of my little brother faded, and all I could see in my mind was the last time I'd spoken to him over FaceTime before he'd left Wisper, before Stuey had come along and Dixon had dropped his kid like a hot potato.

Dixon had called me in the middle of a workday up in Sheridan, but I'd just finished eating my lunch and had a few minutes to spare, so I answered. Just the fact that his name had appeared on my phone's screen should've clued me in that something was really wrong with my brother. He rarely called or touched base with any of us. I'd heard Merv make a comment here or there when I talked to her occasionally.

Abey had openly worried about Dixon back then, and Bax had been alone in his own world after the sudden loss of his first wife.

And I'd been so wrapped up with my own worries and business that I didn't see it. I didn't see how thin Dixon had become, or how distracted. He'd called just to tell me he missed me. There were several awkward silences during the call, but still, all I had been able to think about was getting off the phone so I could finish whatever task I'd started before lunch.

I should've known he was crying out for help, that he had an addiction, and the guilt I felt now stole my breath.

If I'd just talked to him. If only I'd taken the time to really listen to him, maybe he wouldn't be a ghost in our family. He could've died, and we would've had no idea.

I thought about that fateful FaceTime call while I continued down the gravel lane that led to the center part of the property, and how, after Abey told me her fear that Dixon had become addicted to heroin, I'd tried to throw money at the problem. I offered to pay for rehab, but I hadn't bothered to call my brother back to tell him I was there for him, that I still loved him no matter the mistakes he'd made.

Maybe I could've driven home and gone on a walk with him like the one I was taking now. Maybe then he would've told me his secret and I could've done something to help him.

I hadn't gone for a walk just to walk and enjoy my time maybe ever when I was up in Sheridan. I jogged. I worked outside, but I never took the time to look around.

It felt good. The blood pumping through my lungs and legs got my brain working again. Thoughts of Dixon tucked themselves neatly away where they couldn't hurt or cause me shame, and then I heard some kind of commotion near the barn over by Bax's house, so I headed that way, completely forgetting my original intention of checking on the inn project.

When I got there, the barn and the exercise paddock were empty of humans, as was the mostly unoccupied new bunkhouse Bea and Clay had thrown up over the summer. Next year, it would be full of cowboys.

I said hello to a couple horses, a group of cows loitering near the fence gate, and one lone, black goat, Pekoe. I thought it was what Athena had named him. I wasn't one hundred percent on that, but the name was weird, so it fit my darling niece and the quirky need she seemed to have to name every living thing she met.

The sound of the barking dog I'd heard on my walk over carried through the gate that led to a grazing field. Rye's horse, Blue, wasn't in the barn, nor Bax's, but Athena's mare, Tulsa, munched hay in her stall, so I saddled her, hoping I remembered how to do it properly, and set out slowly to investigate.

When I approached them, Rye, Bax, and their lead cowboy, Presley, all sat in their saddles in a line in the field, looking past a grouping of trees in the distance.

Tulsa and I sneaked up beside Rye and Blue and stopped. When Tulsa chuffed, Rye turned his head and stared at me for a beat, a look of confusion tugging his eyebrows low over his eyes.

He adjusted the hat on his head and clicked his tongue. "Well, if this ain't the curious case of Brand Lee. I didn't know you could tell a cow from a horse, let alone saddle one."

"Ha. It's been a while," I said, "but it's all comin' back to me now."

"Bax tells us y'all found that girl last night. Good on you, man."

"Thanks. It wasn't just us. There were teams of people searchin'."

"Still, I'm glad she's safe."

"Me too. What's goin' on here?" I asked.

"It's Bea's bison," my brother said, pointing to a dark dot on the horizon. "Seems he came to say hello."

"What? None of the words you just said go together."

Bax handed a pair of binoculars to Rye, who handed them to me, and I looked through the lenses carefully, still not understanding until I saw a humungous buffalo staring back at me. He was alone. His herd had to be further past the trees to the east. Or maybe he'd wandered this far west on his own?

"Bison don't usually travel solo, do they?" I asked. "And why do you call him Bea's bison?"

"She met him last year on her way into Wisper, when she came to finish the houses and cabins for you."

"*This* bison? How can you know it's the same animal?"

Out of the corner of my eye, I saw Bax's shoulders lift. "Guess I can't, but it's intuition. We've seen him a few times now. You can just look in his eyes to know it's him. Bea calls him Wally."

"Okay, but why are y'all sittin' here starin' at him? Is he on our property? Should we call Game and Fish?"

"Naw," Rye drawled. "He was, but Fig chased him off. His herd is further east. We must have a breach in the east fence. We heard Fig barkin' like a madman, so we came to see what the fuss was all about."

The German Shepherd in question, Figaro, who lay at Blue's front hooves, rolled on his back in the grass at the mention of his name, his long tongue lolling, like he wanted belly scratches for his good deeds.

"That still doesn't tell me why you're not doin' somethin'."

"Bison are majestic animals," Presley uttered. "He knows this land better than any of us. It was his before we stole it. We're just takin' the moment in." He leaned forward on his bay mare and looked past Bax and Rye, his coal-black eyes narrowing at me. "You still can't relax, can you? Same as when you were a kid. Gotta control everything."

I'd known Elvis Decker since I was probably thirteen, but not once had I heard anyone refer to him as Elvis. He had always been just Presley. He'd come to the area from Texas to work on Rye's dad's ranch but had followed Rye when he set out on his own last year and we'd all gone in together to start up Spitfire Ranch at Lee Valley.

Crude tattoos covered his arms and chest, and they showed now because he'd ripped the sleeves off his button-down. A blade of wheat or dried field grass jutted from the side of his mouth, and his black hat shrouded his eyes in shade. The man rarely spoke. He was a mystery, and he was the absolute epitome of what people probably thought of when they pictured a cowboy in the Wild West.

Pursing my lips, feeling annoyed my latent anxiety was so obvious to Presley, I said, "I'm workin' on it."

CHAPTER ELEVEN

ROXANNE

AFTER I DROPPED Brand at his mama's house, I drove back into town.

I should've gone home to my duplex to shower and sleep, but instead, I parked behind my best friend's bookstore and let myself in through the back door, narrowly escaping knocking over a human-sized stack of boxes piled near the entryway.

"Who's there?" Aubrey called from the front main room.

"It's your best and most beautiful friend."

Peeking my head around the corner, I saw her standing behind the cash register, closing the drawer as a customer walked out the front door, a tote bag loaded to the brim with the latest bestsellers dangling from their hand.

"Any other customers?" I asked.

"Nope. Just you, but I doubt you're gonna buy anything."

Aubrey had recently decided to change her hours of business. She'd been switching up a lot of things to try to increase business. It seemed to be working. Tourists spent Sunday mornings eating breakfast in town and then a lot of them would pop into Your Local Bookie to grab a paperback to read during their vacation or on their flight back to wherever they called home.

"You are correct. Not today, but I've got somethin' better for you than revenue."

She spun to face me with her hands on her cute, little five-foot-four hips. "What?"

I couldn't hide my smirk. "A heartbreakin' tale of a lost girl alone in the mountains, vicious wolves, the brave man and woman who saved the girl, and their tawdry sex affair after it was all said and done in a motel off Highway 191."

"I heard they found the girl. That was you? Wait. Did you say *sex affair*?"

I backed up into the storeroom and wilted down to the cold, hard floor, spreading my arms and legs wide like a tab of butter melting on a hot pan.

"You know I haven't mopped that floor in ages. Get up. You're gettin' dirty."

"Oh, Aubs," I breathed. "I'm already dirty. So, *so* dirty."

"Roxi! You had sex? With whom?" Her eyes narrowed in skepticism. "Seriously, who? And skip the rescue part for now. You can come back to that later."

"So much sex! I think my hoo-ha might be broken."

"Does that mean it was *good* sex?"

Using my core, I sat up and could feel my hair frizzing out behind me. "The. Best. Sex. I've. *Ever*. Had."

Aubrey pulled her rolling desk chair toward me and sank into it. "Tell me and start with a name. Do I know him?"

"Uh, I think ya might."

She stomped her supportive and cushy Hoka's on the floor in rapid succession.

"I slept with Brand. Well, 'slept' isn't exactly the right word."

"Brand?" Aubrey's eyebrows rose to her hairline. "Brand *Lee*?"

When I nodded and purred satisfaction in the back of my throat, she gasped and covered her mouth with her hand. "Does Abey know?"

"No! Not yet. It literally just happened."

"Why are you makin' me drag this out of you? Spill right now!"

"Well, he was kinda flirtin' with me while we looked for the girl, but then we found her. It was crazy, like somethin' you'd read in one of your books. Anyway, but then they whisked her off to the hospital and everybody lived happily ever after. The rescue teams and cops went home, and it was just Brand and me on the trail.

"He came onto me. I swear to you, he would've screwed me up against a tree if I'd let him."

"*If?*"

"I told him no."

"Roxanne Rhiannon Fitts, I don't believe you. He's handsome and kind, and I don't know him super well, but somethin' tells me he's just your type."

"Okay, okay, jeez, Ma. Don't go all middle-name on me. You know I hate it. But I did say no 'cause I was armed with all kinds of weapons. I couldn't have sex out in the open air in my uniform. You know I take my job seriously."

She nodded. "Okay, I see your point. Then what happened?"

"God, when he turned his hat backwards and looked in my eyes?" I sighed dreamily. "You're right. He is my type, so you know that little inn by the fill-up station off the highway by Flat Creek?"

She nodded.

"We went there, and while I locked my gun in my truck, he got us a room, and then we screwed our brains out!"

Kicking her legs and stomping her feet again, she squealed.

"Orgasms, Aubrey," I breathed. "So. Many. Orgasms! We did it in the bathroom in front of the mirror." Heat rushed to my cheeks, and Aubrey's eyes got big. "Then he said, 'Let's get you cleaned up,' and he fondled me in the shower.

"And when he carried me to the bed, I thought I'd die. He carried me, Aubrey! Like I weighed no more than a pillow. I felt like a girl for the first time ever."

"Roxi, you *are* a girl. You're a woman. And apparently, one who knows how to get some."

"Yeah, but you don't get it. Men look at all this"—I waved my hand over my torso like a gameshow host—"and they wanna run for the hills. My stature intimidates them or just plain turns 'em off. But not Brand. He said we were a perfect fit."

Like a dreamy eyed teenager, I sighed. "He went downtown then, and I didn't think I had it in me to withstand all the naughty things he did to me there, but oh"—a devil's smile grew on my lips, like Lucifer himself had slapped it on my face—"he wasn't anywhere *near* done."

Aubrey fanned her face with her hand. "No?"

I shook my head slowly, remembering my legs hooked over Brand's shoulders and the almost-feral look in his eyes while his balls slapped my ass and he pounded into me, but then the jingle bell on the bookshop's front door tinkled.

Aubrey stood. "I have to get this, but we are *not* done here. Don't you dare leave."

"I won't."

As she greeted her customer, my phone rang in my back

pocket. I pulled it out and saw my daddy's face flashing on my screen.

Popping up off the floor, I leaned around the door again. "It's my dad. Call me after work later and I'll fill you in more."

Aubrey shot me an angry glare as the two women in the store meandered down the aisles.

I blew her a kiss. "Promise."

She rolled her eyes but smiled, and I answered my call as I left the way I'd come in.

"Hi, Daddy. How're you and Mama?"

"This is your mother, Roxanne. Daddy's drivin' us home from church, which is where I expect you've been this mornin' too?"

Uh, that's a hard no.

"Mama, don't start. No, I didn't go to church this mornin'. I was… workin'." That was close enough to the truth. And besides, what forty-something woman was required to report her whereabouts to her mama and daddy?

"Daddy was on the Facebook last night, and he said y'all had a missin' girl up there."

"That's why I was workin'. We found her though. She's okay."

"Praise Jesus. You know, that's just one more reason you need to go to services. And who knows? You might meet a man there, a God-fearin' one."

Right. The last "God-fearin'" man I dated wanted to paint my toenails and suck on them while he jacked off. Another hard pass.

Mama didn't bat an eye at my silence. "You could bring him home for Thanksgiving."

"I told you I probably can't come home for the holidays this year."

She tsked. "You say that every year."

One-two-three.

"I know," I said as I opened my door and slid into my truck. "I'm sorry, but my job is really important to me, Mama. And my coworkers have young families. I like workin' the holidays so they can spend time with their kids. It makes me feel good.

"And it makes me feel even better if an emergency call comes in on Christmas or Thanksgiving and I get to be the one to help. Bad things don't stop happenin' just 'cause you made pimento salad and bought way too many gifts for your grandkids."

Mama clucked her tongue, then under her breath, she said, "You should be doin' that for a family of your own."

I started my engine, and my phone transferred to Bluetooth. "Mama, I heard that. I am forty-one years old. Kids are not in the cards for me, and if I never marry, well, you're just gonna have to figure out a way to accept it. I will not hitch my cart to someone I don't love just to make you happy."

I heard my dad in the background, grumbling for Mama to put me on speaker. When she did, his gruff voice was like a bullhorn in my truck cab. "This is your father, RiRi. Don't you upset your mama today. Now, tell us about the case."

I held in my derision, smiling to myself. They made such a big deal about my life and the lack of a husband in it, but my dad was always interested in my cases.

My uncle Al had been on the OK City police force all of his adult life. I had a feeling Daddy regretted not following in his brother's footsteps. Instead, he'd gone the suit route and had recently retired from his job as a bank manager, so he lived vicariously through me and Uncle Al. He'd never admit it to Mama, but he was proud of me for becoming a deputy, helping and saving people and protecting my adopted home of Wisper, Wyoming, and he was proud that I'd left home and found my own piece in the world.

"You know," I tried to tempt them, "y'all could come out here for the holiday. I can cook for you." I was certain Aubrey could talk me through turkey preparation, or maybe she and Rye could even join us and my parents could get to know my friends.

"We can't do that, and you know it. Cecily's helpin' me cook this year, and Bridget and Ramona and their families will be here the week before. *All* my grandkids will be here for Thanksgivin' dinner. I'm not givin' that up to sit in some cold, lonely mountain town with the daughter who does everything she can to make me sad."

While that dig worked its way beneath my skin, my dad asked, "Can't you drive down this year? Just for a day or two?"

I tried not to scoff. Had they listened to anything I'd just said? "It's an eighteen-hour drive, Daddy. You know I don't like to fly, so that's two days there, two days back, and two days with y'all. That's a week off work. I can't do it. Everybody's already put in for their time off. I'm sorry. Maybe I can come next summer for your anniversary. Everybody will be home then too, right?"

"If we're not dead by then," Mama mumbled.

"Doris," Daddy scolded. "Don't start with that morbid stuff."

"Fine," she intoned, and I could picture her swiping lint off her church slacks, her lips fixed in a hard line. "But is it too much to ask for the daughter I spent thirty-seven hours in labor with to come see her family? I don't think so."

One-two-three. Breathe.

"We're pullin' into the OK Corral for brunch, RiRi.

Mama will call you back later. Good job findin' that missin' girl, baby."

"Thank you, Daddy. Love you both," I said and barely got the last word out before Mama hung up the phone.

CHAPTER TWELVE

BRAND

MERV WORKED up a belch and let it rip at the dinner table. Athena giggled, and Stuey growled, trying to imitate the sound.

"Mama!" Abey scoffed, and Devo made a disgusted face across the table in Merv's open-concept great room. Since Merv had moved into the new house, the family had been trying to eat together on Sunday nights like we used to when we were kids.

I'd been quiet. That was normal for me, but tonight it wasn't because of my old man or feeling out of place in my own family. Tonight, I was finding it hard not to think about Roxanne, and what it had felt like when her mouth was on my body. My mouth on hers.

When she came and I caught the fountain of liquid on my tongue, I had nearly come all over the motel bed. *Goddamn, that was hot.*

My mother burping next to me pulled me right out of the sexy memory, and I dropped my fork. It clattered on my plate loudly, and I cleared my throat and looked around, hoping no one had noticed my distraction.

"I apologize," Merv said. "I've got awful indigestion lately. It's makin' my ribs burn."

"You oughta go to the doctor, Mama," Bax said before he shoved a heaping forkful of mashed potatoes into his mouth.

"I'm fine. Just gotta eat slower."

Stuey looked around the table, babbling and catching everyone's attention. With a devious smile, he brought his sippy cup to his mouth to take a drink but then threw it to the floor with what sounded like the force of a tree hitting pavement.

He squealed and giggled, and Bea lifted her face to the ceiling, trying to hold onto her composure. "Lord, give me strength." She looked at Stu pointedly. "You're s'posed to *drink* the milk, Stu. Not hurl it."

"No want," he said with an impish grin.

"Yes, want," Bax said, and he picked up the cup and set it in front of the kid again.

A pile of stewed beef, carrots, smushed potatoes, and green beans littered the floor in a halo around Stu's booster seat. I wasn't sure he'd actually ingested any of it. Merv didn't care about the mess. She gazed adoringly at the little devil, like she always did, and I wondered if, in her mind, she was blocking Dixon's face and replacing it with Stuart's.

Dixon's absence tonight was probably causing her a hell of a lot more pain than her heartburn. She'd never give up on her youngest son though. If he was out in the world still, he had a home to come to whenever he wanted. Maybe someday he would, but Bax and Bea were planning to adopt Stu in the new year, whether Dixon showed or not.

When Stu threw the cup again, Bax groaned. "That's it. Dinner's over. C'mon, Athena. You've got homework to finish anyway." He lifted Stu out of his seat, and more food that the little stinker had hidden between his legs and in the top of his diaper slopped to the floor.

"I'll clean this up," Bea said, standing and collecting all their plates and glasses.

"Child," Bax complained, "I swear you're a tornado on two legs."

"Don't worry about it," Merv said. "I'll get it."

Before she could argue, Bax hitched Stu on his hip, grabbed Bea's hand, and hauled them both toward the exit. "Thanks for dinner, Mama. See y'all tomorrow."

"Thanks, Merv," Bea called as Bax dragged her through the door.

"You're welcome," she said as they left.

Athena had her nose stuck in her phone, and she bumped into the wall on her way out and barely even noticed. She tossed a wave back at the rest of us before the screen door clattered shut behind her.

"I've got the mess," I said, standing to stack all the dirty plates and silverware. "Mama, your new car will be here in a couple days. Why don't you make a doctor's appointment, and you can drive it and show it off?"

"Well now," she said. "There's a good idea. Betty Johnson will be so jealous!"

Devo snorted, and Abey rolled her eyes.

MONDAY MORNING, Tab showed up at eight forty-five on the dot and waited for me outside in her car so we could go check out some properties for rent.

Lee Construction needed a new home base. We usually worked out of a trailer we could transport to each build site, and I was still planning to do that when possible, but I'd been thinking it might be nice to have a main office we could fix up for meetings with potential clients. Somewhere we could display pictures of previous projects or models of upcoming builds. I was already tired of working out of Merv's house. I needed a place to call my own, and Tab needed a better office than the kitchen table in her new rental. I needed to hire a local HR manager and other positions, and they'd all need somewhere to work.

It was just an idea at this point. I wanted to see what we could find in town before I made the decision. I could always build something if the available properties didn't meet my needs.

The plans I'd had drawn up for a home of my own sat tucked away in a corner in my room at Merv's, waiting for me to be ready, but it wouldn't be built until next summer, and it was just a small two-bedroom log A-frame, definitely not big enough to incorporate offices. Besides that, part of what I thought needed to change in my life was my work-to-relaxation ratio. If my office was inside my house, I'd never shut off my brain.

"Morning," Tab said when I opened her passenger door and sank down into her sporty Nissan's bucket seat.

"Morning. You need a truck. This car's too low."

She laughed.

"You're laughin' now but get back to me after you live through your first blizzard around here and have to drive on all these curvy, windin' roads with no four-wheel drive or underbody clearance." She rolled her eyes, so I pushed on. "What's on our agenda today?"

"We're meeting Mrs. Brooks from Wisper Realty. She's got a few places for us to see. Oh, and before I forget, Gina Scott emailed. She wants to set up an appointment with you to go over the new build we're in contract for here in the spring."

Holding in a groan of annoyance, I said, "I forgot she was the lead architect on the project." I shouldn't have forgotten, but I tried to repress any memory or interaction I'd had with Gina Scott.

"She said she'll be down this way in a couple weeks, so she wanted to get something on our books. She suggested dinner."

"Great."

I said it like, *"Great, that sounds fine,"* but I meant it like, *"Fucking great, I can't wait to see that slithering snake of a woman. Maybe she'll try to harvest my sperm so she can tie me down for good this time."*

Unfortunately, Gina Scott was the go-to architect for the company that had hired Lee Construction to build their new residential project when they heard I was moving back home.

Based out of Sheridan, Wy Not Homes had projects going up all over Wyoming. I wasn't surprised they wanted to build in Jackson Hole. Their usual MO was luxury homes, but they were savvy businesspeople and knew that if they started in the area with affordable and subsidized homes, they'd build a good rep before they started buying up land for their chance to make gazillions off rich tourists and celebrities who wanted to vacation in the Tetons.

Also unfortunately, Gina Scott was my ex-girlfriend. The three months or so we'd dated last year had been some of the least sexy or fun times of my adult life. We had sex and ate dinner together two or three times a week, and she'd sat at my dining table talking about how she wanted to redecorate my house, with her eyes on her phone the whole time, checking emails or Instagram.

When I'd finally called it off, she'd tried her hardest to

hold onto the joke of a relationship. It had started out great. There had been mutual attraction, but it quickly turned disappointing, just like every other relationship I'd had to date.

Something's missing.

Ninety days later, I barely knew anything about her, and she couldn't have cared less about my wants and desires. All she'd cared about was money and status. She had plans to make us the Wyoming building community's new "it" couple, whatever the hell that was, and when I'd started talking about moving home, she told me it was a mistake I'd regret.

I disagreed strongly. And I realized then that her opinion didn't matter to me, which was the night I broke things off.

If I'd tried to wrap my hand around her throat when I'd fucked her, she probably would've called the cops. I imagined Roxanne showing up to the call and snorted out loud.

Tab looked at me out of the corner of her eye, like I'd just grown a second head.

So, yeah. Great. *Super* excited to see Gina Scott again.

"And then," Tab went on, dismissing my outburst, "after we're done touring properties, I'll start reaching out to the crews who worked for you last year and see if I can drum up some more interest. The guys who've signed on to build the inn and those who worked on the barn and the bunkhouse this summer have already said they'll work any job you offer them."

"That's great. Thanks, Tab."

"Welcome. So, tell me about this weekend. I saw your sister on my way to pick you up, and she told me you went up there to help search for that missing girl. I'm so glad you found her. God, can you imagine if you hadn't?"

I could imagine, and the nightmare of that exact scenario had played out in my dreams and kept me up half the night.

"Actually, Deputy Roxanne and I found Natalie. She was

only a couple miles from the trailhead, but she fell and broke her ankle so she'd veered off course. From what her dad said, he was really close to where we found her when he looked for her earlier in the day, but apparently she wandered aimlessly for a while, and in those woods, you can get disoriented really fast. But a broken ankle was the worst of it.

"She's at the hospital. I imagine they'll release her today or tomorrow if she's doin' well. Bax said he talked to her dad and they've extended their stay at the cabin a couple days so she can rest, but they're eager to get her home. She broke her arm at volleyball camp last year, so they want the same surgeon to treat her ankle."

"We should buy them dinner or something before they leave. They've got to be exhausted."

"That's a good idea. I'll find out when they're comin' back to the cabin and set it up. The diner in town caters. I'll give them a call after we're done this mornin'."

Tab drove into downtown Wisper, right past the diner in question, José's, but we didn't have time to stop, so I set a reminder in my calendar to call José later as Tab pulled up and parked across the street from the sheriff's station.

"Why are we here?" I asked.

"I told you, we're meeting Mrs. Brooks. This is the first property." Tab nodded at an empty storefront across the street from the station, then looked at her phone, clicking the screen a few times. "She's already inside. Come on."

"Right." But my attention wasn't on the rental property. It was fixed on the station, and I was hoping for a glimpse of Roxanne.

I didn't get one, and Mrs. Brooks met us in the open door of the Main Street building, shook our hands, and introduced herself. We walked through the space she wanted us to see, but it was small and not really the right floor plan for my purposes.

The community center next to the sheriff's station was buzzing with activity when we were done, and I waved to Devo when I saw her trying to wrangle a couple little kids through the big, open front doors, but the sun was shining on the station's windows next door. If Roxanne was in there, I couldn't see her.

The sharp pang of disappointment I felt surprised me.

Tab and I followed Mrs. Brooks to the next available property, but it was an old house ten miles south of town. Technically, it could've worked. It was big enough, but it would need major renovations if it was going to be used as offices, and I figured if I wanted to go that route, I could just build the offices on my family's land and make it exactly how I wanted it from the get-go.

That idea had me thinking and imagining family offices, where we could run the ranch, the rentals, and Lee Construction all from the same building. I'd kept my business separate from my family for so long, but now I found myself wondering if things needed to change. Maybe being hands-off wasn't suiting me anymore. I wasn't sure how I felt about it though. It was a bigger deal than just relocating Lee Construction.

The third property Mrs. Brooks showed us was another house, but it was north of town, closer to the highway and more accessible. The size was right, and I could picture a big Lee Construction sign facing Highway 20, but I couldn't muster any excitement about it now that the image of the family offices had invaded my mind.

I told Mrs. Brooks I'd think about it and we'd get back to her. In fact, I had *a lot* of thinking to do. She thanked us, gave us her business card, and then Tab drove over to José's since we had to pass through town on our way back to Merv's anyway.

The Monday lunch crowd was small but boisterous and loud when we walked in. José himself greeted us at the counter. I hadn't seen him in a long time. I'd heard he'd gotten married a few years back, but he looked the same as he had when I was a teenager and he made my brothers, sister, and me milkshakes on the weekends.

I asked him about catering a dinner for the Manning family, explaining who they were, and he shook my hand and said, "It's on the house, kid. Don't you even dare pull out your credit card."

He'd heard about Natalie already, of course. The news of her ordeal had probably circulated through town like a stiff wind over the weekend, and José seemed glad for the opportunity to pitch in and help. Since he had dinner covered, I put another reminder in my phone to talk to Bax and Rye about offering the Mannings an all-expenses-paid stay at the cabins next summer and *guided* Teton tours, and then added another reminder to call Carey's wife, Frannie, over at the bakery to see if she had time to make dessert for the family.

I told José I'd call him later with a firmer time once I'd talked to Bax, and as Tab and I turned to leave, I got the glimpse of Roxanne I'd been craving like air.

She sat facing the door across a booth from Rye's girl-friend, Aubrey, and my mouth watered when I pictured the gun most likely strapped to Roxanne's thigh below the table.

The two women had their heads together over their table, whispering to each other as Roxanne looked at me. Had they been talking about me? I couldn't help my smile, and I lifted my hand in a discreet wave.

Roxanne blushed. I would've seen it a mile away, her cheeks pinking like a sunset, and she smiled back. Aubrey turned in her seat, and as she looked me up and down, her smirk seemed way too knowing.

They had been talking about me! What had Roxanne told her friend? I hoped it was all good things, but a sudden rush of uncertainty pulsed through me. Had Roxanne enjoyed our time together as much as I had?

I decided I wanted to know the answer to that question, so when I pulled open the door for Tab and she walked through, I lifted my hand to my ear like a phone and mouthed to Roxanne, "Call me."

She nodded and I found myself blushing now, too, and a new rush of anticipation burned through me as I followed Tab back to her car.

CHAPTER THIRTEEN

ROXANNE

"YOU GONNA CALL HIM?" Aubrey asked as Brand and his office manager left the diner.

Watching him through the window, my eyes were glued to his ass in his jeans as he walked to Tabitha's electric-blue Nissan. They spoke for a minute over the roof, then got in.

"Roxi?" Aubrey said, waving her hand over the table in front of my face.

"Huh?" I shook my head to clear it of lust and focused on her.

"Oh my God. You've got it bad for that man, don't you?"

"What? No! Shh. Keep your voice down," I whispered, glancing around the restaurant, but no one seemed bothered. When I looked at Aubrey again, the smirk on her face was so smug. I wanted to smack her hard on her back and make the silly grin stick there forever. Leaning closer, I said, "It's just his ass... I was rememberin' clutchin' it and my fingernails diggin' into that firm—"

Aubrey cut me off. "Thanks very much for that visual."

Tabitha backed slowly out of their parking spot in front of José's, like she was afraid of some imaginary rush of traffic, and for a brief second, Brand's eyes met mine through the windshield.

I lifted my phone high enough so he could see me typing, but instead of calling, I texted him:

12:37 PM

417 Tacoma Ave

9pm

If he showed, that would be enough time after my shift to hydrate, shower and shave my legs, and do something with my hair.

Brand's phone must have alerted him that he had a new message. A hint of a smile showed on his lips, and he looked down.

I could see Tabitha's mouth moving as she said something to Brand and put her car in Drive, but his eyes lifted to mine after he read my text, and right before she hit her gas pedal and drove off, he nodded once through the passenger window, then turned his head and looked away.

And I shivered from head to toe.

How could one tight movement of some guy's head be so sexy?

AT 9:10 when Brand knocked on my door and I opened it breathlessly, I said, "You're late."

Thank God he showed. I was starting to think he wouldn't. If he hadn't, my self-esteem would've taken a hard nosedive.

After changing six times, I'd become a sweating, flus-
tered mess, even though I'd finally ended up in a pizzazz-less
jeans-and-tank-top combo with no bra 'cause every single
one I owned kept digging into the skin above my ribcage and
pinching me. My boobs were pretty small though—and still
high and tight, thank you very much—and jogging most
mornings kept me pretty fit, so I never worried about turning
into Drooping Dolly.

My hair had looked so cute at one point. I used my special
curl cream and scrunched till my fingers were sore and my
diffuser all but gave up, but now, the sweaty mop hung limp
and barely wavy, the sad victim of overexcited body heat.

And now I was worried about my house. My duplex
rental was nothing to write home about. It was old, the finish-
ings outdated, but it was just me. I couldn't afford any of the
fancy, newer homes northwest of town, and I wasn't one to
waste money on that kind of thing anyway.

My place was clean though, so I had to hope Brand didn't
care about that kind of thing. But he was a billionaire. Surely
he was used to nicer accommodations.

"I'm sorry," he said in his low voice, and it sent vibrations
right to my clit. "I wasn't sure what to wear."

He couldn't have responded more perfectly. Thoughts of
my haggard house disappeared, and I yanked him inside by
his jacket, slammed the door shut behind him, and
kissed him.

Mr. Begley next door would complain about the noise
tomorrow, but I knew for a fact that he wore hearing aids and
kept them turned down or off most of the time unless he was
watching World War II documentaries, and then his TV was
louder than I'd ever been.

There was no pretense between Brand and me. No small
talk. Just tongues in mouths.

He growled and kissed me back, and after I pushed his jacket off and to the floor, he unbuttoned his jeans and yanked one side of my tank down roughly, exposing my breast. Pushing his face against my chest, I smothered him, my fingers raking through his hair, and he sucked my nipple into his mouth and slipped his hand between my legs.

"I love when you do that."

"Mm," he moaned, trying to back me to my couch.

I redirected him. "Bedroom."

We made it there, but it was touch and go for a minute because he slipped the same hand inside my jeans and found that I was already wet for him. He played in the wetness, stroking me with sure fingers, and bit down on my nipple, and I probably could've come right there in the hallway.

He tried to take charge like last time, but I was feeling a little bold, confidence flowing through me since he'd shown up, so I clasped his wrist in my hand and spun him, then pushed him down on his back on my bed like a feast on a platter, waiting for me to devour him.

He stared up at me, mouth open, breath shaking out of him. Want in his eyes.

Dipping my head, I said, "Take off your clothes."

He did, slowly, and I watched as every inch of his skin was exposed to me, every muscle tight with anticipation, his cock hard and jutting away from his stomach, pointing right at me. I wanted to impale my body on his, but he kept glancing at my bedside table.

I'd locked my weapons in my safe, but my flashlight and handcuffs sat there, the metal gleaming and reflecting the light from the hallway.

"You can't use those on me," I said as he pulled off his socks and dropped them off the far edge of my bed. "I'm afraid that's against the rules, but if *you* were interested…"

Technically, I probably wasn't supposed to use my hand-cuffs on anyone when I wasn't on duty. I was pretty sure I remembered that little tidbit from my training, but for some reason, Brand Lee made me want to forget all the rules. I'd clung to them by the very tips of my fingernails the last time we were together.

But tonight?

"Yes," he said breathlessly, and he raised his hands above his head, wrists pressed together.

What rules?

I used to think my bed frame was ugly and outdated, but now I loved it, and I'd never been so glad that it had been made of metal and had a slatted headboard. It was an old one, a hand-me-down from my sister, Maureen, but God knew I wouldn't be telling her how I was about to use it.

"It's your turn," Brand said as I walked around the end of my bed to the table and lifted the cuffs. "You still have way too many clothes on."

I tsked my tongue. "Look at you, tryin' to be all bossy." I wrapped a cuff around one of his wrists, the zipping-metal sound loud in my room as it locked in place. He tried to lift my shirt with his other hand, but I gripped it tight. "Nuh-uh. Tonight, Deputy Roxi's in charge, and you don't get to tell me what to do."

I threaded the second cuff behind a slat on the headboard and lifted his other arm above his head. His bicep flexed as I shackled his wrists, and he pulled against the handcuff's hold and adjusted his body to the position.

When I had him how I wanted him, completely naked and chained to my bed like my very own sex prisoner, I said, "Test them. Can you wiggle free?"

The metal clanged against the headboard loudly when he

tried to pull his wrists out, but he shook his head and moaned softly.

"Good. Wait. You know this is all pretend, right? Like, you know I'm not actually a deputy right now? I have no authority over you."

"The hell you don't," he argued.

"No, really I don't. You don't have to do what I say just 'cause I'm law enforcement. It's not—"

"I will do *everything* you want me to because I have never wanted anyone more than I want you right now." He licked his lip and slowly scraped his teeth over the wetness.

It took me a moment to let that comment sink in. God, the power it gave me!

"You know, I didn't expect this when I invited you to my place. I'm pleasantly surprised. Have you ever been hand-cuffed before?"

He shook his head again against my favorite feather pillow as I dragged one finger down his chest and abs, loving how his coarse body hair abraded my skin, and when I wrapped my hand around his hard-on and squeezed, his whole body tensed, and his cock jerked and throbbed in my grip.

"Good boy. I'll be your first."

He groaned, "Fuck."

"Not yet, loverboy. Like you said, I'm wearin' too many clothes."

He nodded tightly, and I unbuttoned my jeans.

Pushing them to the floor, I hooked my fingers beneath my undies and let them drop too. "Hm, but if you can't touch me, how will you make me ready for you?"

In a low and carefully restrained voice, he said, "Touch yourself. I need to watch."

My pussy clenched and pleasure shot through me like I'd

been defibrillated. I shivered as I lifted my tank over my head. My hair fell down around my shoulders, and Brand's eyes followed the barely waving strands.

"I can't see you," he said.

"No?" I cupped my breasts with both hands, thumbing over my nipples softly, and his nostrils flared as he inhaled, and when I faced him fully and lifted my foot onto the mattress, spreading my leg wide open so he had an unobstructed view, he stopped breathing.

"Breathe, Mr. Lee. If this becomes a homicide, it won't be much fun for either of us."

His eyes rose to mine, and together we took a deep breath.

"I'm gonna make myself come now while you watch," I whispered. "And then I'm gonna ride your cock raw."

"*Yes.*"

Resting one hand on my raised knee, I let the other slip down my stomach till my fingers touched slick, wet skin.

Brand gasped and the handcuffs scraped against the bed frame as he flexed his shoulders, his arms straining and trying to pull his hands free so he could touch me.

His eyes on me had me feeling all kinds of bold. His attention heightened the silky buzzing feeling between my legs when I rubbed and circled my clit, and when I pushed two fingers inside my pussy, my eyes rolled closed because it was unlike anything I'd ever felt before.

I'd never felt so desired.

"Yes," he whispered. "Again."

I pumped and rolled my hips softly to chase the pressure.

"*Again*," he demanded this time. "Harder and faster. Imagine it's my fingers inside you." His voice rasped dangerously when he said, "I'd be rougher."

Doing exactly what he wanted, I imagined him finger fucking me roughly. I pumped and pumped, my thumb pressing against my clit, heightening the pleasure so much that I moaned.

"Roxanne," he groaned, "you're makin' me insane."

I smiled. Oh, I liked that.

"Make yourself come and then get up here and fuck me."

Stilling my hand, I let my fingers slip from my body.

He growled at me. "Don't stop. Why're you stoppin'?"

"Stop givin' me orders. Want me to duct tape your mouth?"

A darkness passed through his eyes. He watched my mouth for a moment, and I almost thought he'd say yes, but he shook his head.

He groaned his frustration and flexed his hips deeper into the mattress as I touched myself again.

Dipping my fingers inside my pussy, I pulled them out slowly, then held them over his lips. They parted and I waited for his tongue to reach for them. When it did and he pulled my fingers into his mouth and sucked, I climbed onto the bed and over his stomach, and I kneeled above him and fucked myself with my other hand, trapping his cock between my legs, letting it bump against my hand occasionally.

His chest heaved with breath as he watched me, and I reveled in the power he'd given me. I felt like a goddess, moaning and rocking above him and rubbing myself to ecstasy, while his thighs tightened below me and he tried to pull his wrists free from the restraints so he could take charge, and this time, my height and stature only added to the powerful feeling inside me, running through my veins like an electrical charge.

That confidence and his masculine display of competing strength pushed me over the edge, and I rubbed my clit hard, rolling my hips to orgasm, gasping and practically purring. Every nerve ending inside me fired and buzzed. My head tipped back, and I sighed as I came and then lowered my body to his and took his cock inside, not allowing him one second to prepare.

He groaned. "Goddamn, you feel so good." He bucked his hips, trying to fuck up into me, but I rose on my knees, not letting him reach the depth he was desperate for.

"*Roxanne*," he begged.

Or was he… scolding me?

When he spoke again, the sound was coarse and held a command. "Fuck me. Take all of me."

"Like this?" I lowered my body, my hands splayed over his chest, taking him deeper just like he wanted, rocking us both and making the bed frame creak.

His response was tight and so quiet, I almost couldn't hear him. "Yes. Just like that. Faster."

I let him have his way for a few minutes and increased my pace, my knees digging into my mattress, my body enveloping his rhythmically.

He watched me, watched my body take his inside, his hips moving in tandem, and he squeezed his eyes shut. His oblique muscles popped as he breathed faster and faster, and I knew he was close, but I wasn't done with him.

Lifting up on my knees again, I released him, and his breath hitched and stopped. He was ready to come.

"Tsk, tsk, tsk. Not yet."

He growled again, and I smiled. He had no idea the power his need for me had given me and the way it made all my anxiety and inhibitions bleed away.

Coated in my cum, his cock looked especially slippery, so I lowered myself but this time let it settle between my pussy lips, and I rubbed myself on him, teasing him and working myself into a frenzy with the rolling pressure on my clit.

Quick, shallow pants were his only source of oxygen. I

thought he might pass out, but he was in exemplary shape, so I closed my eyes and worked him harder. My fingertips dug into his pecs, and my core spasmed on emptiness, begging to be filled again.

I closed my eyes, letting the rush take root deep inside my body once more. The bed creaked louder, and Brand grunted. I heard an odd snapping sound, metal bending, and then his hands were on me, still cuffed together, but when I opened my eyes, the middle slat on the headboard had been bent just enough for him to break free.

A smug smile appeared on his lips. "I'll buy you a new one," he said, and then his hands slid down my body and between my legs.

I lifted up on my knees in surprise, and he sought any hole he could find. Pushing three fingers inside me roughly, just like he'd promised, he watched my face as I climbed closer and closer to release. The pad of his thumb found my clit and he tapped quickly, until I had no other choice but to explode.

He hadn't forgotten how I'd tortured him before. That was obvious when with his next breath, he stole his fingers away, bent his knees beneath me, and lifted my body above him with the brute strength in his thighs. And when he dropped the backs of his knees to the bed, my body slammed back down on his cock, but the man's aim was true.

"Yes!" His head fell back on my pillow, and he bucked up into me.

My breasts bounced with each thrust. Breath punched out of my mouth, and before I knew what he was doing, he flipped me and pressed my chest to the bed with his still-cuffed hands on the middle of my back. He grabbed the cuff key from the edge of my bedside table and held it between his teeth, braced himself on my back again, and spread my legs open with his knees.

With the key still gritted between his teeth, he slapped my ass and commanded, "Up." The harsh smacking sound of his hand on my skin and the sting it left there made a shot of lust rush through me, and I moaned. "That's enough of playtime," he said. "I'm in charge now, Roxanne. You gonna do what I say?"

Nodding as fast as I could, I bent my knees and raised my ass up in the air, and as he pushed inside me again, he slipped his arms over my head, leaning over me now, his hot chest to my back, his cock teasing me slowly. The smooth strokes of his body inside mine felt like pulsing velvet, and then he spit the key next to my arm on the bed.

"Uncuff me," he breathed next to my ear. "I need to touch you now."

My entire body felt like it had caught fire, the gritty, raw sound of his voice like the striking edge of a matchbox. His dominance was what I'd always wanted. Someone to take charge, to control me like I wasn't the authority in the room.

Someone to make me feel like a wanted woman, and right now there was no mistaking how much Brand wanted me.

I lifted the key from the bed and uncuffed him, tossed the cuffs and key over the edge, hoping I could find them later, and rubbed my lips over his red wrists, soothing them with my tongue and apologizing silently for my earlier disobedience.

His arms and then the heat from his body over mine disappeared. He pulled out, but soon, I felt his lips on my ass, his tongue, and then his teeth when he bit me possessively. He lapped at my hot core, dragging his mouth over the slick slowly.

I shivered and mewled like a cat in heat. Nothing had ever

felt so good, but then he straightened and rose behind me on his knees, centering his hard cock between my spread legs.

"Say it," he commanded, his voice a rule I never wanted to break. "You know what I wanna hear."

Hiking my ass higher with one hand cupping my pussy, he had me how he wanted me, and he held my body in place with his other hand gripping my hip and punched his cock inside.

I grunted at the punishing fullness, but I smiled. I did know what he wanted to hear. The way my words had made his eyes come alive the night we met and again on the trail the night we'd found Natalie hadn't escaped my careful notice.

Nor had his need to control everything around him, including me.

Lifting my ass even higher, my pussy grasped his dick and sucked him in deeper. His entire body stilled behind me in expectation, and when my eyes met his over my shoulder, something passed between us:

A reversal of power.

I obeyed and breathed, "Yes, sir."

CHAPTER FOURTEEN

BRAND

I CAME SO FUCKING hard I saw stars and worried for a moment I might lose consciousness.

When she said it— The *way* she said it, the wanting sound of her voice…

Yes, sir.

Roxanne's surrender eased my body in ways I'd never felt before. The power. The intimacy. The thought scared me, but I wondered if this was how Dixon felt when he did drugs, because already I was hooked.

And once I'd taken back control, the way Roxanne *begged* me to make her come?

Fuck.

"What did you just do to me?" I rolled off of her onto my back and pulled her against my chest, my spent cock softening between our bodies.

"Me? That was all on you, sir, and it was hot." She moaned, her eyes still closed in bliss, and she hitched her leg over my hip.

"Have you ever done anything like that before?"

"No," she said earnestly. "You brought it out in me. Have you?"

No, but it was the sexiest thing I've ever experienced and your obedience made me harder than I've ever been in my life.

Shaking my head against her pillow, all I could manage to say was, "Again. I want that again."

"Right now?"

"Well, yeah," I said, chuckling, "but I don't think my body's on the same page yet. Give it a minute."

She shivered, the chill in the air making her nipples bead and poke my chest, and I pulled her covers over us and snuggled deeper into her comfort, letting her sweet honeysuckle scent lure me closer. She tasted like wild honeysuckle too.

"Roxanne?" I asked, stroking my fingers down the outside of her thigh beneath the covers and staring up at her dark ceiling, watching the lights from a passing car outside travel its width quickly. She tucked her head into the crook of my neck, and it felt… right.

I was a little afraid to know the answer to the question I wanted to ask. What did it mean that I got off on controlling her? God, so many images flooded my head. Ropes and leather restraints. Gags and bindings.

Just thinking about it was making my body fight through its hard-won fatigue.

"Yeah?"

"Are you okay? I was a little rough there at the end."

She lifted up on her elbow, her eyes searching mine because she'd heard the unsure tone of my voice. "Brand, I'm more than okay. That was… I don't even have words. I loved every second of it."

"Honestly?"

She breathed, "Yes," and she leaned in to kiss me, her hot tongue convincing me what she'd said was true.

"Good," I said when we came up for air. "Got any rope around here?"

"No, I don't think so. Why?"

"Because." I pulled her on top of me, letting her feel what she was doing to me again. "I wanna tie *your* hands to the bed." I could already picture the type of knot I'd use. Bax and Rye would be proud that I hadn't forgotten all my roping knowledge.

Roxanne froze and lifted her head. Strands of her hair caught between her lips, and fire danced through her brown eyes in burnt oranges as I tugged the soft wisps free.

A moment passed as we stared at one another, me requesting her consent to do all the things in my head I suddenly needed to do to her, and silently she gave me the yes I wanted desperately. And this time, she held my gaze and kept it.

"I don't have rope," she said, "but I have a silk scarf my mama gave me to wear to church." She smirked. "But lucky for you, I don't go to church."

Gripping her ass cheeks in my hands, I yanked her body harder against mine. "That's even better. Get it and then get on your knees at the end of the bed."

She blinked, dipped her head, offering me the sexiest smile I'd ever seen, and dropped her eyes in obedience.

"Yes, sir."

WAS it possible to fuck yourself bowlegged?

If it could be done, I figured I'd probably managed it last night. I'd never gone so hard for so long. I found I liked it best when Roxanne let me pleasure her and I denied my own desire for as long as I could. The orgasms at the end of those sessions had felt otherworldly.

And *damn*. The way I'd worn her out? I felt like fucking Superman.

She fell asleep face down on her bed after our last go, her knees still bent and her ass in the air, her wrists bound behind her back with the silky scarf. I'd adjusted her so she could breathe, untied her and rubbed her wrists and arms softly. I left her house with a kiss on her forehead and my handprint on her ass.

I also left her two ibuprofen and a full glass of water on the table next to her bed because she was sure to be sore after the battering I'd given her pussy. But she'd said she loved it, and the harder I fucked, the harder she came.

Exploring the control… exploring *her* was all I could think about.

I pulled up an incognito page on my phone and searched BDSM gear, and the results made me drop the phone, and then Merv knocked on my door and pushed it open.

Shit!

"Son? You awake?"

"Yeah."

She stepped inside my bedroom, and I adjusted the sheet over my erection, again like I was fifteen.

"Can you drive me to the doctor? My appointment's at nine. The new car is nice, but I don't wanna go by myself."

"Y-yeah. You feelin' okay?" I grabbed my phone from between my legs on the bed and clicked off the screen as quickly as I could.

"Just a little lightheaded."

"Yeah, Mama. Let me change and we'll go."

"Thank you."

She stepped into the hallway and closed the door, and I stripped and threw on clean boxers and jeans and grabbed the flannel hanging off the back of my desk chair, and when I met her in the kitchen, Merv stumbled as she walked to dump her coffee in the sink.

"Mama?"

She set her mug on the counter, and it almost tumbled off the edge, but I reached forward and nudged it further back. She turned toward me, and the fear I saw on her face scared me down to my bones.

She stuttered, "I th-think... think somethin's wrong."

———

THE AMBULANCE WOULD'VE TAKEN TOO long to get out to her house, so I ransacked Merv's bathroom and found a bottle of aspirin and made her chew two, and then I drove her and met the paramedics at Dr. Whitley's clinic in town, the whole time begging silently for her not to have a stroke or a heart attack. For her to live.

I'd wasted so much time being antithetical, thinking I was better and different from my family, resenting my dad and what he'd done to us all. The way he'd darkened the light, happy family we used to be. I'd barely had time to patch what had been broken between us, but I wanted to. Desperately. I wanted my family back in my life. I wanted them to want me back in theirs.

I was so fucking pissed at myself, and the anger ran through me now as I thought about the contempt I'd felt for my mama all these years. I'd never spoken to her about how life had been for her married to the son of a bitch.

Would she die now and I'd never know?

"Brand?"

Dr. Whitley operated his clinic out of a house in downtown Wisper, and I'd been pacing the waiting area since I'd carried Merv inside and the doctor and his assistant had helped her onto a rolling bed and wheeled her away, but when I heard his voice, I turned on a dime. The soft smile I saw on his face dropped me to my knees because I couldn't decipher its meaning.

Abey and Bax were on their way, but it felt like hours since I'd called them. I'd never needed them more. And I'd never felt more alone.

"Your mother is stable now, but she had a heart attack," Dr. Whitley said. "I suspect it's not the first. She may have been having small attacks she didn't even notice; she reported pain in her neck and jaw and bouts of heartburn and other things that could be symptoms of small myocardial infarctions.

"We'll need to send her for testing, but a cardiologist will be able to discern if it's connected. Thankfully, this time it was mild. You did the exact right thing, giving her aspirin. I've given her medication to help dilate her arteries until a specialist can assess her and come up with a treatment plan. I'm having the paramedics transfer her to the hospital in Jackson."

He laid his old, frail hand on my shoulder, and I lost my careful composure. All the bullshit I'd held inside for so long rushed out of me in sobs. I felt like the worst son for denying my mother for so long when all she'd wanted to do was love me.

"It's okay, son. You got her to help in time."

Dr. Whitley waited for me to sop the mess off my face with my sleeve.

Finally, I stood. "Can I see her?"

"Of course. Sylvia and Cord will be ready to transport her soon, but you can have a few minutes."

"Thank you."

He led me back to his exam room, and when I pushed open the door, Merv's eyes were closed, her breathing a little uneven. She lay on the rolling bed still, and when she heard my boots on the floor, she turned her head toward the wall, probably to hide tears from me, but she said, "I fucked up."

I had never heard my mother utter the word "fuck." In fact, she'd smacked me more than once for saying it, and hearing it now from her mouth nearly knocked me right back down to my knees.

"Mama?"

Her choked voice and tight throat told me she was holding back tears. "I spent years smokin' and abusin' the one body God gave me and look what happened. Look what I did to myself. I could've died."

"But you didn't."

"But I could've. What if you hadn't been home?"

I shuddered at the thought. "But I was."

She nodded and finally looked at me, and we both cried.

"I'm so sorry I haven't been here," I whispered. I grabbed the back of the chair in the corner and dragged it to her bedside, then sat and reached for her hands folded together over her stomach. I gripped them tightly. "I won't do that to you again."

"It's okay, Brand. You needed space. I understood. I didn't blame you."

"But my absence hurt you. I'm sorry. I love you. I don't know what I would've done if—"

"I love you too, son." She squeezed my hands in hers. "Thank you for savin' my life."

I DIDN'T KNOW where else to go, but when I pulled up in front of 417 Tacoma Avenue after Merv had fallen asleep in her room at the hospital, I hadn't even thought to call or text Roxanne to make sure she was home. Her truck sat parked in the driveway, though, and her living room light glowed behind the curtains hanging in her front windows.

As I opened my door and stumbled out of the SUV I'd bought for Merv, the curtains rustled, and three seconds later, her front door opened, and there she stood, Roxanne's tall, steadfast frame and warm arms exactly the balm I needed.

"Brand? I heard about your mama. Is she okay? Are *you* okay?"

I shook my head. I couldn't speak. The knot of fear still lodged in my chest had worked its way up to my throat and was choking me now too.

With feet covered in pink, furry slippers, she stepped down her cracked, poured-concrete porch stairs.

This goddess deserved better than cracked concrete.

I didn't need to speak. She seemed to understand that I was not okay, and when I reached her, she held my face between her hands, warming away the chill I thought I'd feel for the rest of my life.

She looked into my eyes, conveying to me without a word that whatever I needed to say or do, I'd be safe with her, so I lifted her silently and carried her inside, and until well into the night, she let me release my fear inside her body.

CHAPTER FIFTEEN

ROXANNE

"WHY DID YOU LEAVE WISPER?" I asked, and Brand hid his face above the swell of my naked hip, dipping his head below my rumpled covers, rubbing his soft lips over the skin beneath my rib cage and soothing the fingerprints he'd left there.

"I'm not sure I know how to explain. My old man was a piece of work. The biggest asshole you've ever met, and I needed to get away from him. Bax wasn't my dad's biggest fan either, but he loved workin' the land. He hated sheep." Brand laughed, and his breath tickled over my skin. "But he always knew this was where he needed to be.

"Not me. I wanted out. I needed to be somewhere else, somewhere the smell of sheep shit and desperation didn't cling to my clothes, somewhere I could breathe. If I had stayed, I'd be a different man now. Maybe not a good one."

"Do you regret leavin'?"

He nodded. "I regret that I stayed away so long. My dad's been dead nine years now. I knew things here weren't great. Knew my brothers and sister were strugglin', knew Merv was unhappy, but I was selfish, and I pushed it from my mind and focused on the things *I* needed." He curled into a ball beside me, his arm draped over my stomach. "What if I hadn't come home? What if Merv had been alone today?"

Stroking my hand lazily over his tanned shoulder, connecting the faint freckles there with a finger, I whispered, "But you did come home, and she wasn't alone."

"Thank God. I never would've forgiven myself if…"

"Hey." I tugged a lock of his soft brown hair between my fingers, and he looked up my body. God, his eyes held so much pain. It wasn't something he often let others see, of that I was sure. "Don't go there. It doesn't help you or your mama if you wallow in the what ifs. She's in good hands up in Jackson. The doctors will come up with a plan to get her healthy again, and you and Abey and the family will be there to help her."

He nodded. "I know you're right, but there was an hour today when I didn't know if she'd make it. I can't describe the feelin' inside my body while I raced her to Dr. Whitley and waited for him to tell me if she was dead or alive."

His arm around my body tightened, and he slipped his other beneath my back and held onto me like a lifeline. Like I was the only port in his shitstorm. His grip was almost painful, the tips of his fingers burrowing into my skin, but I let him cling to me because I loved the violent way he needed me.

I had never felt more wanted or needed than the way Brand had made me feel over the last week.

Not within my family, not at work, not in any of the pitiful excuses of relationships I'd had. No one had ever held me the way Brand was, like he'd crawl inside me if he could.

He'd given me power over *him.* He'd opened up to me about things that weren't easy to talk about, and knowing he trusted me enough to be vulnerable was just as tantalizing as it felt to be under his command and his body.

"There's still so much left unsaid, you know?" he whispered. "Today, I could've lost my chance to tell her. To explain to her who I am and why I left. And I think that's what scared me the most."

"So, you'll say it now."

He nodded and asked, "What about you? You said before that your family has a lot of expectations."

"Yeah. I love them fiercely, but I think you and I have more in common than we know."

"How so?"

"Mm. I was different than my sisters. I've never wanted what they did. And I'm... anxious. You know?"

"You fidget."

I blushed, embarrassed he'd noticed. No one ever had before, besides Aubrey. "Yeah. Always have. I don't know. I guess I see the negative around me. I can get obsessed about it. I don't try to, but I do, and I guess I try to distract myself from all the bad stuff I see every day."

"I imagine in your job, that could be pretty depressing. Traumatic even."

"Yeah. But I wouldn't change it. I wouldn't give up my job for anything. After high school, I knew I wanted to be in law enforcement. My uncle Al is a cop, and I've looked up to him since I was ten years old. He worked the Oklahoma City bombing. He's a hero. He helped so many people." I smiled, thinking of Al and what he'd curse at me if he heard me call him a hero. "But in our family, girls get married. They pop out kids and make a home. I didn't want that.

"Don't get me wrong. There's nothin' wrong with that life. And actually, I'd love to be married, to know my husband was at home, waitin' on me. I respect my sisters and how hard they work at home with the kids. But I needed somethin' different.

"I've got this… *thing* inside me. I need to help people too. It's what fulfills me, you know? It's who I am." I shook my head against the pillow. "But my mama still calls once a week to nag me about bringin' a man home for the holidays and the kids I'll never have."

"Hm. And if you did bring someone home? Tell me what that would look like."

"Well, if I had *my* way, he'd show up on his valiant steed and shut my mama up, but then he'd back me up and tell her how proud he is of me and the job I do." Massaging my fingertips through Brand's hair, I said, "He would of course be the *most* handsome man in the world, he wouldn't care that I'm weird, and he'd be head over heels in love with me. He'd probably propose in front of the whole family, and we'd ride off into the sunset and they'd all be left speechless."

Brand smiled up at me. "You've given this some thought."

"Yeah, well, I've had the time. And I've dated enough Mr. Wrongs to know what I don't want."

We were quiet for a while, and I kept up my slow tousling of his hair. Whatever weirdness or difference I had inside me seemed to be calmed when I touched him.

"Roxanne, do you know what neurodivergence is?"

I shrugged. "Not really. I mean, isn't it like autism?"

"That's one form, but neurodivergence just means that your brain works a little differently than most people's. One of my project leads, Tweety, is neurodivergent. It makes him uncomfortable when he has to deal with people he doesn't know, but the man is one hell of a lead. He's only twenty-six, but he's already well on his way to runnin' my whole company."

"Tweety?"

"Yeah. His name is Jason Kendrick, but he wears cartoon T-shirts every day, so the crew started callin' him Tweety."

Brand's hands still clinging to me began to move. They slid from beneath me and to my knees slowly. He spread them and moved his body between them, kissing my thighs, tickling the backs of my knees with his tongue, and the barely controlled need in his eyes when his gaze met mine again began to clear away the conversation between us.

"Is that... unappealing? My quirks. Am I not who you want?"

He shook his head. "It's who you are. There's nothin' wrong with bein' different. Haven't you noticed I'm a little different too? I think it's why I'm so drawn to you."

He couldn't have answered any more perfectly. "Really?"

He nodded, pushing my bent legs down to the mattress. "This is who *I* am, Roxanne," he said, my name a rasp from his mouth. "And you are what I want and what I *need*." His elbows dug into the tender skin of my thighs, pressing them harder to the bed, and he spread my pussy lips open with his thumbs and fixed his eyes on the part of me other men had barely glimpsed, but Brand stared at my body like he wanted to memorize the sight of my wet, pink, swollen skin.

He'd already dragged me to sweet perdition and back tonight, but there was no mistaking that he was ready to do it again.

He bent his head, and his tongue peeked out of his mouth before he took a long, slow lap between my legs. Goose-bumps rose all over me, and I cried out in ecstasy.

"What a mess I've made between your legs, beauty," he whispered, and his tongue entered my body, wet and hot, collecting the cum he'd left inside me the last time he'd fucked me.

Curling it onto the flat of his tongue, he rose above me, his biceps flexing and holding him up. He worked our cum in his mouth, mixing it with his saliva. Pursing his lips, he let it drip onto my belly, and he rubbed his spit into my skin with one hand while his other sought things inside me I had no words for.

But we didn't really need words anymore. Not tonight.

His calloused fingers worked me, the hilt of his hand pounding my pubic bones with every pump.

His eyes met mine again, possession and some kind of depravity I'd never seen before shining through his blue irises. "I want to break this pussy. Wreck it so no other man can have it. No more Mr. Wrongs. Tell me yes."

"*Yes*," I consented instantly, but in my head thought, *but we may need to set some boundaries and come up with a safe word.* "Basketball," I blurted and he stilled, probably thinking I'd lost my mind. "That's my safe word. If I say basketball, stop what you're doin'."

A curt nod was his only response before he descended again and euphoria rushed through me as he proceeded to indeed wreck my pussy with his wicked, *wicked* hands and mouth.

YAWNING WIDELY, I leaned back against the headrest in Dan's cruiser.

Most days, I prided myself on my astute dedication and my ability to be engaged on the job no matter the things going on in my personal life, but today my whole body felt like it was being dragged behind Dan's truck by a rope tied to the bumper.

I'd never been so tired, but I giggled to myself when the words "rope" and "tied" passed through my head.

My phone pinged with a text from my youngest sister, Cecily, and when I looked at my screen, I saw the meme she'd sent: a picture of Betty White from the *Golden Girls,* holding two light sabers, and the text read "Always be yourself, unless you can be a Jedi Betty White."

I snorted, and Dan bristled next to me.

"What's goin' on with you?" he asked, depressing his right turn signal, and he veered onto Highway 10, heading southwest. "You seem different today."

We'd gotten a call at the station about someone messing around an abandoned house, but it was so far out in the boonies, we knew we needed to go as a team, just in case real trouble lurked, but we were both expecting to find Teton Tom, an old Army vet who had been camping and living off the land since he'd returned home from the Iraq War. Occasionally, he'd wander through Wisper, and some folks didn't like the sad, dirty look of him.

I would've preferred to take the call on my own, but maybe it was a good idea to have Dan as backup and a distraction, so I couldn't get carried away with the memories swirling around my head of last night and Brand's possessive debauchery.

But *oh*, his sins against my body had been so sweet.

Until Brand, I'd had no idea I could feel so utterly satisfied. Sex with other men grew boring after the second or third time, but not with Brand. I had no clue how it was possible for him to treat me like a princess but pound, scratch, and smack at the same time, all the while demanding my obedience, and I hoped it would never end.

And the way he cared for and replenished me afterward was so thorough and touching. A full water bottle was never far from my hands, and he insisted on us finishing our escapades in the shower so he could cleanse us both. And he loved to brush my wet hair after our showers and rub lotion all over me, which then led to more sex and more showers.

When I arrived at the station this morning, a text from him appeared on my phone, asking if I'd taken my vitamins or had eaten.

He said he'd ordered something for us that would arrive at my house tomorrow, and the mystery excited me so much that I was getting wet in Dan's truck, just imagining what it might be… fluffy, non-county-issued cuffs? A blindfold? I had no idea, but limitless and darkly seductive possibilities raced through my head.

He forbade me to open the box when it arrived. I was to wait for him to—

Dan's voice jerked me back to reality. "Roxi?"

"Huh?" I rolled down my window so the cool fall air rushing in could bring my body heat down a notch or two, and I pulled my hair into a low pony, so it would be out of the way when I put my hat back on when we arrived at the call.

"I asked if you're okay. You're distracted."

"Oh." I straightened and ran my hands over my vest to make sure all my tools were still attached and at the ready. I hadn't realized I'd begun to slide down the seat a little, my body relaxing and becoming pliant already for the domination Brand would inflict on me soon. "No. I'm fine, just thinkin' about some stuff."

Dan's covert wellness check when he snuck a glance at the expression on my face made a laugh bubble out of my mouth. Could he tell that I was imagining being whipped and chained to my already broken bed?

To steer him far away from that subject, I asked, "You hear about Abey's mama?"

"Yeah," he said, seemingly relieved to have something to chat easily about. "I was outside the station with Sylvia and Cord when the call came in. I followed them over to the doc's place, but my help wasn't needed. Abey was on another call, but she got over to the clinic quick. Her brother drove their mom from her house so they didn't have to wait on the ambulance to get out to their property. It was a pretty tense time for him, I'd bet, but seemed like he had things under control."

Another laugh hiccupped out of me. It was wildly inappropriate, but the word "control" when relating to Brand would forever make me blush.

Dan pulled off the side of the highway and parked, a look of real concern now marring his face. "Seriously, Roxanne, what's goin' on with you? You're actin' weird. It's not like you to laugh at someone's misfortune."

"Oh God, I'm sorry! No, that's not— I wasn't laughin' about Abey's mama's situation. It's somethin' in my personal life. I just can't get it out of my head today."

"Oh." He pulled back onto the highway to drive the last mile we had to go to get to our call. "Do you wanna tell me about it?"

And now a cackle burst from the back of my throat. "Definitely not," I said. "Since when do you and I discuss personal stuff?"

He shrugged. "We could. You're my partner. I... care about you. If you need someone to talk to, it would make sense for you to talk to me."

"Thanks, buddy," I said, and I mock-punched his arm. That was about as touchy-feely as I was going to get from Dan Draven. "I appreciate that, but it wouldn't be appropriate. It's... private."

When he turned onto the gravel drive leading to the abandoned property, he parked and looked over at me again, his shrewd eyes roaming my face, trying to figure out my secrets. Dan had come to Wisper from the military, which was another reason I was glad he was with me today. He understood Teton Tom.

He'd balked and complained about the small-town gossip at first, but now he was just as guilty as the rest of the town. A good, juicy secret was the lifeblood of Wisper. No one was safe from it, but I was so not ready to be at the center of it.

I saw the wheels turning in his head, so I cut him off at the pass. "C'mon. Let's go find Tom, or maybe it's a robber, and we'll get to shoot somebody today."

Dan rolled his eyes, but he pushed open his door, finally ready to work.

CHAPTER SIXTEEN

BRAND

MERV CAME HOME the next evening.

I drove her from the hospital in the new Explorer, and she ran her swollen, arthritic hands over the door and the dash, admiring for the first time the luxury of the model I'd chosen for her, while my sister led us down Highway 20, two car-lengths ahead of us in her cruiser, like we were carrying gold bars in the back seat. Abey just wanted to help, to be there for Merv however she could.

"Thank you again for this car, son," she said, adjusting her seat temperature and fussing with the onboard computer. "Don't think I've ever owned anything so fancy."

"You're welcome, Mama. You deserve it," I said, and I smiled, but inside guilt for abandoning my family gnawed at my stomach. I'd bought the car for her to assuage that guilt and the guilt I felt about Dixon and how I hadn't helped him until it was too late.

I had a lot of guilt for a lot of reasons.

How the fuck had I ever thought a car could make up for it all?

It felt odd to be thrust into Merv's life in such a vital way when I'd been gone from it for so long. But my siblings had busy lives; Bax and Bea had the kids, so they'd already learned to lean on me where Merv was concerned, and I had to admit it felt good.

When I'd come home to visit in the past, it was always a quick trip. The obligatory Christmas eve and morning every other year, a birthday here and there, usually Athena's. But I'd been avoiding home for a long time, and now that I'd moved back, it made me happy to blend in with my family so easily, at least in some aspects. Not all. Relating to my mother was still not an effortless feat.

But the guilt was at war with the happiness I'd felt the last two weeks, and I didn't know how to fix that particular conflict.

"Everything has to change," Merv said as she peered out her window at the passing trees and the cold and gloomy sky. "The way I eat. I'll have to start exercisin'."

"Yes, all of those things are important, but first you need to rest. You have four stents in your heart. You need to heal."

"I just feel so anxious. It feels like I'm out of time."

"I understand, Mama, but you're gonna have to ease into this new life. You heard the doctor."

"Yeah," she mumbled. "But I…"

"What?" I asked, looking away from the road, trying to read the expression on her face. "What's botherin' you?"

"Your brother. What if I die and I don't get to see him again? Will he blame himself like he did when Candy and the baby died? I don't want my heart to be the reason his breaks again."

It damn sure broke my heart hearing her say it. Bax's first wife's aneurysm and death and the subsequent death of their unborn son were not Dixon's fault, but the facts had never mattered to Dixon. He'd blamed himself from the second

Candy had drawn her last breath because he'd been with her in her truck that day. Bax tried to get through to our brother, but Dixon had refused to listen.

"Mama, Dixon's demons, his addiction has nothin' to do with you."

"It does though," she said. "I raised him. I sat back, watchin' when your daddy hollered at him and punished him for bein' weak. I knew I was babyin' him and holdin' him too close. I shouldn't have done that. But I did, and the damage is done. Maybe if his head hadn't been so messed up with all the alcohol back then, he wouldn't blame himself."

I had no response to that. What she'd said was true, and it had been part of the reason I'd run from home the first chance I got after high school.

"The last time anyone heard from him was a year ago," she said quietly. "Do you think he's still alive?"

She clutched her hand to her heart, but it had nothing to do with the organ or the new hardware holding her arteries open. I had the information that would ease her worries, but I'd promised Dixon I wouldn't say a word, so I grasped her cold fingers and held her hand in mine for the rest of the drive. I might not have figured out how to relate to her yet, but I let her know I was there.

Both my brother and sister were at the house waiting when we pulled up, Athena and Stuey, and Devo and Bea, too, but Merv said she didn't want to be fussed over and that they should all go home, so they did after I promised them outside her bedroom door that I would stay with her and take care of her. They didn't need to worry.

Once I'd gotten her settled in her bed, I made her a cup of chamomile tea and handed her the remote to the TV mounted on her bedroom wall, and I stepped back into the hallway and grabbed my phone from my back pocket.

When my sister answered my call now, she sounded freaked out, like she was ten years old again, looking up to her brothers to protect their family. "What's wrong? Is Mama okay?"

"Oh, sorry. Yeah, she's okay. She's in her happy place, watchin' *Forensic Files* in her room, but I wanted to ask you about somethin'. I didn't mention it when you were here in case she overheard."

"Ask me what?" Abey said.

"Who's the woman I remember hearin' about who finds people? She lives around here, married a rancher, if I remember it right."

"Billie Cade."

"Do you think she could find Dixon? Merv brought him up on the drive home this afternoon. She's scared of dyin', scared he'll blame himself the same way he did when Candy died."

"Shit."

"Yeah. Don't tell Bax. The last thing he needs to be reminded of is his dead wife and kid. He and Bea are happy. I don't want Dixon to fuck it up. He's not even here and he still has the power to break us. Just like Dad."

"Ain't that the truth," my sister said and then mused, "I don't know what Billie can do that I haven't, but it's worth a shot. Billie's kind of a mastermind. If anyone could find Dixon, it'd be her. I'll call her."

"Tell her money's not an issue, if that matters."

"Not to Billie. I'll let her know, but she and Carey are good friends, and she's in my book club. She probably won't take your money."

"Okay, but offer it anyway."

"I will. I'll let you know what she says."

"Thanks, sis."

"You got it. I'll talk at ya tomorrow."
"Night."

———————

BECAUSE OF MERV'S heart attack, I had completely forgotten about bringing dinner to the Manning family. Natalie had been released from the same hospital Merv had just been discharged from, and the family was resting at Cowboy Court, gearing up for their drive home.

When Bax, Bea, the kids, and I finally visited with them, I offered to fly them home and hire someone to drive their vehicle back to Nebraska, but Xavier had declined. Maybe it was pride, or maybe it was just that the father needed to find some kind of control after what happened to his daughter.

I could respect that, and I damn sure understood it.

So, instead, we ate José's food together from paper plates, all of us crammed into the Mannings' cabin, and then pigged out on dessert made by Carey's wife, Frannie. Natalie said she was in a chocolate coma because Frannie had heard that Natalie loved hazelnut chocolates. The rich indulgences Frannie had made for the Mannings had crispy, candied hazelnut centers surrounded by dark-chocolate mousse and a milk-chocolate ganache coating, and they were the most decadent things I'd ever tasted. They could've been served in the most expensive restaurant in the world and wouldn't have been out of place.

I'd invited Roxanne, but she and my sister were busy at work and couldn't get the time away. But Roxanne promised to see the Mannings before they left town the next day. Natalie wanted to say goodbye to the woman who'd found her when she was lost.

Plus, there was still the issue of our time together being a secret. The Mannings wouldn't have cared, but if Bax and Bea knew, they'd tell Abey, and Roxanne wasn't ready yet.

I'd started to wonder when she would be ready. But whatever this thing was between us, it was still new, so I didn't push.

Over the last several days, I found myself missing her, but work caught up to us both, and in the blink of an eye, a week had passed. The Mannings had made it safely back home to Nebraska, and life seemed to be moving on.

Abey called her friend, Billie, but after a few days, Billie had reported back that she'd found no sign of Dixon, wherever he was, but she wasn't done searching. It would of course take time, but Billie was some kind of computer genius, so she'd set up programs to do the work for her when she couldn't focus on Dixon.

I didn't hold much hope, but I'd kept the truth to myself. For the purpose of her searches, I'd told Billie what I knew when she called to get more information from me, that Dixon's last known location was Redding, California, but Abey still had no clue. If she knew, she'd tell the rest of our family, and then all hell would break loose.

Maybe it was self-preservation that made me withhold possibly the most vital piece of information concerning Dixon, but like a coward, I had hoped Abey's friend would find our brother, and then the decision to come clean to my family would be taken out of my hands.

Would I ever feel clean where Dixon was concerned?

Before I knew it, Tab was rushing me out of Merv's house because we were meeting Gina Scott at the coffee shop downtown, and then she and I had reservations at a restaurant in Jackson to discuss the new affordable-housing project we'd both been hired to build in the spring.

I hated the feeling inside my chest as I dressed, thinking I knew Gina well enough to be comfortable around her, but I also wanted to be nothing but professional with her. There would be no ambiguity about who we were to each other. We were coworkers and colleagues, nothing more.

And when Tab and I entered Coffee Shot and saw Gina waving across the café at us, even colleagues felt like too much.

I'd forgotten how striking Gina was, with her long, black hair, blue eyes, and perfectly toned body, but I felt no attraction to her anymore. All I felt was uneasiness and exhaustion, knowing how much I'd come to dislike working with her.

Warring against that, wild anticipation rushed through me because Coffee Shot wasn't far from the sheriff's station, and I hoped once again for a glimpse of Roxanne.

Looking over my shoulder and out the café window, I thought, *Just one glimpse. It's all you need. One secret smile.* Just seeing Roxanne would fill me back up after a week of taking care of Merv, of paperwork and glaring computer screens, phone calls, and decision making, and now this meeting with Gina.

One look from Roxanne would wash away the guilt that ate at me every damn minute of the day.

But I saw no sign of her, so, resigned, I moved across the café, and Gina stood as Tab and I approached her table.

She didn't extend her hand to Tab, but she took mine and held it a little too long to be appropriate or comfortable, looking in my eyes and dipping her chin. When she let go, she smoothed her hand over her ass, tucking her skirt as she sat again, but she was also trying to force my attention to her body. It was a move she'd used on me many times.

My eyes tracked Gina's as I held a chair for Tab and then sat next to her. But I wasn't looking with interest. It was more like I was a rabid guard dog, getting ready to growl and bite if she pushed me too far.

"Gina, nice to see you again," I said.

Tab dove right into work. "I printed out the files you sent, Ms. Scott." She handed a thin file folder to Gina, and Gina took it from Tab's hand, but her gaze never left mine. She was studying me, trying to ascertain what had changed with me. Since we last spoke, everything had changed in my life.

"Thank you."

"Okay," Tab said, probably sensing the tension between Gina and me. "Well, I guess that concludes my duties for this meeting. Enjoy your dinner."

Tab stood, and Gina flashed her a curt and impatient smile.

"Thanks, Tab," I said, interrupting the possessive stare Gina had fixed on my face. "I'll call you first thing tomorrow. We need to check in with Bea and Clay at the inn site, and we can start scheduling interviews."

"Sure thing, boss," Tab said. She saluted me and walked to the counter to order a green tea latte, her usual.

Nodding at the folder in front of Gina, I said, "Shall we go? We can have a look at that at the restaurant."

"Of course," Gina purred. "It's so good to see you, Brand. I've really missed your smile."

If she only knew that the smile she was professing dramatically to miss was a practiced one. It wasn't the same smile I reserved for Roxanne or for my family when I was truly happy.

As we stood, Gina grabbed her purse and the laptop case she'd hooked over the back of her chair with the housing plans she'd soon be showing me and came to my side. I reminded myself to be a gentleman, and I guided her toward the exit with my hand at the small of her back. She smirked and straightened, pushing her breasts out in front of her and arching her back just enough to make every man in the café take notice of her ass.

I held the door open for her, but just before Gina stepped over the threshold, a woman rushed in.

Roxanne's name left my mouth when we made eye contact, and my heart began to race.

I had been wrong that just one look would be enough to sustain me, because as I took her in, noticing the flicker of our secret flashing through her brown eyes and a tinge of excitement blushing on her cheeks, the need I felt to hear her say my name and cry out when I made her come nearly knocked me on my ass.

Roxanne's eyes traveled the shape of my face, but then they landed on Gina in front of me and my hand still held out toward her.

I wanted to tell Roxanne how much I'd missed her all week, but I didn't. That would've been inappropriate in this business setting, so I said, "Hello, Deputy, nice to see you," but I hoped she could hear the need I felt for her in my voice and read it on my face.

She opened her mouth but said nothing, and as Gina sighed with annoyance at Roxanne blocking her path, Roxanne focused once again on my hand at Gina's back.

I nodded at her, knowing she'd understand my silence. After all, it was what Roxanne wanted, and I followed Gina into the bright, autumn afternoon.

But it felt like fifty kinds of wrong not to reach for Roxanne, not to push Gina out of our way and kiss her in the sunshine.

The last place Roxanne belonged was in the shadows.

CHAPTER SEVENTEEN

ROXANNE

'HELLO'? *'Nice to see you'?*

What the fuck was that?

Thoughts of finding Teton Tom out at the abandoned house when Dan and I had driven out there and how he was now enjoying ESPN on Dan's couch while he rested his twisted ankle dissolved from my head.

Plopping down in a chair after Brand and his... *date* left Coffee Shot, I felt the wind leave my sails. The whole fucking boat sank, and I stared out the café's big Main Street window as the man I was pretty sure I'd been falling in love with and the painfully beautiful woman walked away. Her sexy, flowing black hair shone like obsidian in the sun and fluttered lightly in the wind, and it only highlighted further that she was probably only five-six.

Her high heels, though, they gave her a step up and accentuated the most perfect ass in a pencil skirt I'd ever seen on a woman. My own ass beneath me felt like a flubbery seat cushion that had always had a very distinctive heart shape, and in my uniform? Forget about it. There were no perfect, round globes on my backside. The only way to obtain those bouncing orbs would be butt implants, and just thinking about two of them digging into my glutei maximi during a stakeout made me cringe.

Brand held his hand behind the woman's back to guide her where he wanted her to go, not touching her, but fucking close enough!

One-two-three.

Dear God, the man looked *fine* in a suit jacket. The deep charcoal color made his eyes almost glow blue, and it fit him like it had been made specifically for him. Maybe it had been. He could afford bespoke business wear.

And goddammit, he'd worn a cowboy hat. A fucking cowboy hat and it was so hot, I hadn't been able to speak!

For her?

Why had he never worn it for me? Because if he had, there were things hidden in my mind I'd read about in book club and imagined alone in the dark of my bedroom on lonely nights, and those things he would earn simply by showing up in that smoke-colored, felt, sex hat.

I hadn't even known he owned one, but that woman got the corporate cowboy version of Brand, and I didn't? Why? 'Cause I was a cop? 'Cause I wasn't gorgeous like her? Probably.

One-two-three.

His jeans hugged his thighs like I wanted to, and the crisp, white shirt beneath his jacket molded to his chest. The jacket itself was a perfect fit, and it wrapped his biceps and pecs like a present.

He'd worn brown snakeskin, square-toed cowboy boots, but they were expertly worn in. Even they were sexy, and the brown belt around his waistband and his flashy, silver belt buckle made my mouth water when I imagined what he could do to me with that strap of leather and what the imprint of the buckle would look like on my skin.

My hands fisted on the café table, and I wanted to bang my head on it. What the hell had I even been thinking? There was no way a man like Brand Lee would want me. Sure, maybe for a few hard pokes of his stick, but not for the long haul. He had money. Connections. He needed a woman like Miss Laser Hair Removal. She probably wore designer crotchless panties.

"Ughhh."

As I tried to curb the obsessive need I felt to tap out "The Star Spangled Banner" on my leg, I felt a presence standing just behind my shoulder. Whoever it was smelled like Cinnamon Toast Crunch cereal, but I couldn't be bothered to turn to find the source of the delicious breakfast scent.

From my reaction to Brand and his raven-haired mistress, the whole town of Wisper probably already knew Brand and I'd had a fling, or a three-night stand, or whatever the hell the gossip mill would call it.

So then they shouldn't be surprised about the ugly, flat-out jealousy I felt toward the woman crossing Washington Street with Brand, now hanging on his arm and laughing, like they were lovers who'd just met by happenstance but couldn't believe their luck, and now they would go to her car, and he'd drive to a hotel. Not a motel. No, there would be no cheap, discounted room in the middle of the night. They'd drive to Jackson, and Brand would whip out a stiff, black credit card at the fanciest joint in town, probably with teardrop-shaped crystal chandeliers, and they'd spend whole days and nights ordering room service and fucking politely.

Not like me and Brand. Every time we'd been together, our sex was the opposite of polite. It was messy and hard and possessive. It was the kind of sex you had with a... secret. With a mistress.

Wait, am I the mistress in this scenario?

"Of course that's how this story ends," I whispered to myself, giving in and letting my fingers tap to their heart's desire. I rolled my eyes and tried to breathe undramatically, but my lungs wouldn't seem to cooperate. Air wheedled its way up my throat, like a stubborn five-year-old being pulled through a department store by her mama, but a loud breath finally squeaked out of my mouth when the person behind me spoke.

"Gina Scott."

"Huh?" My head whipped itself around at the female voice belonging to the person now bent and peering over my shoulder. "Oh, Tabitha." I acknowledged her, but my head turned right back around like a scene out of *The Exorcist*. Great, now Brand and his hussy had stopped on the sidewalk. His date used her hands to talk, as if she couldn't waste one precious ounce of her kinetic energy in case it might turn him on too. "Hi."

Completely deflated and trying not to whine like a wounded dog, I sighed. And had Tabitha never heard of personal space? She was practically cheek to cheek with me. I hadn't even noticed she and her eerily perky double Ds had been in Coffee Shot with Brand and the mystery woman, but could the universe send me any more hints? *You're not good enough. You're too old. Too tall. Too imperfect. Not pretty enough. You're not interesting enough to be CEO girlfriend material.*

One-two-three.

"Hi," Tabitha said brightly, and she pulled the chair opposite me closer and sat next to me, so she could watch the almost-PDA down the street too. She set her to-go cup on the table between us and flicked her fingers toward the window. "Call me Tab. Everybody does, and that wretch of a woman is Gina Scott, Brand's ex-girlfriend."

There was my confirmation. Old lovers. "I knew it."

"He can't stand her."

"Oh right, it sure looks like he hates her," I said miserably, watching as Gina leaned closer to Brand and brushed her lips against his cheek. To his credit, Brand didn't react, but it still made me want to murder them both.

Tabitha shook her head. "He's being professional. Gina is the lead architect in charge of the subsidy homes project Lee Construction is contracted to build in the spring."

Really? Oh.

My face must've shown my irritation because Tabby Cat laughed. "They're not together. I promise."

"Yeah, but then why did he act like he didn't even know me, like we haven't—" Heat crawled up my neck and lit my face on fire. I was sure flames had burst into existence on my cheeks and a big, flashing text bubble had appeared above my head. It probably read: *I'm having sex with Brand Lee, but I'm not good enough for him. Wisperites, discuss!*

Tab didn't flinch or react. She shrugged. "Brand doesn't talk to me about his personal matters. We're close, but he has firm boundaries about that kind of thing. Although, he's loosened up a bit since he's been back home. But I'm a very observant person. It's part of what makes me so good at my job. I have to anticipate what my boss wants before he even knows he needs it."

I raised my eyebrows. Sounded like a whole lot of boundary crossing to me.

"Not like *that*," Tab said, and she swatted my hand on the table. "But I pay attention, and my keen observations tell me that Brand really dislikes Gina. You have to understand though. Brand has put his entire life into Lee Construction. He wouldn't do or say anything to jeopardize his company, including saying no to Gina Scott.

"Especially now. He's taken a big gamble, moving the company to Wisper. It's a whole new ball game down here. New rules, new nuances, and new asses to kiss in order to win bids for jobs he wants. Gina is one of those asses. Or her bosses are."

"How long did they date?" I asked as Brand and Gina Scott disappeared down the road. I leaned forward in my chair, craning my neck and hoping for a few more seconds of visibility, but they were all the way down by Franklin Street now.

"For a few months last year. Brand ended it." Tab sipped her frothy, pea-green latte and licked the residual foam from her lip, and the investigator in me came out.

"Why?"

"Officially, I have no idea. Like I said, he doesn't usually talk to me about that kind of thing. But unofficially?"

I rolled my eyes and nodded. Of course I wanted to know what she thought. "Unofficially, Brand and this Gina Scott broke up because…? Fill in the blank, please, Tabitha."

"Because she's a shallow asshole."

Hm. I liked that answer.

"Go on."

"Brand has a type." She looked me up and down. "Or he used to, and Gina is it. I've only worked at Lee Construction for a year, so I wasn't around before Gina, but from other employees, I learned that he's always dated… mm, professional women. Not like you and me."

"What?" How offensive! "You don't think I'm professional?"

"No!" Tab rushed to say. "Of course I do. I meant, like, white-collar, architect, business-y kind of professional."

"Oh," I said, tapping my leg again. Okay, a tiny bit less offensive. "But you and I are nothin' alike."

"Really? You don't think so?"

I shook my head. Tab was all seductress, Instagram Reel perfection, with a tiny frame, big boobs, sixty-watt smile, and I was... nerdy Roxi. Awkward, too tall, and too middle class for Brand. Okay fine, low, *low* middle class.

"You're from Oklahoma. I'm from Missouri. Bible-Belt central and Tornado Alley. My guess is that you come from a small town and a big family. I have three brothers and a sister."

"I have five sisters."

She nodded. "Do your parents still go to church every Sunday morning and Wednesday evening?"

"How'd you guess?"

"'Cause mine still do too."

"Okay, but people from small towns can still be CEOs."

"You're right." She flipped her auburn waves over her shoulder and took another sip of her drink. "I guess I just meant that Gina isn't exactly what I'd call 'down to earth,' not like you and me."

"Oh."

I wasn't sure how I felt about her comparison or the many, glaring differences between Brand's ex and me. Tab wasn't wrong that we were clearly different. And while I berated myself silently for being the opposite of what Brand usually wanted, I didn't wish I was more like this Gina Scott. I liked who I was. I loved my job and my family, and if having Brand meant changing my identity, then we really were a no-go.

When I realized it was true, a weird confidence flowed

through me because I knew myself well, and surely that was an attractive quality.

I didn't think he wanted me to change, but I couldn't stop my brain from hanging onto the image burned into it of Brand escorting the fancy-schmancy vixen out of the coffee shop. And now my retinas were burning, too, as they pictured Brand and Miss Boyfriend Stealer ensconced in their fancy hotel together, her perfectly toned calves wrapped around Brand's neck while he went to town on her expertly waxed, rich-lady bits.

Arghh!

My phone dinging with a text from Brand cleared the jealousy from my body, but only for a few seconds. I just couldn't stop seeing Gina Scott writhing in the throes of passion with my… What exactly was Brand Lee to me?

5:32 PM

Tonight. Be ready for me. 10pm.

I didn't respond. Why would I? What would I even say? *Yes, sir. I'll be waiting so your girlfriend can turn you on but then you can act out all your fantasies on your white-trash booty call after she squeaks through her elegant orgasm and falls asleep in the chic, trendy hotel you paid for.*

CHAPTER EIGHTEEN

ROXANNE

"HOW WAS YOUR *DINNER*?" I asked when Brand showed up at my duplex at 10 p.m. on the dot, the top three buttons of his shirt open, jacket missing, his blue baseball cap now shading his eyes instead of his cowboy hat.

As much as I loved that Lee Construction cap on him, it didn't escape my notice that he hadn't worn it around Gina Scott, and no matter how hard I tried, I couldn't disguise the jealous tinge to my voice.

His careful gaze caressed my face, lingering on my mouth for a moment, but as it lifted to take in my expression, his intelligent eyes missed nothing. They narrowed the littlest bit, eyebrows furrowing for half a second as he stepped inside my door.

"It was fine," he said. "Just business. I'm glad it's over."

Turning away from him, I walked to my kitchen. I needed a drink. "I'm sure you are."

"I missed you this week," he said, his gaze now following mine as it roamed my living room. I looked everywhere but at him. He tilted his head. "Roxanne? Are you... *jealous*?" His voice was a low hum as he tracked me, almost menacingly so, but when I finally glanced at him, a smile lifted the edges of his lips.

I turned to face him. With a jut of my chin, I said, "No," and I spun away.

"Don't lie to me." He touched my arm with the tips of two fingers, but when I tried to yank it away from their warmth, they slid to my wrist, and his hot hand closed around it.

"I didn't lie."

"Yes, you did, and if you do it again—" He paused, and his voice was dangerously seductive when he finished his sentence. "I may have to punish you."

Reaching above the fridge, I grabbed the bottle of whiskey I kept for special occasions, though the bottle was still sealed. What special thing had happened to me in the last two years?

There was nothing until I met Brand.

Annoyance and desire fought for control inside me. I didn't want to admit that I'd been more jealous today than a fifteen-year-old girl watching her boyfriend flirt with a sixteen-year-old bombshell at the weekly football game, but it was true, even after Tab explained. But the images my mind conjured of just how Brand might punish me made my whole body shudder.

I wasn't a liar, though, at least not a very good one if I wasn't interrogating a suspect at work, so I let him turn me with a tug of his strong hand.

"Fine. I was jealous but then Tabitha told me who Gina was."

"And that settled it for you?" he deduced, searching my face, like a detective himself, looking for clues of deception.

Without blinking, my eyes met his, and I stood tall. "Yes."

"Liar."

I scoffed. "You're awfully sure of yourself. Why should I care who you date?"

Turning away, I jerked my wrist out of his grasp, intending to escape to my bathroom with the whiskey and slam the door in his face, just for dramatic effect. I didn't need to use the restroom, but I could see no way to end the conversation without admitting I cared for him. In private, I could let my tics and my anxiety run wild. I could let my insecurities roar in my head and admit to myself without shame that I'd been so jealous when I saw him with his ex today that my whole world had turned green.

But Brand had no intention of letting me storm off to prove my point, whatever that was. And it seemed he was not about to let me wallow.

He seized both my wrists this time, and his hands slid slowly up my arms. He took the bottle from my hand, set it on the counter, and pulled me against his body, nuzzling his nose into my hair at the back of my neck and letting me feel his erection against my ass.

"Would it make you feel better if I told you that throughout the entire dinner, all I could think about was you?"

"Now who's lyin'?"

"Roxanne, if you're under some kind of impression that there isn't one moment of my day I'm not rememberin' our time together, you're wrong."

"Right," I said, sarcasm dripping from my mouth, "'cause you're all about dollar-store merchandise. Everything you do, everything you own is top shelf. I'm not good enough, and you proved it when you acted like you didn't even know me at the coffee shop."

"Because *you* said you wanted to keep this between the two of us," he growled in my ear, almost betraying his normally perfect composure. "Half of Wisper was in that café. I did that for *you*."

"Yeah, right. You did it for her. You did it so your beautiful girlfriend wouldn't know you'd been slummin' it with me."

His hands tightened around my upper arms. "*Ex*-girlfriend," he said, a warning clear in his tone. "You are *more* than enough, and she's nothin' compared to you. Not in my eyes. I broke it off with her because when I looked at her, I felt apathy. I could barely get it up around her in the end. She may seem beautiful on the outside, but inside, she's vacant and manipulative, and I wanted more than that in my life.

"*You* are so much more." He thrust his hips once. "Do you feel that?"

Oh, I felt it all right, his dick hard as steel and digging into my non-bouncy, heart-shaped ass.

"You do that to me. I've never been so hard in my life."

"So I'm good enough to get you hard, but can you honestly stand there and tell me I'm your type? I'm not the kind of girl you take home to your mama."

"You've already met my mother."

"Not my point."

"What will it take to convince you?"

He rocked against me, his hard cock trying to tunnel out of his jeans and between my shaking thighs, and all my jealous thoughts and the blatant lust I felt for him became a swirling tornado in my mind. They reminded me of what Tab had said, how we were both from Tornado Alley, how I wasn't Brand's type, and how I was too "down to earth" for him.

"What is it you need from me that will show you I want you, not just here in secret, not just at some nondescript motel? That all I think about is you?"

"Dunno," I breathed, pushing back against him and realizing his touch, no matter how soft or hard, calmed the twisting of my mind. And I imagined him taking me right here in the middle of my dingy kitchen.

"That's the third lie you've told me tonight."

Suddenly, I was spinning. The kitchen walls swirled around me like I'd boarded the Tilt-A-Whirl at the county fair. His hands on my hips, Brand guided us to the counter behind me and pressed me against it. The rounded, Formica edge dug into my low back, and his cock did the same to my front.

My old, threadbare, red and white Oklahoma Sooners T-shirt split up the middle like a book being ripped open at the spine, and Brand's hands jerked wide with the fabric still bunched inside them.

He didn't speak, but his pulse hammered away in the thick artery traveling up his neck, and his chest heaved with quick breaths.

Reaching for the whiskey, he uncapped it and his other hand wrapped around my neck. He tilted my head toward the ceiling with the pad of his thumb and let the amber liquid trickle over my aching breasts. It ran between them and down to the waist of my sweats. They soaked up the silky moisture as he leaned over me and licked at the whiskey.

Nipping the tender skin on the side of my right breast with his teeth, he yanked at my sweatpants like he was trying to break into a bank vault on a time crunch. He made quick work of the rope ties at the top, and the sweats fell to the floor.

"Are we definin' our relationship right now, Roxanne?" he asked, his strong grip on my hip possessive, his eyes burning me where his mouth had just been, but his question was clearly rhetorical. "Because if we are, you're the one who needs to set the rules. You didn't want the world to know you were fuckin' me, but now you're jealous of a woman I don't give two shits about because we walked down Main Street together? So tell me what you want from me. Be clear, 'cause I'm inclined to give it to you."

From the red mark he'd left on my skin, he lifted his eyes and fixed his lightning-blue irises on mine, but indecision crossed his face, and he stepped into me. His nice shirt was ruined as it sopped up the sticky liquid and he touched his stomach to mine, his chest rising and falling and training my lungs to breathe with him, and I swore I could feel his heart-beat pulsing beneath his fancy jeans.

He kissed me, moaned into my mouth, and anchored a hand behind my head, his fingers threading through my hair, holding my lips to his. "Tell me now, Roxanne, 'cause I want this, whatever it is. I need it. I need you."

What I wanted—what I *needed* was entirely too bold to say out loud.

In the past, if I had been confident enough to tell a man what I wanted from him, very soon after, I had to figure out how to pick myself up and dust the dirt off my ass without inconveniencing anyone, without causing a commotion. Roxi Riri Fitts didn't deserve a commotion. Her anxieties and inse-curities were a burden. She was the middle sister. That tall daughter of Mr. and Mrs. Fitts. The one without a husband or kids. Her heartache didn't merit a commotion, not like her sisters'.

I whispered, "I want to be the only woman you touch. The only woman you kiss." Looking him straight in the eye, I spoke loud and clearly. "You only fuck me."

"Done." His hands left my body needy and cold, and he backed into my living room with the bottle of whiskey, taunting me to follow as he unbuckled his belt, unbuttoned his jeans, and turned his hat backward, the CEO of Lee Construction fighting for dominance against the farm-raised country boy he used to be.

I followed him slowly, knowing full well the power my naked skin had over him. The only articles of clothing he hadn't yanked off my body were my ripped shirt and my stretchy black pair of bikini-cut underwear.

"You know what I think?" Something inside me wanted to defy him, to argue and push him to some limit I could feel but couldn't see, and oddly, my near nakedness gave me courage.

He shook his head, his eyes tracking my path toward him like a tornado chaser ready to face the big, bad storm. "I'm waitin' with bated breath to hear exactly what you think, Roxanne."

"I think the fact that this is a secret is the only thing makin' you want me. If we came out, told everyone our secret, you wouldn't feel the same."

"And *I* think you're feelin' unsure, and your insecurities are makin' bullshit come out your mouth."

Stopping in the middle of my living room as he lowered to sit on my couch, my mouth popped open, and I gaped like a fish out of water. I had no response to that.

He was right.

"So what's gonna make you sure?" he asked as he reached forward and took my hand, then pulled me so I stood between his legs, looking down at him.

Grabbing the bottle from his hand, I gulped down a shot and swallowed, trying not to let him know how much it burned my throat. The liquid sloshed against the sides of the bottle as I lowered it and let it hang from two fingers next to my thigh. "Take me out."

"Out where?"

"Where everyone can see us. I want you to *not* be professional. I want you to claim me."

He considered me for a moment. I *was* asking him to define us. "You sure you're ready for that? For my sister to see us?"

Arching an eyebrow, I dared him. "Yes."

He stole the whiskey from my hand and took his own shot. "Alright then."

"And your girlfriend too. I want her to hear the gossip. She's still in town, right?" I asked the question, but I could already guess the answer because if Brand were my ex and I thought he was unattached, I wouldn't leave town without at least trying my hand at getting him back.

"*Ex*," he growled, his eyes still tracking me above him. "We'll go out tomorrow night. Agreed?"

I nodded.

"Good," he said. "Now that's settled, where's the package?"

He swigged another mouthful, but he seemed to be having a hard time looking away from my bare chest and my breasts peeking out from behind the ripped fabric of my T-shirt. He pulled at it gently, tugging it off my body, and let the wet, ruined cotton drop to the carpet.

I looked between his legs, at the erection straining to break out of his pants.

"Not *that* package, Roxanne. The one I had shipped to your house."

"Oh." My face heated, and I giggled like an embarrassed teenager. "It's in my bedroom."

"Did you open it?"

"No. You told me not to."

"Good girl," he breathed, shifting his hips on the couch cushion, the movement the only physical sign he'd liked my answer. He let go of my hand. "Go get it and come back to me. I'll wait." He leaned back, relaxing on my couch with his hand slung over the back, the whiskey still dangling from his grip, and he crossed his ankle over his knee, like he didn't have a care in the world. But as he waited for me to do what I'd been told, a little glint sparked in his eyes. "Be quick about it. Don't make me wait *too* long."

Crossing my arms over my breasts, I cocked a hip.

In the lowest growl of a voice, he warned, "You can act like a brat all you want, but if you make me wait much longer, the punishment you'll earn will only get more intense."

The gasp that slipped through my lips was loud.

Brand smiled, and I narrowed my eyes. I couldn't let him know that just the thought of him punishing me was making arousal drip down my thighs.

He gripped his leather belt, let the open strap slip across the palm of his hand. I had to bite back a moan, and I ran. Not because I didn't want him to use the belt on me, but because I didn't possess the self-control to wait for him to put his hands on me one second longer.

The length of my hallway was maybe ten feet, but I sprinted like an Olympic runner in a relay race holding the baton.

The mystery box still sat in the chair in the corner of my bedroom where I'd left it days ago.

I was kind of surprised I hadn't already opened the damn thing, but work had been busy the last week, and when I'd gotten off shift every night, I'd been exhausted. Plus, the excitement of opening it with Brand and the mysterious antic-ipation of discovering the kinks in his head had given me the chill I'd needed to let it sit untouched in the chair.

I grabbed the box and tossed it on my bed, and then

scoured every surface in my room, looking for something sharp to cut through the packing tape, but there was nothing!

My heart raced with anxiety, my breathing fast and unsteady. The urge to please Brand and get my punishment pushed me, made me feel panicked. Whatever it was he intended to give me, I wanted it *bad*, and like a rush from a drug, I wanted the calm that his touch inflicted on me.

I was addicted to it. To him.

Whimpering at the frustration of not being able to find anything sharp enough to cut through the tape, I balled my hands into fists, but then warm hands slid over my hips and between my arms hanging at my sides.

"Let me," Brand said softly, and he reached around me for the box, lifted it in front of me, and ripped the thick, stiff material with his bare hands. The sound of splitting cardboard filled my bedroom, and many wrapped items fell to my bed along with a bunch of six-by-six-inch air-filled, plastic shipping puffs.

A packing slip appeared last, and it fluttered onto my comforter as he tossed the box to the floor next to the bed.

"What is all that?" I asked, but he didn't answer.

Instead, he lifted a sealed and discreet black plastic bag in front of my chest, and his breath rushed over my shoulder.

A dark urgency laced his voice when he whispered, "Bend over."

CHAPTER NINETEEN

BRAND

KNEELING BEHIND ROXANNE, I watched as she leaned forward slowly.

With her torso laid out on the bed and her tits smashed into the comforter, her head turned to the side, lips parted in anticipation, my view was nothing but the backs of her supple thighs and grabbable ass cheeks. My mouth watered to taste her as I dragged her panties down her long legs to the floor and pushed them away.

She smelled sweet, like soft roses and vanilla and the smoky bite of whiskey. I smelled her need, too, and it over-powered the alcohol.

Wrapping the restraint I'd bought for her around one thigh, I tightened it. The leather was as soft as butter, and it slipped easily into place. Her skin spilled over the top, and my dick jumped, still locked inside my pants. Holding her arm next to her leg, I wrapped the smaller Velcro cuff attached to the leather, belt-like restraint around her wrist and secured it.

She tugged her arm, testing the power and connection

between the two pieces, but she couldn't get free, not without my help, and I had to work to not moan at the sight.

When I had the matching restraint secured to her other thigh and wrist, I swiped the other items I'd ordered for us off the side of the bed, and I sat back on my heels to take her in.

I knew from the first moment I met her that she'd be beautiful dressed only in something black and leather, and I was right. I'd wanted her like this since that first night on the highway, with her gun holster hugging the sexiest thigh I'd ever laid eyes on.

Now, it was all I could do not to push down my jeans and fuck her hard from behind, but I hadn't forgotten she'd lied to me, and the restless need I felt to punish her for that itched beneath my skin.

I wanted to bring her as close to orgasm as I could and then take it away. A relentless tease, over and over. It was a reprimand in a way, stopping her from feeling the euphoria of release she craved, but I had a feeling denying her would make it that much more exquisite when I finally allowed her to come, and that was what I really needed from her.

I wanted her shaking, aching, sweating, and I wanted her to scream my name.

I wanted her to know the immeasurable lengths I'd go to please her, that she was the *only* woman I wanted, and that I'd deny myself to give her everything.

She seemed to believe the lies she told herself, that she wasn't as beautiful as other women, or that somehow she didn't measure up. I had no idea where those beliefs had come from, but I wanted to push them from her mind.

In fact, I wanted to slap them out of her.

Standing, I positioned myself on one side of her body. She hadn't spoken since I began strapping her up in black leather, and she was quiet now, but her breathing had quickened, so I explained all the things I wanted to do to her.

"You lied to me, Roxanne," I said, my voice almost a whisper because I was so fucking turned on, I could barely control it. "You've earned my punishment. Do you consent?"

A pulse of air rushed out of her mouth, and riding it was the "Yes" I wanted.

"Good. Remember your safe word?"

"Basketball," she breathed into her duvet.

"Good girl. Don't forget. I'm gonna slap your beautiful ass twice for each lie you told."

She nodded silently, her forehead hitting the mattress eagerly. God, this woman! She wanted whatever I had to give, even though I had no way to explain to her why I wanted to punish and restrain her.

I just... *needed* it.

I licked my lips and dug my teeth into the wet skin, watching her from behind as she began to tremble.

"Are you afraid, Roxanne?"

She stilled. "No, sir."

Goddamn, my heart beat so fast. My chest heaved. The trust she gave me was intoxicating.

Lifting my arm, I tightened my muscles, wanting to hit her hard enough to see my handprint flare on her skin, but I didn't want to hurt her. Not too much. Not so much that she'd make me stop. I'd lose my mind if she did and beg on my knees to fuck her.

She pressed her ass back and higher in the air, inviting me to smack it, so I did. I brought my hand down hard, watching her skin ripple and react to the sudden pressure.

She moaned, and my whole body hardened. Pleasure shot through me like a drug.

The second time was even better; she spread her legs

wider, and I caught a glistening glimpse of her pussy and the arousal now rimming it.

My hand rubbed circles over her skin, smoothing the redness away. "That's one lie punished."

She nodded and wiggled her ass a little, seeking pressure, so I pressed against her, the fly of my jeans soaking up her wetness and rubbing her roughly. She moaned and pushed harder against me, trying to ride the hard ridge of my cock beneath the denim.

She pulled at her restraints, and I smiled when they left her frustrated.

"You wanna touch yourself right now, don't you, Roxanne? Rub your tight clit round and round and get off?"

"Yes, sir."

I slapped her ass again, harder this time but on the other cheek, and she tensed and surged against the mattress.

"Would you like me to finger fuck you? Slide one inside your wet pussy? You're practically drippin' for me now."

"Yes. *Please*."

"Have you earned it yet, Roxanne?"

She whimpered and shook her head, her face rasping against her bedcovers. "No, sir."

My hand cut through the air again, but when it made contact, my ring and pinkie finger slapped her cunt. She gasped and groaned, and a flash of heat pulsed off her skin.

Fuck.

"Did you like that, beauty? You liked what I gave you?" I asked, my rough, calloused hands molding over and caressing the soft, round mounds of her ass.

"Yes, sir," she breathed, her hips now grinding thin air.

Two more. I wasn't sure I could last.

"How 'bout a little reward then?"

"*Please!*"

I thought a tease would give me a moment to compose myself so I didn't explode in my jeans before I'd even finished spanking her, but when my hands gripped her thighs below the leather, I had to bite the inside of my cheek to stop myself coming. The restraints had been padded on the inside, so they weren't pinching her, but the pressure left red lines on her soft, pale skin, and I'd never seen anything sexier.

I crouched behind her and spread her legs wider. I'd brought the whiskey into her bedroom, and it sat next my boot on the floor, so I lifted the open bottle slowly, watching the glowing liquid reflect the light from the streetlight outside as it shined in Roxanne's window.

When I tipped the bottle over her lush ass and a fat drop dripped onto her skin, she gasped softly.

The whiskey sloshed against the sides of the glass, tinkling and flowing out of the mouth of the bottle as I poured out more, and it ran between her ass cheeks and dripped down her pussy, mixing and spicing her cum, and when I licked the liquid from her ass cheek with the pointed tip of my tongue and dragged it to her clit, sucking my new favorite cocktail from her skin, her whole body writhed on the bed. She began to quiver, need shaking her down to a cellular level.

I wanted to shove my tongue inside her, get drunk on her, and drown in her jealousy and insecurity. I wanted to eat her out and take all that doubt inside me so she'd never feel it again, because what I'd told her was true.

She was the only woman I wanted. The only woman I could remember ever wanting so badly that my soul ached for her.

But no. She needed to earn my tongue.

Retreating, I sat back on my heels again, taking her taste with me. The whiskey sweetened it, and my eyes rolled closed when the rich taste hit the back of my throat, and I licked the sloppy wetness from my lips like an animal licking blood off his muzzle after a kill.

I felt like an animal, like a wolf, and she was my Little Red Riding Hood.

I thought if I breathed her in one more time, I might die of euphoria. She was so wet, cum seeped out of her pussy, trying to tempt me to fuck her.

I would. I'd fuck her hard enough to mark her insides, but not yet.

"That's two lies, Roxanne," I whispered, my voice tight and barely discernible as want raged through my body and the alcohol began to bloom in my gut.

She nodded, so I smacked her ass again, this time immediately rubbing the sting away with the hot palm of my hand, while with my other, I reached inside my jeans and fisted my cock.

My zipper was loud when I lowered it, and Roxanne gasped at the sound. I pushed the jeans down, and my dick sprang free and stood up straight against my stomach, my punching breaths making it bounce and dance.

I wanted her to feel the hardness I planned to ram inside her, so I stood and pressed my cock against her swollen lips, letting it slip between them and rub her tight, pink asshole.

The grunt that came from the depths of her lungs made me insane. It raised the hair at the nape of my neck, and my cock swelled and jerked against her.

Picturing breaking into that hole made me shake with desire, but not tonight.

Tonight, I wanted something else from her.

"One more, good girl. Can you take it?"

She moaned and turned her head into her comforter as I

grabbed her hip and held on, clutching her skin and loving feeling it between my fingers.

"Tell me yes," I commanded.

"Yes, sir," she breathed, her voice low, rasping and pleading. Fucking perfect. "*Please*."

Her whole body quaked with anticipation, and I lifted my other hand high in the air, then let it fall fast. I slapped her wet pussy, and the contact cracked in the air around us, the rush of slick from inside her thick and heady as it mingled with the whiskey and coated my hand, and she called out my name.

"Three lies," I breathed, both my hands now gripping her hips, but I bent and lifted the whiskey again. Slowly, I pushed the neck of the bottle inside her.

She gasped, "What?" and looked over her shoulder at me, but the restraints kept her from turning as much as she wanted to.

When she realized what I'd done, she eased back onto the cold glass bottle, her body accepting it easily. She tried to fuck it, but I pulled it out after two pumps of her hips, and I lifted it to my lips.

"More, please, sir," she begged as I deep throated the bottle, and she moaned when I wrapped my lips around the neck and sucked her cum off of it, then tipped my head back and let the rush of alcohol mix with her juice in my mouth.

I drank deeply while I filled her pussy with my cock in one thrust, taking her hard as I swallowed.

"Yes!" she shouted, and she clutched the bedcovers tight beside her thighs, pressing her ass back and flush against my skin.

The bottle slipped from my hand and landed on the floor with a *thud*. I leaned over her, my hips like hinges allowing me to fuck into her in a fast rhythm, and I slipped my still wet fingers beneath her mouth. "Suck."

She ate at my fingers like they were made of pure sugar, rolling her tongue over them, and then sucking them like they were my cock, in and out. In and out.

"*Fuck*, Roxanne."

"Mm," she hummed, satisfaction pumping through her. She knew she'd pleased me, and she loved it.

Cum had loaded at the base of my dick. It pulsed and throbbed inside her and I wanted to release so fucking bad, my whole body ached and begged me for it.

But I needed to make her come first.

She'd already primed my fingers, so I pulled my hand away from her mouth and slid it beneath her hip pressed hard to the bed as I pounded into her from behind, and those wet fingers found her clit.

They sought the hot little button like heat-seeking missiles, and when they found it and pressed and rubbed it, she contracted around my cock painfully. Her body swallowed mine, milked me, and a burning rush began at the base of my spine.

"You're mine, Roxanne." I grunted, "*Mine*."

Leaning lower, I bit the curve of her neck like the goddamn wolf again, claiming her just like she wanted, and she shattered apart beneath me.

I slowed my hips. If I wasn't careful, I'd spill inside her, but I wasn't done with her.

Not even close.

Pulling out, my cock slapped against her ass, smearing the mess we'd made together over her warm, reddened skin, and she moaned and sagged into the bed, but I slipped my arms beneath hers and tugged her against my body.

Stepping out of the tangle I'd left our legs in, I turned her, flipped her over like a rag doll, and let her fall back to the bed on her back.

Her legs bracketed mine when I stood between them at the end of the bed, and she rubbed her bare feet on the outsides of my jeans, trying to work them lower, her eyes fixed firmly on my dick, still as hard as her broken iron head-board, and still wet from her cum and the faint sheen of whiskey that lingered.

She wanted more, but I had one last tease left to give her, and one more gift I needed her to grant me first.

CHAPTER TWENTY

ROXANNE

"COME IN MY MOUTH," Brand ordered, kneeling on the floor, his head between my legs and his tongue wild and working quickly in fast, fluttering strokes over my clit as he doused me in more whiskey.

The liquid soaked my comforter, probably my mattress too, but I didn't care, and it cooled my hot skin as it evaporated, heightening the sensation of his tongue lashing my pussy.

My bent and open legs shook, heels digging into the mattress, my body trying to find purchase wherever it could because my wrists were still bound to the outsides of my thighs.

I tried so hard to pull my arms free from the restraints. I wanted to touch him, to smash his head harder against my body so I could steal the pressure I needed to come again, but he wouldn't allow it.

Pushing two fingers inside me, he pumped them again and again, dragging them in and out, the rough calluses on his hands the perfect texture to make me lose my mind.

He moaned as he sucked at my body, and I thrust my hips

up and down against his face because it was the only movement he allowed me to make.

And when he curved those fingers deep inside, the tips
kneading something that tingled and buzzed from his touch,
my body released into his mouth, and the bizarre squirting
thing happened again.

I barely had a chance to wrap my head around it before
Brand licked it, lapped it up with his tongue, and drank it
down, like that naughty rush of liquid was his prize, the ulti-
mate goal he'd been working for.

Sexy boots and jeans still on, he kicked and pawed at
them, trying to wiggle them off. He was frantic, his control so
far gone, he was almost a different man, but I didn't mind.
Wild Brand was so turned on by me that he could barely
catch his breath.

Something happened then, when he couldn't wriggle free
from the traps on his legs and feet. He stood and took a deep,
clarifying breath. He reached down one hand at a time to free
himself from his own restraints, and then he entered my body
slowly and carefully, like it was sacred to him.

And he began to make love to me.

I thought I might have whiplash from the dizzying
changes in his demeanor, but it felt like he wanted it all.

All of me.

And he wanted to show me all of himself. He needed me
to understand him, but he didn't know which part of himself
to expose, so they all showed. The man now caressing my
face with his hands, his elbows digging into the bed and
holding him above me as he moved inside me slowly, almost
reverently, was at war with the dominant man who got off on
punishing me and restraining me while he smacked my ass
raw and fucked me with his mouth and a whiskey bottle.

And then there was the country boy, with his backward

hat and his mountain twang, the man who couldn't seem to believe I wanted to give him this forbidden thing he'd only just realized he needed.

He was the one moving inside me in a slow and steady rhythm, and I loved him the most because he was mine. I knew that now.

He released my wrists from the Velcro holds, lifting my hands one by one to his ass as it clenched and he glided in and out of my body.

Looking in my eyes, his were backlit by the moon glowing behind my gauzy window shades. "There's no one else, Roxanne," he breathed. "Only you. Do you know why?"

I shook my head. I couldn't speak because the vulnerability etched into the lines around his eyes mesmerized me.

"Because you see me. All of me. Every part. No one's ever known the parts of me you know."

Sweat trickled down his face, the drips catching in the hair darkening on his cheeks and chin and above his lip as the night wore on. He touched his forehead to mine, and his thrusts became stronger. My hands smoothed up his back and I held him, letting him fuck however he needed to.

It didn't matter to me as long as he was mine.

"I promised I'd take you out tomorrow night," he whispered, "so will you come to dinner with me at my brother's house? I wanna take you home."

"Yes," I breathed, my heart filling to the brim.

It was all I'd ever wanted, for someone to want me so much that he showed me off to the people most important to him. I just never expected to be in love with that man.

But I was. I was in love with Brand Lee.

He kissed me then, sealing the moment so no one could ever take it from me, and I cried out softly into his mouth as another wave crashed over me, my body clutching and responding to his as he came inside me.

CHAPTER TWENTY-ONE

BRAND

THE NEXT MORNING, drinking coffee with Merv at her kitchen table, she came right out with what she wanted to know.

She'd been watching me, wonder written all over her face. The heart attack and her brush with death had her questioning the world around her.

Merv wasn't usually so direct, but she looked at me and asked, "Why'd you stay away all those years, Brand?"

"I…" She'd caught me off guard. "It's not important."

She'd switched to decaf, and I was already wishing she hadn't, but not because it put her in a bad mood. The lack of caffeine made *me* feel off kilter.

After last night with Roxanne, I needed it. We'd made love again and again, and then I'd cleansed her in the shower, washed her hair, combed it, dressed her in pajamas, and tucked her into her bed.

A text came through from her as Merv worked up the courage to ask me more.

7:15 AM

Did you take my front door key?

I'd already ordered her a new bedroom set, mattress, and linens from a local furniture boutique in Jackson, and they'd be delivered and assembled later today while she was at work. I'd stolen her front door key from her key ring before I left, but her door locked automatically, so her place wouldn't be left unsecured all day. She just wouldn't be able to engage the deadbolt, and by the time she got home in the evening, the new bed would be ready and waiting for us, and the key would be tucked beneath the pot of pansies next to her front door.

Yes. Something's being delivered today. I needed access.

You could've asked.

I did, but you were passed out.

A meme popped onto my screen of some actor tapping his chin and looking at nothing inquisitively, with the words "Gee, I wonder why" flashing above the image.

I sent a responding smiling devil emoji, but Merv's voice jolted me back to her inquiry, and I set my phone face down on the kitchen table and sipped my coffee again, almost groaning at the lack of caffeine this time.

"Yes, it is important," Merv said, "and yes, you do know why. I do, too, so just say it."

"Mama—"

"Say it."

"Fine." It wasn't a secret, I supposed. I'd just never said it to her face. "I stayed away because of Dad." I paused. I wasn't done, not by a long shot, but I didn't want to hurt her, and the truth would do just that.

"Go on," she said. "I know there's more."

"I don't know if anyone else remembers, but *I* remember how different Dad was when Bax and I were young. Dad was happy. He loved us. He played. He smiled and laughed. But then... I don't know what happened to him. He changed, and I hated him after that. I hated the way he treated Abey, the way he treated us like hired help instead of his kids. The way he badgered Dixon and yelled at him all the time. I hated the way he treated *you*."

Sadness seeped out from her soul. It settled into the corners of her eyes, and she nodded for me to continue.

"And I hated the way you let him."

She smiled softly. "There. Now you said it. Abey says we can't keep secrets about how we feel anymore, and since you're home, that applies to you too. I'm sorry, son. Sorry I didn't stand up to your daddy. I'm so sorry for the way he treated your baby sister and brother and for not standin' up for them. And I'm sorry we both hurt you and made you feel like you needed to run."

The fear I'd felt since I was fifteen years old crept into my voice, and when I spoke, it slithered out of me, like dirty air. "I'm afraid I'm like him. There's a... darkness inside me. A need to control."

Merv nodded. How could I have ever thought she didn't see it?

"You know?"

"I suspected. But Brand, your dad, he *wasn't* in control. That's where his anger came from. You're not like him at all. You've made such a success of your life. We're all proud of you. That need you feel isn't about bein' like your daddy. It's about *not* becomin' him. But you don't have to worry 'cause you're already twice the man he was."

She smiled again, but the curve of her mouth trembled. I'd never heard her speak ill of my father. When he was alive, it would've been disobedient and almost blasphemous for her to talk about her husband this way. And I knew from my sister that it had taken Merv almost losing Abey in her life for her to admit how she'd felt all those years ago, but she finally had.

"I never stopped to think what life was like for you," I said. "If you want to tell me, I'll listen."

"It's not— There are things a mother doesn't talk to her kids about. This is one of those things."

"Mama, I can take it. I'm not twelve years old anymore."

But she wasn't listening. There was a far-off look in her eyes. She gazed out the window, but the mountains could've disappeared into thin air and she wouldn't have noticed.

BEA AND CLAY were at the future site of Spitfire Inn, waiting for me when I rode Bax's ATV out there, trying to shake the conversation I'd had with Merv earlier in the morning.

There was so much left unsaid, but I couldn't tell her any of it, not without risking telling her the truth. That I'd spoken to Dixon. That I'd given him money.

And Bax might never forgive me for not telling him and Bea that Stuey's birth mother was dead. I wasn't sure I'd ever forgive myself for holding onto that secret. I still remembered the phone call when Dixon told me. When he blamed himself again for someone else's choices and fate.

"*Kel's dead,*" he'd said. "*The mother of my child is gone,*"

Brand. I don't know what to do with that. It-it's my fault. I should've protected her better. I should've done… somethin'. And now she's just gone, and I'm alone, and there's a kid in the world who'll never know his mama. Why the fuck do I keep killin' mothers?"

"Dixon, you didn't kill anyone. Are you safe? Where are you?"

"I'm nowhere," he said. "Not anywhere you can find me."

And that was the last I'd spoken to him until he called to ask me to get him into another rehabilitation program, which I did. And now I was clueless again. Was he sober? Was he alive?

But Dixon had begged me not to tell the family about Kel, and I owed him.

WE'D CHOSEN the perfect spot for the inn. The field three-quarters of a mile from Merv's house butted up against our mountain, and it was naturally flat but raised up above Lee Lake. I could see the lake from almost every vantage point, so future guests would have that as a perk, and out back, the meadow stretched out for a mile to the west, and wild animals traveled through it during the day, elk, deer, occasionally moose, and even bears once in a while.

The inn would be far enough away from the cattle farming areas of the ranch so the stench wouldn't be strong. Most days, thanks to the wind coming down the mountains, it was almost completely indiscernible, but the cattle would be visible during certain parts of the year as my brother and Rye circulated our herd from field to field.

"How's everything goin' out here?" I asked as I climbed

up onto the huge concrete slab. I reached my hand out to Clay and he shook it. "How's my number one ball buster?" I asked Bea.

"What's up, brother-in-law?" she said. "You know, since I married Bax and he's older than you, I think that means I'm your boss now."

I snorted. "In your dreams. Seriously, how's it goin'?"

"Good. Clay and I were just talkin' about the accessibility ramps. Clay saw the plans, and he thinks he's got a design in mind that will flow better with the aesthetic of the inn, if you're open to suggestions?"

"Of course," I said. "I'd love to see some mock-ups."

"Sure," Clay offered, excitement lighting his eyes. "I can get them for you. Your brother said he'd draw some up for me."

"And the berm side of the building," Bea said, "we were talkin' about that too. We're kind of excited to work on that. Neither of us have any experience with berms, though, so you might want to bring in an outside expert."

"I have a little experience with them," I said, "but you're probably right. Just to make sure we don't screw it up. I think I know a guy I can consult with. But don't forget, this is an *inn*, not a hotel. It's basically a humungous house, and you're a rock star when it comes to buildin' those."

"True. I am pretty good," Bea said, and she and Clay laughed. "Anyway, we've laid the foundation and all the infrastructure. Now we just have to wait till spring so we can finish this bitch. I'm not real good with interior crap, but Bax, Athena, Aubrey, and Rye have been makin' plans. Seems like they've figured out how they want to decorate."

"That's good," I said. "Yeah, it's not my forte either."

I looked around the site, picturing what it would look like next year when we finished the inn. It would be beautiful and grand, and the excitement I felt about seeing it come to fruition surprised me. Every building or house I'd ever built gave me a sense of satisfaction, but this inn would be different. It was a big part of my family's future, and that made it personal.

Clay left to get started on his proposal, and Bea took my arm as we walked back to the ATV. Clay was her ride, so I told her I'd drop her back at her house.

"You're still comin' to dinner tonight, right?" she asked.

"Yeah. Actually, I'm bringin' a date."

"A date? You?"

"What? You've known me three years. You've seen me with women before."

"Yeah," she said, "but we never talk about it. Who is it? If she's from around here, do I know her?"

"Probably. She was at your wedding."

I watched as she thought about it, trying to remember the single women who'd attended her wedding, but she came up empty. "Who?"

Before I could deflect, my phone rang in my pocket. I pulled it out and looked at the number, but I didn't recognize it. I smiled. "Saved by the bell. Give me a minute?"

Bea narrowed her eyes but then rolled them. "Fine. Keep your secrets. I'm callin' Bax. He'll remember who was there."

I shook my head and answered the unknown caller, "Brand Lee."

"... Yeah, it's... Dixon."

My eyes flashed to Bea, worried she'd be able to tell who'd called me from the look on my face, but she was already on her own call, smiling at whatever Bax was saying to her. I walked further away, just in case she might hear.

"Dixon. Where are you? H-how are you? It's so good to hear your voice."

"Kel's dead," he said flatly.

"I know. You told me before you went into rehab."

"I did? I was pretty high then."

"You did. I'm so sorry, Dix. Are you okay now? Are you… high now?"

"No," he said. "Been sober almost five months now. Look, the reason I'm callin' is to tell you I'm off the grid. You can't track this phone, so don't even try. It's a cheap, piece-of-shit burner I borrowed from some junkie at NA."

It wasn't the only reason he'd called. Dixon, no matter how many times he told me he wanted to be left alone, still wanted and needed a connection to our family, and I was that connection. He and I had lived in hell together. I was his safest bet.

"I'm in California still, but I ain't sayin' where. I've got a place to stay while I get my head straight. I can't do it with a bunch of assholes around me all the time. Sometimes, bein' around people is too much."

"Okay, I mean, that's good, I guess. I'm glad you're better. Can I let the family know now? Can I tell them you're better?"

"No! You said you'd keep this shit to yourself."

"You're right," I said, trying to calm him down. "I did. But I thought you just didn't want them to know about rehab or Kel."

"I don't. Listen, how many times have I been through this? I don't want them to know until I'm good." The line went quiet. More than a minute passed, and I had begun to think he'd cut the call. "I-I'm *not* good right now, Brand. Not even close. I'm sober… for now. I wanna stay that way, and you have no fuckin' idea how bad I wanna see my kid, but if I can't keep this up, I can't put that on him. I can't hurt him like that. You understand?"

"I do," I said, though I was sure the family wanted him home no matter the condition he showed up in. "How can I contact you?"

Guilt and panic ran through me like a runaway train. I needed to see my brother. I wanted to hug him and show him how proud I was of him. And selfishly, I wanted our family to see him sober and healthy, too, so they wouldn't hate me for keeping his secrets.

"You can't," he said. "I'll come home when I'm ready. But Brand?"

"Yeah, little brother, what do you need? Money? A car?"

"Naw, man. Thanks, but I just need you to do somethin' for me."

"What? Anything," I offered, though, as I said it I winced. Maybe offering "anything" was going too far.

"Can you give my kid a hug from me? Squeeze him tight? Tell him his daddy loves him and misses him, but make sure no one hears you, okay?"

My eyes filled with tears, and the choke in my throat made it hard to respond, but I swallowed my guilt and pushed out the words. "I will, Dixon. I promise. You know he's—"

"No. Don't you tell me nothin' about him. I can't handle that. I can't… I just can't be there right now. It'll break me, Brand. All those precious things I'm missin'. I can't. But it's for the best. I promise. I'll get better, and I'll come home. I dunno when, but I'll… be better."

"I know you will, Dix—"

But before I could even get his name out of my mouth, the line went dead.

CHAPTER TWENTY-TWO

ROXANNE

"YOU LOOK BEAUTIFUL," Brand said when he picked me up for dinner at Bax's house with his family.

I'd had an easy shift at work. It was a long day, six to six, but we'd had no more reports of missing people, Teton Tom, or old ladies in a tither because someone parked too close to their mailbox. I was more tired than I could ever remember being, though.

Last night was exhausting in the best way. I'd never been so happy to be wrung out.

Figuring out I'd fallen in love took a lot out of me, too, and now, as I looked at the man in question walking up my porch stairs to take me on a date, it occurred to me that maybe I should tell him about my midnight revelation. But maybe waiting for another time would be better, when we weren't both exhausted and about to out our relationship to the world.

Lifting my hand as we descended my porch steps, Brand placed a soft kiss across my knuckles and then guided me with his other hand low on my back. He held the truck door open for me as I admired his crisp, light blue button-down and tight jeans, then climbed up, trying not to flash him when my pink-and-purple floral sundress rode up my thighs. Static cling—the struggle was real.

Mr. Begley watched from his front stoop as he enjoyed his evening cigar, but when Brand shoved the fabric higher and smacked my bare ass because I'd worn a thong, Begley huffed and slammed his door shut when he went inside.

Brand leaned down and bit my ass cheek. I yelped and flopped onto the seat, and he leaned over me to adjust the dress and make me pious again, or at least appear that way.

Reaching for the seat belt next to my arm, he tugged it down and stretched the strap across my chest. When he clicked it into place, his eyes met mine, and I had to hold in a moan because all I could think about was how his body fit similarly inside mine, with a click. And now, I was imagining him using the seatbelt to bind my wrists and eating me out right here on the street curb, with Mr. Begley watching from his window.

Get a grip, Roxi!

Brand had worn perfectly casual clothes, but it was the *way* he wore them, the way his jeans molded to his butt like Levi Strauss himself had crafted the damn things. And his shirt was close-fitting. Not too tight, but snug enough that I didn't have to imagine the shape of his pecs or biceps. His charcoal suit jacket had been tossed on his back seat, and I thought if he put it on, I might pass out from the sheer sexiness.

I felt underdressed. And I was utterly turned on.

He'd shaved, but already I saw the hint of stubble growing back in. And God, he smelled good, like fresh-cut wood and some kind of warm musk that had me inching closer to him. I wanted to burrow into his skin, become part of him so I'd never forget the scent and the way he looked tonight.

When he was sitting next to me, he put his big, fancy white truck in gear and grabbed hold of my hand as he headed west out of town. "You nervous?" He'd asked an innocent question, but I couldn't put my finger on the change in his voice.

Something was different today.

"A little," I said, trying to discern what could have changed the shape of his face and the sound of his voice in less than twenty-four hours. "Are you okay?"

He nodded but didn't actually answer me.

My nerves kicked up as we drove. I'd meant to call Abey to warn her that I would be her brother's date for dinner, but I chickened out. I truly didn't think she'd mind, but there was a little part of me that was terrified she would and it would cause a rift between us.

When I talked to her on the phone so she could help me decide what to wear, Aubrey yelled at me. She felt Abey deserved the warning. I agreed, but insecurity made the decision for me.

What if this was just a fling for Brand?

If he dumped me and moved on, things with Abey would go back to normal. But now I was freaking out that Aubrey was right. What if the fact that I hadn't come clean to Abey was the thing that caused the rift and not that I was sleeping with her brother?

My hands itched to grab my phone tucked away in my purse and text my boss, but I didn't because now I was worried that the change in Brand was because he'd realized I'd fallen in love with him and he didn't want me like that.

God, why can't I shut my mind off? My fingers tapped

one-two-three over and over against my leg next to my door so Brand couldn't see.

"Are *you* nervous?" I asked him.

He looked the picture of calm with his hand resting on the top of his steering wheel, not gripping it, but there was a buzzing beneath his skin, like the sound of an old radio when the volume had been turned all the way down, but the thing still crackled somehow.

"I've never brought a woman home," he said. "So yeah. Maybe a little nervous."

"Never? Why not?"

He shrugged. "I wasn't here. And when I did come home, it was as brief a trip as I could make it. Plus, none of the women I dated were what you'd call family oriented."

"Like Gina?"

His eyes slid to mine, and there was a warning in them. "Exactly like Gina." He didn't like me talking about his ex and didn't want me comparing myself to her. But if he didn't love me too, why would he care?

I babbled because the look in his eyes sent butterflies screaming in my stomach, the sexy kind *and* the nervous kind. "Well, I don't have kids and I'm too old for them now, anyway. I'm forty-one, you know. I saw your birth date on your driver's license that first night, so I know I'm four years older than you.

"But I'm a family girl. Kind of have to be with five sisters and brothers-in-law and fifteen nieces and nephews. Can I tell you a secret? I think my sister Maureen is in an open relationship with her husband Drew. I mean, I think they're screwin' other people, or they're, like, swingers or somethin'."

"So?"

"Well, I mean, I don't care, but you know, in small-town

Oklahoma, it's a big deal. If my parents found out? Yeesh. The whole family would implode."

"Mm. And if they found out I tied you up, fucked you with a whiskey bottle, and smacked your ass and your pussy to make you come?"

Instantly, my face felt hot, and the little squiggle tugging at the inside of my stomach made a laugh tumble out of my mouth in a breath.

"I would die. Full stop."

"Roxanne, you're a grown woman. Why do you care what they think?"

"I don't. I don't care what their opinion is, but I don't want them to know that I..."

We turned off the highway onto Old Fish Creek Road and shortly thereafter onto Bear Lane, but Brand pulled off to the side, into a little divot a fallen pine had made in the tree line. He left his engine running but put the truck in Park.

"That you what?" he asked, and he turned to face me and let go of my hand.

"That, you know, that I like..."

His voice was a low murmur when he asked, "What do you like, Roxanne?"

"You know."

"I do not. I need you to say it."

"I-I— No. You're teasin' me."

"I am most certainly *not* teasin' you." His hand dropped to his lap, and he fisted his hard-on beneath his jeans. My eyes followed the movement, and a soft moan slipped from my mouth. "Tell me now, and maybe you'll be rewarded later."

An impending reward made the words rush from my lips. "I like when you tie me up and spank me. When you control me."

"And did you wear a thong tonight to tease *me,* so I would be forced to punish you?"

My mouth dropped open. "No. I—"

He raised one perfect eyebrow.

"Yes, sir, " I said, my eyes cast down and my voice easing out of my mouth like smoke, thick and curling, and just like that, the butterflies in my stomach stilled.

With one finger under my chin, he lifted my gaze back to his. That was all it took. One touch from him. One look and my anxiety bled away. All those intrusive thoughts and doubts disappeared, as if my submission to him allowed me to feel confident and not second guess myself.

Brand saw the desire on my face, and he closed his eyes and inhaled deeply. When he opened them again, he stared at my breasts beneath my dress.

Growling low in his throat, he reached over and tugged the square neck of my dress down, then leaned closer and slid his hand inside my bra cup. Before I knew what he was doing, the dress was down around my waist, and he ripped the bra in two, tore it right where a little blue bow had been sewn between the cups. Silently, he dragged one strap off my shoulder and down my arm, and then the other.

Discarding the tattered fabric onto his back seat, he leaned closer and licked my nipple into his mouth. Goose-bumps rose on my arms and at the back of my neck, and then he was lifting the dress up my thighs, his hot fingers searching between my legs.

"When we're together, you will not wear a bra. Do I make myself clear?"

"Yes, sir."

"You may wear one when you're workin', but if you're off the clock and in my presence, I don't want these beautiful tits bound. Ever."

I nodded. What else was there to say to that? A thrill rushed through me. Knowing that I would be braless around him and that he'd demanded it of me but no one else would know it was for him made me smile.

I had begun to think every single thing I did was for him.

"I think now's the perfect time to discuss your limits."

"M-my limits?"

"Yeah. What you'll let me do to you. Restraint is okay?"

I nodded. Restraints were more than okay.

"Say the words, Roxanne."

"Yes," I said, "restraint is okay."

"Good girl. And bondage. Rope. They're okay?"

"Yes, sir."

"May I gag you? Blindfold you?"

"Um," squeaked out of my mouth, and his eyes lifted from my breasts.

"Does that make you nervous?"

"A little, but I'm willin' to try with you."

"And," he murmured, "clamps?"

"Clamps? Like nipple clamps?"

"Yes, and they make them for *other* parts of your body."

"We'll see about those," I said, doubtfully. He could bite my nipples and pinch them all day long if he wanted to, but metal clamps? And on *other* body parts?

"Fair enough," he said. He leaned down and licked my nipple again slowly. "Paddles? Crops and whips?"

I moaned. I couldn't help it. Had he been doing research? Or maybe he hadn't been truthful when he said he'd never done anything like this before. The dominance in his eyes and the sound of his voice told me he knew exactly what he wanted.

Brand smiled deviously, and his breath washed over my skin when he said, "God, look what you do to me." He closed his mouth over my nipple and clamped his teeth around it, then grabbed my hand and led it to his dick. When I gripped it though his jeans, he was as hard as stone. "You've wrecked me again. Do you think it should go unpunished?"

He bit down hard, his teeth digging in around the tight bud, and I moaned wantonly and so loudly that I thought I'd probably scared the birds in the trees.

"No, sir," I breathed. My head tipped back against the headrest as he pushed my thong's thin strip of fabric out of his way and slipped a finger inside me. It glided in easily, and I tilted my hips to give him better access. "Punish me."

His mouth came down over mine so hard, my head snapped back against the seat. My legs fell fully open and my arms dropped to my sides like overcooked spaghetti noodles as he added another finger and kissed me.

Pumping slowly, his other hand snaked behind my head. He gripped my hair in his palm, not letting me move. I rode his hand as best as I could in the seat, my hips rolling against his wrist, and my hands lifted to clutch the collar of his shirt.

"When you're with me, you're on my time. This is how I want you." His fingers inside me massaged and pumped possessively, and his thumb came down over my clit. His whole hand owned me. "Tell me yes."

"Yes."

"I want you wet and ready for me to fuck you whenever I want. However I want."

"Oh God."

"Do you want to come, Roxanne?"

"Yes, sir, *please*."

He said nothing more, and my eyes popped open when he stole his body away from mine. After he sucked the fingers that had just been inside me, he put his truck in Reverse and backed onto the dirt lane, adjusting himself beneath his jeans as he drove.

He didn't look at me again until we parked in front of Bax's and Bea's yellow house. "I should make you suck my cock for teasin' me."

The scene played clearly in my mind: Brand sitting on my couch in my living room, his jeans and boxers pulled down to his thighs, and me on my knees between his legs, my wrists secured together behind my back and my head bobbing above his lap. His strong hands would hold me down, make me take him deeper. His cock in my mouth would choke me, and I'd suck his cum down my throat like a vanilla milkshake from the Dairy Dream when I made him come.

I moaned and pressed my thighs together, trying silently to convince myself not to do it right here in his truck in front of his brother's house.

"That's your punishment, Roxanne," he said, turning and finding satisfaction in the desperate need splashed across my face. "You will imagine givin' me head all night, and later, I won't let you come until you've sucked me dry. Now, get out of the truck and go say hi to my baby sister."

I couldn't look at him. If I did, I'd jump him, so I couldn't see his smile, but I heard it in the sound of his voice.

"Yes, sir."

"ROXI?" Brand's niece, Athena, greeted me when we walked into her house, and the *one-two-threes* started up again. "What're you doin' here?"

Abey's head appeared around the corner of the wall dividing Bax's kitchen and living room. "Rox? Is there an emergency? My radio hasn't gone off."

I shook my head. I was at a loss for words, but I gripped the hem of my dress and squeezed to stop myself from tapping.

Brand reached for my hand, detached it from the fabric, and held it. "Roxanne is my guest. My date."

His gentle touch on my skin eased my nervousness, and a rush of relaxation pulsed through me from my hand, where he rubbed soothing circles into my palm, to my heart and my head.

"Oh." Athena smiled. "Didn't see that one comin'."

Abey moved into the kitchen, her wife Devo following behind her. "Your date?" Abey said to Brand, and then she looked at me, eyebrows furrowed, probably confused, like two plus two didn't equal four anymore. "And how long's this been goin' on?"

"Since the search for Natalie," Brand said easily, like there weren't three sets of eyes staring us down.

At least their mom hadn't shown up yet. I could just imagine the look of disapproval Merv would aim at me. Abey told me last year when Bax and Bea had first gotten together that her mama didn't like any woman who dated her sons.

"Actually," Brand amended, "it started the first night I was back home."

It felt like he had injected sunshine straight into my heart hearing him say it. He wanted his family to know how much he liked me.

"And why am I just hearin' about this now?" Abey asked. There wasn't anger on her face, just confusion, but she aimed it at me, not her brother.

Bax and Bea joined everyone in their kitchen, Bea holding little Stuey on her hip.

Brand tensed next to me. He could tell me till he was blue in the face that everything would be fine when we outed our relationship, but his hand flexed around mine, so I squeezed back, trying to convey to him that he could be my support, but I'd be his too.

"What's goin' on?" Bax asked.

Great. The whole fucking family. And now I needed to explain, except I realized I didn't really know how to. *What should I say? Brand and I are dating? Fucking? It's a tryst? A one-night stand that wouldn't quit? I'm totally head over heels for him, but I'm scared it's a one-sided thing? Oh, and your brother likes to boss me around and tie my hands to my thighs so he can have his wicked way with me and fuck me with liquor bottles?*

But none of that was appropriate in front of Athena and Stuart.

Brand leaned forward, like he was going to take the problem out of my hands and fix it, but it was my confession Abey wanted.

I squeezed again, tugging him back to me.

"We haven't exactly defined this," I said, wagging a finger between the two of us. "It happened, and I was afraid to tell you, Abey. I didn't want it to mess up our friendship or our workin' relationship. I-I"—looking around the room at all the people Brand loved, I sighed—"I was just scared."

"Rox, you're family," Abey said. "There's no need for your fear. If you and Brand have somethin', I can respect that."

Instant relief. "Thank you."

Brand rumbled something beside me. Probably, "I told you so."

Abey smiled. If I wasn't wrong, there was a little glint in her eye. "But you should've told me."

Standing beside her, Devo snorted loudly. "Oh, book club is gonna hear about this. You're really in trouble now, Roxi."

Abey grabbed my hand out of Brand's, and I followed as she pulled me into the living room. I sat on the couch while the whole family, including Brand, formed a semi-circle in front of me and stared at me.

Just then, the kitchen door banged open behind us.

"Where y'all at?" Merv hollered. "I brought a surprise."

Bax turned toward the sound of his mom's voice. "Mama? I was just about to come pick you up."

"No need," Merv replied.

She entered the living room. A big meddlesome smile clogged her features as she dragged someone with her by their hand. Someone with long, shiny, black hair.

"Brand, look. I brought your friend, Gina."

CHAPTER TWENTY-THREE

BRAND

INSTANTLY, Roxanne deflated.

That was unacceptable. She sat, still on the couch but now looking defenseless and defeated after she'd just stood up for herself. For us.

It wouldn't do. She deserved better than to feel belittled on our date.

She could already tell something was bothering me, and I hadn't said a word about Dixon's phone call. No one else could tell. Not Gina standing five feet away, not my family. Roxanne already knew me better than all of them combined.

I held my hand out to her, and she looked up at me, uncertain and insecure, the lines around her smile tight, her beautiful brown eyes careful.

My family gawked, all of them looking back and forth between my ex and Roxanne.

With the exception of Bea, they'd never met Gina before, had no idea we'd dated, but the coy smile on Gina's face and the way she ate me up with her eyes told them all they needed to know.

Roxanne took my hand. I tugged her up and to my side,

and she relaxed a fraction as I tucked her beneath my arm, like a weapon.

"Gina. Nice to see you again," I said. "Why are you here?"

She had dressed to kill in a short, black skirt and a soft, pink top that accentuated her tan complexion. The deep neckline showed hints of her breasts and black-lace bra, and she'd worn expensive, high, black heels, which were utterly ridiculous on a ranch.

"Brand," Merv admonished. "Don't be rude. Gina came to see the new the cabins you built. She was thinkin' of rentin' one, and she knocked on my door earlier to introduce herself." Merv looked at Roxanne, confusion clouding her blue eyes. "But you didn't tell me your friend would be stoppin' by, and you failed to mention you'd be bringin' someone tonight."

I had to stop myself from snorting out loud. Gina in a cabin alone, treating herself to a rugged getaway? *Right*. "That's because I didn't know."

"Oh." Merv seemed completely befuddled now, her excitement at surprising me quickly waning.

"Didn't I mention it?" Gina said. "I'm sure I brought it up when Brand took me to dinner the other night." She let out a breezy laugh, but I knew her game.

"When you *met* me for a work dinner, Gina, to go over the plans for the new contract."

Fixing her eyes on Roxanne, Gina waved her hand in front of her. "That's what I meant."

When I lowered my arm and wrapped it around Roxanne's hip, Gina's eyes followed.

"I feel like I'm missin' somethin'," Merv said.

"Mama, Gina, say hello to Roxanne, my *girlfriend*."

Roxanne and I hadn't discussed the label, but I felt her

confidence rising as I said it, so I knew it was okay. I wanted her to be my girlfriend. If I was being honest with myself, she was fast becoming my everything.

Gina flashed a smile. It appeared genuine, but I knew better. The rigid set of her jaw gave away her true feelings about seeing me with Roxanne. She wasn't pleased. Roxanne had become the fly in Gina's ointment tonight.

"Deputy," Mama said, nodding at Roxanne, but then she turned back toward Gina. "But I thought—"

"Who's hungry?" Bax interrupted loudly. "It's such a nice evenin'. We set up the table outside on the fantastic patio my wife just built for us. We can eat and watch the sunset by the fire."

A knock on the kitchen door startled everyone, and then I heard Tab's voice. "Hello? Bea, Abey, are you in there?" She squinted through the mesh screen. "Y'all said seven for dinner, right?"

———

BEA GRABBED my arm and pulled me to a stop around the side of my brother's house as everyone followed Bax out back. Abey had taken Roxanne and Tab by their hands and dragged them away from me.

"What's *Gina* doin' here?" Bea asked in a whisper. "I thought you broke that off a long time ago."

Bea and Gina had only met a few times up in Sheridan, but Bea probably remembered Gina stomping around my office, rearranging everything and tapping her high heel impatiently while I hurried to finish whatever I'd been working on so we could get to the important things in life, like eating at expensive restaurants, but only if they were Michelin-starred, which posed a problem since there weren't any in Sheridan. None existed in the whole state of Wyoming, which led me to charter a helicopter to Montana twice in the beginning of our relationship, when I'd still been in the wooing phase. It died quickly, not surprisingly.

"I did," I whispered back. "She's here 'cause she's the lead architect on the project we're startin' in the spring, but she's *here*"—I looked around my brother's back yard and at the big cedar table in the middle of the brick patio Bea had just finished—"because she saw an opportunity."

Bea glared at me. If there was one thing she hated, it was disingenuousness. She didn't play games and didn't suffer others who did.

"So how do you and my son know each other?" Merv asked Gina as everyone sat and Abey poured red wine in a glass in front of Gina and one for Tab. Everybody else drank beer or water. Bea kept her eyes on Gina, ready to claw the woman's eyes out if she tried to cause a scene.

"Oh, we go way back," Gina said, smiling. "Don't we, Brand?" Of course she'd chosen the seat directly across from me that would give her the best view of Roxanne. She wouldn't risk losing our attention.

Tab answered for me. "Gina and Brand worked together up in Sheridan," she said. "Gina's an architect, and she's been the lead on a few of the projects Lee Construction has built for Wy Not Homes. Oh, and they dated a few times."

Gina huffed a laugh "'A few times'? We were practically living together."

Roxanne hadn't said a word, and now she pulled her hand from mine and dropped it into her lap, and out of the corner of my eye, I saw her fingers begin their tapping.

"No," I said, lifting Roxanne's hand again, yanking it from her lap and into mine, where it belonged. "We weren't."

"I mean, basically," Gina said with an awkward laugh.

She'd never known me to be argumentative. "Anyway, now we're working together again on Brand's new project here in Wisper, so you'll be seeing a lot of me."

Merv must have picked up on the tension between Gina and me. She was side-eyeing Gina. She probably didn't like that I'd brought a date to dinner, but if you fucked with her sons, Merv would break kneecaps for that offense.

It looked like Merv had been about to question Gina, but then we heard a deep voice coming from the front of the house.

"Hello? Anybody home? Sorry I'm late."

How many fucking people had been invited to this family dinner? But I'd been lucky to find Clay Marveaux last year, and he was one of my favorite foremen. He appeared around the side of the house and dabbed at the drops of sweat on his face with an old-fashioned, white, cloth handkerchief when he saw the big group of us all sitting around the table.

"Oh. There y'all are."

Merv's face turned beet red, and she stared daggers at Bea, who was turning out to be just as meddlesome as her mother-in-law.

Bea stood and smiled widely at Clay. "Clay, so glad you could make it. Grab a chair. You're not late. We just sat down."

Clay looked uncomfortable, but he grabbed the only open seat left, the one next to Merv. He gripped the chairback, pulled it out, and sat, smiling at my mama like a love-struck idiot.

BAX AND ATHENA SERVED DINNER—CAESAR salad, garlic bread, and lasagna, but only salad and grilled chicken breast for Merv—while Gina watched Roxanne and me, studying the dynamic between us, and Clay watched Merv.

Tab chattered away with Abey and Devo, thanking them again for inviting her because she had been feeling a little homesick, something she'd failed to mention to me. I would've invited her if I hadn't been so wrapped up in Roxanne.

Bea jumped headfirst into the awkwardness. "You know, Merv, Clay here organized a walkin' club through the community center. I hope he won't mind me sayin' so, but Clay has heart issues, too, so he wanted to do somethin' to better his own health and offer a friendly face for people who wanna exercise but don't know where to start. Isn't that nice?"

And now I was sure Bax and Bea had somehow planned for the only available seat to be next to Merv's. I watched Clay nodding and smiling at Merv, and I realized he had stars in his eyes for my mama.

"That's nice," Merv said, and she glanced at Clay, but her eyes dropped quickly back to her plate.

She seemed a little nervous, but we'd had several conversations about how she could get started on an exercise routine. I'd offered to buy her a treadmill or an elliptical machine, or both, but she'd balked at the expense. Clay's walking club was the perfect alternative. He said the small group hiked easy trails around the area or downtown, and in the winter, the community center offered the use of its meager gym and two treadmills. If she agreed to join Clay, I was already planning on donating more exercise equipment to the center. Shit, if she'd use it, I'd build an entire fitness center inside Ace's House for Merv.

Devo would be giddy since she worked as the community

center's assistant director and was a staunch advocate for her community.

"That's a great idea, Bea," Devo said. "Merv, you should join Clay and the others. They walk four times a week."

"Oh, I dunno," Merv mumbled. "I'm not much for big groups."

"It's not big, Mrs. Lee," Clay offered. "There's only three of us. If you join us, you'd make four. We'd love to have you."

Truth be told, Merv was probably shy. She didn't really have friends, and she hated relying on people for anything. Except for my little sister.

Maybe it was because Abey was a woman, but Merv had no problem expecting Abey's help with whatever she needed: a ride, someone to go grocery shopping with, someone to accompany her to a doctor appointment. It was unusual for her to depend on one of her sons, though, lately that seemed to be changing. But secretly, I knew Abey loved it. Despite their differences, she and Merv had a closeness Bax and I didn't have with Merv, but now that she and Devo were married, Abey couldn't always come running when Merv called. It was right that Bax and I picked up the slack.

"I'm not a Mrs. anymore," Merv mumbled to Clay. "Call me Mervella."

"Yes, ma'am," he said, blushing. "Mervella."

"So, Deputy," Gina interrupted, and she pegged my date with her hard stare. "You work for Brand's sister?" She smiled at Abey at the end of the table, but then almost scowled at Roxanne.

Roxanne replied simply, "Yep," popping the "p" at the end of the word.

Abey seemed confused by Roxanne's short reply. "Don't be modest, Rox." To Gina, Abey explained, "Roxi's a fantastic investigator. We don't get a lot of cases needing investigation around here, but when we do, she always comes through, and the community loves her. They've taken her in like she's lived here her whole life."

Roxanne didn't reply. She smiled uneasily, and that was the last straw.

Beneath the table, I squeezed her hand hard, even felt her bones strain in my grip. "Please excuse us for a few minutes," I said, and then I hauled Roxanne out of her chair. Even before we made it into the shade of the house, I spun her in front of me, lifted her, and slung her over my shoulder.

She yelped, and I smacked her ass. She smacked mine in retaliation, which made my hands grip her bare thighs harder under her dress. I hoped my fingerprints would leave marks on her skin.

No one said a word, but I heard my brother laugh, and out of the corner of my eye, I saw Gina's scowl. Good. I wanted her to witness the passion between Roxanne and me. Maybe then she'd respect my choice and my date. I had never been possessive with Gina. She'd never inspired that in me. Not once. If another man had tried to take Gina from me, I probably would've let him.

If he came for Roxanne, I'd take him out.

I carried Roxanne to the big balsam tree by the barn, dropped her to her feet, and pushed her up against its trunk, facing away from the house.

"Tell me what you need," I said, my eyes steady on hers.

"What? What do you mean 'what do I need'? I can't believe you just did that in front of your whole family and your employees!"

"Why can't you believe it? Because I smacked your ass in public, or because it was *your* ass and not Gina Scott's?"

Her eyes narrowed. "Both."

"Tell me what you need from me, Roxanne. What will it take for you to feel confident that I want you and only you? Shall I tell you how beautiful you are tonight? That the settin' sun on your skin makes you glow, and I can't stop starin' at you? Do you need to hear me say that yours is the only body I want to be inside of? That it's all I can think about, gettin' you alone, strappin' you to your bed and fuckin' you till we can't see straight?"

Her eyes dropped to the dirt beneath our feet. "Maybe." Insecurity raged inside her. It pulsed around her body like a second skin.

Lifting the skirt of her dress with my fingertips, I leaned closer. When she looked up at me, I slid my hand inside her thong.

"Brand! Not here. What if they see?"

"Let 'em. I don't give a shit. They'll see how much I want you."

Taking her mouth with mine, I cut off her reply, and I slipped two fingers between her pussy lips, intending to rub her till she was wet enough to take me. I planned to fuck her right here, up against the tree.

She groaned, instantly forgetting embarrassment, and ground herself against my hand.

"Good girl," I breathed into her mouth.

She whimpered into mine, and her whole body went slack when I slid my fingers inside her.

"I'm sorry she's here," I murmured against her lips, leaning into her body, my hand pumping, my eyes open and watching her face as I worked her. "I didn't know she would be, but if you want me to, I'll tell her to leave. I'd fuck you on the dinner table if it's what you want. If it's what you need."

She moaned.

"Tell me what you want, and when we get home, you can take whatever you need from me."

"I don't want you to be rude to her," she said, her breath speeding as she climbed higher and closer to release.

I added another finger and pounded the heel of my hand against her pubic bone. "Liar."

Her eyes opened wide. "And my house is not home. I'm embarrassed by it. You're used to much nicer things. *Gina* wouldn't be caught dead in my run-down duplex."

CHAPTER TWENTY-FOUR

ROXANNE

BRAND GROWLED INTO MY MOUTH. "That's all you want? A house?" He slipped another finger inside me, dragging his whole hand in and out, over and over, claiming me, owning me, and slamming the hard heel of his palm against my clit with every thrust in. "I don't give a shit where you live, but baby, if a house is what you want, I'll build you the finest fuckin' home in all Wyoming."

Were we really having this conversation up against a tree, not two-hundred yards from where his family still sat eating cheesy pasta?

But between panting breaths and moans, I said, "I d-don't need the finest, just a nice place. A view would be cool and a g-good kitchen. I need counter space for all the Christmas candies and crafts I send to my n-nieces and nephews. My place has shit counters. There's b-barely enough room for a two-slot toaster."

Watching my face closely so he could see the pleasure when he gave it to me, he curled all four fingers inside me, hitting places that made my heart race and liquid gush all over his hand. "Mm. We can talk logistics later. Maybe we can hire Gina to draw up the plans."

I froze. My hands stilled on his back where my short fingernails had probably left red divots beneath his shirt. "*What* did you just say to me?"

"There she is," he breathed. "Beautiful, argumentative Roxi. Gimme hell, girl."

"That bitch ain't comin' *anywhere* near my beautiful, imaginary house," I said.

His lips were close, so I bit them. Blood welled below his lip where my teeth nicked him, and he licked it away.

He stared at me in amazement. Two seconds passed, and he growled, "Get on my dick. Now." He reached for his zipper.

"No," I said flippantly. "I don't think I will. Not till you make me come and then put the greedy jerk tryin' to ruin my date in her place."

He moaned, and my head hit bark when he slammed his mouth over mine. I bit him again but kissed the pain away this time as his hand resumed its shock-and-awe routine between my legs.

Normally, Brand's kisses were a little possessive, commanding for sure, and intoxicating, but now, his mouth on mine was brutal and unyielding, his tongue like a snake, impossibly strong, but slow and warm and relentless.

His entire family could've been ten feet away, eating buckets of popcorn and sucking fountain pop through straws as they watched us go at each other, but they wouldn't have stopped us.

Suddenly, Brand dropped to his knees and shoved my dress above my navel. He held it to my stomach with one hand and pressed his face between my legs, licking around my thong and sucking the juice from my cunt. He moaned and swallowed it eagerly and slid a slippery finger over my asshole.

"I'm gonna fuck this ass soon," he promised. "You've earned it."

My whole body shivered and stuttered, and when he bit my clit and slipped his fingers back inside, I came, biting my own lip to keep from screaming.

———

IF I'D HAD a collar and leash, Brand would've followed me like a puppy as I sauntered to Bax's front porch, completely relaxed and confident once more.

Brand was addicted to me now, the power struggle between us reversed again.

A little blood and pain was all it had taken.

We used the bathroom inside Bax's house to clean up, and he rubbed between my legs with a cool, wet washcloth while I dabbed at the red bite mark below his lip with the edge of a hand towel.

"I'm sorry I bit you," I said.

His eyes met mine. "Don't you apologize. It was hot as fuck."

I moaned when he cupped the washcloth over my pussy and jerked my body against his.

"Now, let's go finish our dinner," he whispered. "You're gonna need strength to make it through what I have planned for you tonight."

When we took our seats out back, Gina had mysteriously gone missing.

"I apologize," Brand told the table as he laid his napkin over his thigh. "Mama, did your guest leave?"

Merv said nothing, but Athena chimed in. "Gina faked a

call. Said she had to go, but I saw her screen. It was blank. There was no call."

Devo snickered under her breath, and Merv frowned. Good, I hoped Gina Scott spied on us and got an eyeful.

"So," Bax drawled, "do I need to power wash my front porch, or did y'all do it in the barn?"

"Ew, Daddy," Athena complained. "Gross."

Brand tried not to, but he smiled at his brother.

"Sorry, Road Trip," Bax said to Athena. "I'll explain later."

"Double gross," Athena quipped, and she rolled her eyes. "I think I can figure it out for myself, thanks." She stood and lifted Stuey from his highchair next to Bea. "I'm rescuin' Stu from this conversation. You're gonna burn his poor little ears." Athena hurried away with Stuey in her arms, still munching on a piece of garlic bread, and he wiped his greasy hands on the sides of her face. "Stuey! For real? Yuck."

"So," Merv said, wiggling her oddly bent, arthritic pointer finger over her plate, back and forth from Brand's face to mine, "this is a thing now?"

"Yes," I said.

Brand hung his arm over the back of my chair. "Yes, Mama. Roxanne and I are together."

"Okay, well next time, do you have to be so rude?"

Rude? Miss Priss deserved it. *'Oh Brand and I go way back, right Brand?'* Heart eyes, heart eyes, heart eyes.

Ugh. Gag me with a pitchfork.

"There won't *be* a next time," Brand informed his mom. "Gina is a work colleague, and I'd appreciate it if you didn't invite her to any more family dinners, but I apologize if I was rude.

"I didn't intend to be, but Roxanne and I had a few urgent things we needed to discuss." His hand slid from the back of my chair and beneath the table. He gripped my thigh and moved it up slowly, his skin rasping against mine, and he cupped his fingers possessively over my still-soaked underwear.

No one could see where Brand's hand was, but they could guess.

Bea's eyebrows hit her hairline. Bax looked speechless, his mouth open, but nothing came out. Tab slapped her hand over her mouth, and Devo smiled from ear to ear, happy about being a witness to the drama. Poor Clay was avoiding eye contact with every single person at the table. He seemed to have found something really interesting to look at on the roof of the house.

Abey and Merv both rolled their eyes, mother and daughter in sync, though, I was sure Abey would never admit to that.

Merv stood. "Thank you for dinner, kids. Tell Athena and Stuey goodnight for me. I'm goin' home."

"I'll drive you." Brand scooted his chair back and set his napkin next to his half-full plate on the table.

"Sit your butt down," Merv scolded him like a little boy. "I'm not an invalid. I'm walkin'. You're the one who said I need to walk."

"Yes, ma'am." He scooted back in.

Clay jumped at the opportunity. "I'll walk with you, if that's okay?"

"That'd be fine," Merv said. "Thank you."

Everyone waited a minute until Merv and Clay were far enough away, and then Bea, Bax, Devo, and Abey busted out in laughter. Tab still looked shocked. She'd said Brand didn't normally talk to her about his relationships, so I thought it safe to assume he didn't usually go caveman on a woman at the dinner table either.

"Did you see Merv's face?" Bax doubled over and slapped his hand on the table.

"Jeez, you two," Abey said, trying not to smile, "I hope you don't make a habit out of screwin' all over town. Roxi has a professional reputation to uphold."

"Oh, Roxi has a reputation alright," Bea said, giggling, and Abey and Devo busted out in laughter.

I thought I might die of embarrassment, but this was the dinner I'd been hoping for when Brand asked me to spend the evening with his family. The Lees reminded me of my own family, my sisters and the gossiping we got up to when we were all together.

"You're so lucky Rye ain't here tonight, Brand," Bax said. "He would've pulled up a chair to watch you and yelled back commentary for the rest of us. He'd never let you live it down."

Brand shrugged.

"You guys, cut it out," I said. "We didn't have sex!"

"But you did *somethin'*," Devo said. "What, did you bite him?" She pointed to Brand's lip, and he lifted a finger to press against it.

With all eyes on us, the fidgeting was about get out of control under the table. My leg tingled where I usually tapped out my one-two-threes, but Brand understood. He wrapped his arm around me again and pulled me closer, and the urge subsided, like he was my very own grounding wire. "My woman's a little feisty, is all," he said.

Abey chuckled. "I have never looked forward to book club more in my life!"

"What is this book club I keep hearing about?" Tab asked. "And how do I get in on the action?"

CHAPTER TWENTY-FIVE

BRAND

SPENDING the evening with Roxanne and my family had temporarily cured me of the vicious cycle of thoughts swirling in my mind like a cesspool. Even Gina Scott and her dramatics couldn't spoil it.

Roxanne's laughter had been like therapy for me tonight and seeing her regain her confidence and her insecurity melt away helped tremendously.

But now that we were back at her place, sipping the left-over whiskey from last night and watching and listening to a fire crackle on her TV screen, Dixon and Stuey were on my mind again. Dixon's absence tonight at our family dinner hurt, and being around Stuart was like a knife in my gut. He probably misunderstood when I whispered in his ear before we left tonight that his daddy loved him and missed him. He probably thought I had been talking about Bax.

How could I keep lying to the people I loved? To Stuey? He deserved to know his dad was out there, loving and missing him from afar, but I just couldn't bring myself to rat my brother out. If it was the only thing he'd ask of me, I had to keep his confidence. I owed him that.

"Brand?"

"Hm?" I looked at Roxanne next to me on her couch and realized she'd been talking to me, but I couldn't recall one thing she'd said. "I'm sorry. I'm a little distracted, I guess."

"You're tired," she said. "We didn't get a lot of sleep last night."

I nodded. "Yeah, I am a bit, but it's not that."

"No? What is it? You're always asking me what I need from you, but tonight, tell me what *you* need from *me*. I'd give you anything you ask for."

"You would?"

She wrapped her arm around mine between us and hugged me. "Of course, what is it you need, baby?"

"I need you," I said, and I pulled her on top of me, grabbing her glass before it spilled. I set it on the side table next to me, and she straddled my legs.

"You have me," she said, lifting her dress over her head. Her bare breasts bounced, and seeing her in only her thong drove me wild.

She began to unbutton my jeans and then unzip them. She moved to the floor and knelt between my legs, then tugged the jeans and my boxers down my thighs and rubbed her hands over them slowly. She leaned over me, looking at my cock now standing up between us, smiled softly up at me, and descended.

"Roxanne," I groaned when she opened her mouth and took me inside. I was so hard, it hurt. My head fell to the back of the couch, eyes closed in ecstasy. "Is this how you imagined it earlier, when I told you you'd suck my dick before the night was through?"

"Mm," she moaned around my cock and nodded, and the movement made her suck me harder.

"Fuck."

She increased her pace and wrapped her hand tightly around the base of my dick, then added her other hand and squeezed hard.

"Yeah," I breathed, begging for more, watching her head bob above my body. My belt hung from my jeans, the buckle glinting in the light from her lamp, and it gave me an idea.

The flat of her tongue dragging up my shaft and then curling around the head of my cock was exquisite torture. I could barely focus, but I managed to pull the belt from the loops of my jeans. I folded it in half and held it by the buckle, then let the leather fall over her back as she sucked me.

She felt it and she shivered. She thought I wanted to use it on her.

"Beauty," I said, trying not to come, "will you to do somethin' for me?" She looked up my body, but she didn't stop sucking my dick, and the sight of her flushed cheeks and her mouth wrapped around me was almost my undoing. I bucked into her, and the belt buckle dug into my palm when I grabbed onto the arm and the back of the couch for leverage to fuck her mouth harder.

She didn't look away, and neither did I as I lifted the belt above her back and let it fall onto her skin with a soft *slap*. She gasped and sucked harder.

"Goddamn," I panted, trying to catch my breath. Trying to stay in control. "Your mouth feels so fuckin' good."

But I wanted to feel the belt. I wanted *her* to punish *me*.

Since Dixon's call and her bite this evening, I needed it more every passing second.

Draping the belt over the arm of the couch, I sat up and lifted her mouth off me with my finger under her chin.

Her eyes flashed with uncertainty and confusion. "What is it? What's wrong?"

"You said you'd give me what I need."

"Anything," she said. "Tell me."

Without speaking, I slipped my hands beneath her arms and lifted her off the floor. I sat her next to me on the couch and then stood and took off my shirt. She watched me unbutton it slowly, her eyes darting back and forth between the nervous look on my face and my chest as I revealed it to her.

"Brand?"

I shook my head. I couldn't speak. I had no clue what to say except that I wanted her to hurt me. I wanted her to make me pay for all the secrets I'd been carrying around like a fucking disease. I needed someone to punish me for leaving my brother with a monster all those years ago.

When I knelt in front of the couch and handed her the belt, she didn't speak, but I knew the change in my demeanor and the begging in my eyes were probably confusing her.

"Please, Roxanne? I *need* this."

"Why?" she whispered.

Dropping my head and letting it hang over her couch, I said, "I don't know how to explain, but I love you and I trust you, and I need you to do this to me."

Her silence told me she'd heard me tell her I loved her.

I did. I had no clue how it happened so quickly, but it had. I'd fallen so fucking in love with her I could barely see straight, but this nagging, pulling guilt in my core wouldn't let me free. I needed her to release it so I could laugh with her and love her.

"*Please?*"

Wordlessly, she stood, and she moved to my side and angled her body. The leather zipped through the air when she lifted the belt, but when she let her arm fall, I barely felt it.

"Harder."

"Brand, what's happenin' right now?"

"Harder. *Please*."

"No," she said resolutely. She let the belt drop from her fingers, and she knelt next to me and wrapped me up in her arms. "Talk to me. What's goin' on with you tonight? Please, baby, tell me." She held me, and it felt better than the belt or sex or anything. "I love you too, but I don't want you to hurt."

Finally, when I thought I could talk without blubbering, I rose up on my knees and sat back on my heels.

"I lied."

"To me?" She searched my face, her eyes roaming and trying to find the answer.

"To everyone."

She was uneasy when she asked, "About?"

"A lot of things. And I have so much guilt. *So much* fuckin' guilt, Roxanne."

"Because you lied?"

"Yes. No. I mean, yes but I'm guilty of more than lyin'."

She waited. Didn't push me.

I turned toward her, and we faced each other, both of us still kneeling on the floor. She held my hands while I talked.

"When we were kids, teenagers, my father used to whip my little brother. I don't think Abey ever knew. Until she was fifteen years old, she was my father's princess. Nothing bad ever touched her. Bax was the oldest, and he was well suited for farm life. I was… not so much. But I was strong, and I did what our father wanted.

"Dixon didn't. He was rebellious, as most teens are, but he and my father, they just didn't get along. I noticed it even when Dixon and Abey were little. Our father wasn't cruel then, but I'd see him get irritated with Dixon about the dumbest things. But as Dixon got older and braver, our father got meaner.

"Bax and I did our best to protect him, but Merv babied Dixon. He was small and my father saw that as weakness. She made it worse because she coddled him and let him off the hook for things she shouldn't have. That just made our father irate."

"I'm so sorry," Roxanne murmured. "Did he ever hit you?"

"Once. It was enough. It's why I left really, first chance I got, but he was verbally and emotionally abusive, *especially* to Dixon.

"When Bax and his first wife, Candy, married, they moved off the farm to a little cottage in town, and it got worse. Abey was a ghost in our house. Our dad didn't want her working with us by then, after he found out she was gay, so a lot of days it was only Dixon and me with the old man.

"One night, Dixon was fuckin' around with the shearing equipment, and he broke it. My dad lost his shit. He punched Dixon in the face so hard, he passed out. Broke his nose."

Roxanne gasped beside me. From her stories about her parents and sisters, I knew she came from a normal, loving family. I wanted to spare her the horrid details, but I needed her to understand.

"When I graduated high school, the only thought in my head was gettin' out. I ran. Fast. Dixon was two years behind me, so for two years, he was pretty much alone with that man. Merv was no help. Abey was livin' her own hell, and she avoided home like the plague. Who would blame her? And Bax and Candy were in their own little world.

"My dad cared too much what people thought of him. I think that's why he hid the worst of it from Bax. And Dixon wouldn't talk about it.

"But I knew, and I abandoned him. I'll never forgive myself for it. I should've taken him with me when I left, but what could I have done? Dixon was sixteen, but I was only eighteen, and I was tryin' to figure out how to survive on my own.

"But that's when shit really started to go bad with Dixon. He started drinkin'. Smokin'. He didn't care anymore. And why should he have? Everyone who loved him left him or treated him like shit.

"The one person who treated him like he deserved was Bax's wife, Candy. They were friends. She looked out for Dixon. I'm not certain, but I don't think she knew the worst of Dixon's relationship with our father, but it wasn't hard to see how traumatized Dixon had become.

"Candy loved him. And then she died, and Dixon was with her that day. He watched her and her unborn child die right in front of him. He did CPR. He tried."

I shook my head, whispering, "After that..." I didn't need to finish the sentence. Roxanne didn't need to hear me say it.

CHAPTER TWENTY-SIX

ROXANNE

"GOD. THE POOR GUY."

"He called me," Brand said. "Before he left Wisper and disappeared. Before Stuey. It was two years ago. I was so busy with work. We had so many fuckin' projects goin', and I was overwhelmed. Bea was with me up in Sheridan. She was tryin' to help, but we'd just gotten so big and successful, and it was too much all at once.

"So when Dixon called, 'just to hear my voice,' he said, I didn't see what I should've. I didn't see how he'd changed. Or maybe I did and I chose not to notice because that was easier. It hurt less. It was less messy."

"Brand," I said, "I know you know this, but it isn't your fault. You couldn't have stopped your dad. You couldn't have made him love Dixon. It's not your fault Dixon left, and it's not your fault he became an addict."

"I *don't* know that."

Softly, I said, "I do."

Brand shook his head. "He called again, months after he left Stuart with Bax."

Whoa. This was definitely news. Abey had said no one

had seen or heard from Dixon once since he'd left Stuart at Bax's place in a wicker basket last year. "You talked to him?"

Nodding, he said, "He called and asked for money for rehab. I gave it to him. Of course I did. He told me Stuart's mother died. She overdosed. He'd been somewhat clean after the baby was born, but then Kel died, and he couldn't hold it together. I flew to California and checked him into a rehab in Redding. Paid up front. And then I left him again. He said it was what he wanted, but... I should've stayed."

"Abey and Bax don't know? You didn't tell Merv?"

Jesus. Bax was likely to strangle Brand when he finally told his brother that his kid's birth mother had died months ago, and Brand had known but didn't say anything.

And suddenly, the way he had hugged and kissed Stuey after dinner tonight made perfect sense. Not that it was unusual for him to show his nephew affection, but tonight felt different. He hugged longer and harder, and he whispered something in Stu's ear. Now I had an idea what that might've been about.

"No."

"Brand, why not? They've been worried sick about Dixon."

He looked away. "I know. Don't you think I know that?"

"Then why?"

"Dixon begged me not to. I owed him."

"And now? Do you know where he is now?"

"No. He says he's sober, but he called me this mornin', and he said he needs time. He needs to be alone. I don't know where he is now. All he said was California. I asked if he needed money or a car. He said no, and he hung up."

I flopped on my ass and leaned back against the couch. Minutes passed in silence as I thought through all the ways this information could play out in Brand's life. In Abey's. But then I said, "Brand, you have to tell them."

"Don't you get it? I can't. I can't betray Dixon like that. It's the only thing he asked of me. I can't go back on my word. Not with him."

"And if he gets hurt, or God forbid, he dies, what then? What will you tell them?"

"Even if they knew, what could they do? They can't make him stay sober. Merv can't mother addiction away."

"No," I said. "You're right. Dixon has to come to terms with his addiction on his own, but…"

"But what?"

"I just know that if it were Aubrey and one of her boys was in trouble, she'd want to know he was still alive. If it were you, if you were the addict, Merv would want to know if you were still in this world, still breathin'. Even if she couldn't help you, if she didn't know where you were, don't you think she deserves to know that her son's heart still beats?"

He looked at me. He didn't speak.

"Please don't ever ask me to hurt you like that again," I said. "A little pain is sexy, for the sake of sex and arousal, but not because you believe you deserve to have pain inflicted on you to make up for your perceived sins.

"They're not sins, Brand. They might be mistakes. I'm not you. I can't judge 'cause I haven't lived through what you have. But *please*. If you want someone to hurt you, that's what therapists are for. Or dominatrixes.

"I'm neither. I'm a cop. If you want my help, ask me to help you find Dixon. Ask me to hold you. But don't you dare ever ask me to hit you like that again."

He reached for me and pulled me close, wrapping his arms around me and tucking his face against my shoulder.

"You'd do that for me?" he asked quietly, like he couldn't believe I'd offered.

"Of course I will. I love you. There probably isn't much I wouldn't do for you, but if I help you look, you have to promise me you'll tell your family."

"I will. I promise."

———

"I DON'T LIKE TO FLY," I said as Brand buckled my seatbelt on a small Gulfstream his friend from Montana loaned him for our flight to Redding, California. He tightened the strap across my lap and let his hand linger over my thigh.

"Why not?"

"Dunno. I just never have. This is a fancy plane, but on commercial flights, I'm always so uncomfortable. I think it's 'cause I know everyone can see the back of my head over the seat. And it's that feelin', you know? That out-of-control thing that makes you panic when the plane lifts off the ground."

"Are you afraid of heights?"

"No," I said. "I'm afraid of crashin' to my death in a heap of flamin' metal."

Brand seemed nervous, but I doubted it had anything to do with a fear of hurtling toward the earth from forty-thousand feet in the air.

I tried to distract him while we waited for final checks to be completed and takeoff. "Tell me again what she said when you spoke to the director of the rehab center."

"Not a lot. She said she couldn't give out any information, HIPAA and all that." He shook his head. "I tried to lie, told her Merv was facin' a health crisis, and that she and

Dixon were close so he needed to know. I guess that's not totally a lie, but she wouldn't budge."

"Brand, I know what findin' Dixon means to you, but I don't want you to get your hopes up. If someone doesn't want to be found, sometimes they can't be. I don't have any sway in California, not unless we call in other authorities, which would mean gettin' Abey and probably Sheriff Michaels involved."

"No," he said. "We're doin' this my way."

"Your way?"

He looked me dead in the eye and said, "*My* way. Money talks, Roxanne. I'm not proud of it, but I contacted Billie Cade last night and had her do a little diggin' on the rehab center's director, Julie Buckley. She's a single mom, and she's in the middle of a nasty custody case with her ex-husband. She's up to her ears in debt."

"I'm gonna pretend you didn't just say that to me."

"Fine." He straightened and settled back against his seat. "I'm not askin' for your approval. I just want your support." But he lifted my hand and pressed his lips to my knuckles, rolling his head to look at me. "And your love. Can you forgive me my methods?"

"Ask me tomorrow. But you know money doesn't guarantee this woman will betray her clients' privacy and break the law?"

"I have to *try*, Roxanne. I can't keep livin' with this secret. It's tearin' me apart inside."

"I know." I kissed the back of his hand, too, rubbing my lips over his skin, and laced my fingers around his. "So, say we do find your brother. What then?"

He sighed a long, pained release of breath and faced forward. "I don't know."

A woman who didn't look much older than a high-school

graduate walked out of the airplane's cockpit, patting her red hair neatly into its ponytail, and she smiled widely as she approached us. She laid her hand over the seatback in front of me and leaned forward. "We'll be taking off in a few minutes. Please let me know if I can get you anything."

"Whiskey," Brand and I replied at the same time, and I added, "the cheaper, the better."

CHAPTER TWENTY-SEVEN

BRAND

"MR. LEE, you know I can't give you the information you're asking for," Mrs. Buckley said, leaning back in her chair behind her desk in her office. Three framed, black-and-white photographs of redwood trees adorned the wall behind her. She shook her head. "I'm offended you thought you could buy it from me."

Roxanne tensed in the chair next to mine. She hadn't liked my plan to try to bribe Dixon's whereabouts from the rehab director.

"Your brother was here. You already know that since you checked him in yourself and paid for his treatment, but the second he entered our system and you walked out the door, his information became mine to protect and keep.

"I don't know the answer to the question you're asking. Your brother is not here anymore, and I don't know where he went after treatment. I don't know if he's sober, and even if I did know, I wouldn't tell you."

She stood and smoothed her hands down her jeans and an oversized pumpkin-orange sweater. She seemed younger than

I remembered, but her dark hair had already begun to gray at her temples.

"I'm sorry you came all this way. I thought I made myself clear over the phone, but it's your dime. Now, if you'll excuse me, I have a job to do, other brothers to help, other sons, daughters, sisters, mothers, and fathers. Money doesn't make yours more important."

I stood, too, intending to beg harder just as a knock sounded on her office door.

"Come in, Ernesto," she said, and a short man with unhealthy, pockmarked skin entered the room.

The man looked nervous. He bit the inside of his cheek as he looked at me, Roxanne, and then the director. "Carina said you needed me?"

"Yes. This is Dixon Lee's brother. He was just leaving. Would you mind escorting him and his friend to the exit?"

Ernesto's face lit up at the mention of Dixon's name, but then his eyes flicked back and forth between Mrs. Buckley and me. "Uh, sure?"

"Thank you." She glanced at Roxanne and me one last time. "Good day, Mr. Lee, Ms. Fitts, and good luck."

When she was gone, Ernesto swung his hand toward the door. He seemed proud but confused to have been asked to escort us. The rehab ran out of a large house in the center of town. We couldn't really get lost.

He didn't say anything as he led us to the front door, but when we got there, he turned. "You hear about Dixon's baby mama?"

"Uh, yes," I said. "He told me."

"She was pretty fucked up." His eyes roamed up and down Roxanne's body. "Lady, you're tall."

Roxanne laughed, and I wanted to kiss her for reminding me there was good in the world. The dated house was depressing, the lightless beige color of the walls leaching hope from my chest, and the awkwardness of the entire situation festered beneath my skin. As well-maintained as the old house was, I couldn't imagine living here. I hated that Dixon had to. I wanted to be outside in the fresh air and sunshine, and I was sure it was how Dixon had felt too.

I was ashamed that I'd tried to use money to get what I wanted. This wasn't business. But I was even more irritated that it hadn't worked.

"Thanks, Ernesto," Roxanne said. "Do you usually escort people out?"

"Nope. And don't call me that. Name's Nesty, you know, like Postie? This is a first for me, but since we're here and we're both attractive adults, you wanna pass me your digits? I've got twenty-three days sober this time, and my uncle's holdin' a job for me up in Alaska on his fishin' boat. Pays good money. I could take you out."

"Thanks, Nesty," she said. "I'm flattered you asked, but" —she took hold of my hand and squeezed, and when I looked at her, she flared her eyes and nodded suggestively toward Ernesto—"I think my man here might have somethin' to say about it."

"Your man?" he said, looking me up and down in barely muted disappointment. "Pft. This dude seems like a stuffy suit. Dixon was cooler."

Catching on, I said, "Dixon is definitely cooler than me. You guys are friends?"

Ernesto nodded and puffed out his small chest. "The best."

"Well then maybe you can help us. I'm tryin' to contact my brother. Our mama's sick. Dixon needs to know."

"You the oldest brother or the other one?"

"The other one." I held my hand out. It took a minute, but he finally reached for it and shook it. "Brand Lee."

"You're the rich brother."

"I wouldn't say—"

"Yeah," he said, "but you got money. If I tell you what I know, would you do somethin' for me?"

"Yes," I said, as Roxanne squeezed again and said, "Depends on what it is."

But Ernesto was done flirting with her. Now that he knew who I was, all his attention stayed fixed on me.

"I got a kid too," he said. "Two kids actually. I haven't seen 'em in a couple years. They live with their mom's parents. You know how that goes." He rolled his eyes.

"Uh, yes, I can imagine that's hard for you."

"Yeah, well, I deserve it, but they don't. And my ex says they're strugglin'. Her dad took a job at Home Depot on the weekends to help out, but they're older. They're on social security, and you know that ain't shit these days."

"If I sent them some help…" I hinted.

"Then I'd probably feel real friendly towards you. I'd be grateful and all that bullshit."

"Consider it done," I said, fully planning to keep my word, *if* he kept his and told me where my brother was. Probably even if he didn't.

"There's an old logging company. They ain't in business no more, but that's not my point. If you look on a map and find McCaffrey Logging out by Mad River, follow the road it's on with your finger. Go north. And about an inch further up the map, you'll find a house and an old couple. The Coulters. They're hippies if you ask me, but they're good folks. You'll find your brother there. They take in junkies in recovery and give 'em a place to sleep and work till they're ready to face the world again."

"Thank you." Surprising myself and Ernesto, I reached out and hugged him. "Thank you so much. You have no idea how badly I need to find Dixon."

"Yeah, well, just don't tell him I outed him," he said awkwardly as I stepped away. "He won't be happy with me for that. Better to tell him Buckley gave up the goods."

"We won't say a word," Roxanne assured him.

"Your kids," I reminded him. "Where do they live? What are their names?" I pulled my phone from my pocket and typed in a new contact entry.

"Their grandparents are Opal and Marcos Martinez. They live down near Sacramento. My kids are Gabe and Eden. They deserve better than the shit me and their mom gave 'em. A little donation from you could go a long way, but don't tell 'em I had anything to do with it."

"MAD RIVER? Is it a river or a town?" Roxanne asked as she scissored her fingers over her cell phone's screen and zoomed in on northwestern California. "It sounds like somethin' out of a thriller movie. I really hope it's not a cult or some kind of serial-killer camp."

Despite the urgency I felt to get on the road, I snorted.

"What?" she said with an adorable smile.

"I doubt it's either of those things." Pulling up a search for Mad River on my phone, I said, "Look. It's both. There's a river that runs through a tiny place called Mad River. From the pictures, it doesn't look sinister. Just looks remote."

Roxanne rested her head on my shoulder and glanced at the screen. "It looks like the perfect place to go to grieve and come to terms with sobriety. I hope that's what Dixon found there anyway. He's been through a lot."

"Yeah."

"Here you are, sir," a young guy said when he returned to the rental car booth and handed me a set of keys. "We'll see you back here in two days. Drop off time is noon or before."

"Thank you. Do you have a map of the area? Like an actual paper map in case we lose our cell signal?"

"Yeah, there's one in the glove box. Complimentary."

"Thanks," Roxanne said.

On the lot, we found our silver Jeep Compass and settled in.

"I haven't rented a car in a long time," I said.

"No?"

I shook my head. "Tab makes arrangements if I travel, but I've been so busy with work, I haven't really had the time lately. Besides, someone usually picks me up or sends a car."

"What was it you said? 'Money talks'? Sounds more like money chauffeurs you around like a princess."

Laughing, I said, "Yeah, maybe, but you haven't seen me work. Ain't no princesses on my job sites." I ended the sentence with a cocked eyebrow, and Roxanne licked her lips.

"I might like to see that."

"I bet you would."

"Quit flirtin' with me, and let's go find your brother."

CHAPTER TWENTY-EIGHT

ROXANNE

NORTHERN CALIFORNIA, between Redding and the coast, looked like we'd driven onto the set of *Virgin River*.

Aubrey had made me watch it. She liked the heartfelt stories and all the quirky townsfolk in the show. I liked the sex. Or the almost-sex. She'd tried to get me to read the books, too, but I'd only made it through the first one before Brand had come to town and distracted me. But now that I could see the area the books had been set in, I was eager to read more.

Redwoods and fir trees lined two-lane Highway 36, creating a high canopy above the road, casting shadows on the light traffic passing us in the eastbound lane. Spectacular views, high mountain bridges, and small towns interrupted the scenic route every so often, and wooden signs had been stuck into the earth here and there, noting county roads and small businesses.

The weather was cool but sunny, and warm light filtered down to us through the tall trees. Brand wore a pair of sunglasses he'd pulled out of his backpack. He reminded me of James Dean in *Rebel Without a Cause*, my dad's favorite movie.

"What's the plan then?" I asked. "We're almost to Mad River. If I'm right about the road Evo told us to take, it's not far past the town."

"It's late in the day. I was thinkin' we should find a hotel and get somethin' to eat. We can set out early tomorrow mornin' to find Dixon."

"Okay," I said, scrolling my maps app and pulling up lodging options. "How do you feel about yurts?"

"Does it come with granola, or do we need to supply our own?"

I snorted. "Ha ha. But it looks cool. It's got heat and a private bathroom, and look." I held my phone between us so Brand could see the screen. "There's a big window over the bed so we can fall asleep under the stars."

A slow smile lifted his lips. "I'll fuck you under those stars. Wait. Are yurts soundproof? It's basically a big tent, right?"

"I think so. But I'll just have to whisper 'yes, sir' in your ear so no one else will hear."

He groaned. "Don't you start with that now, or I'll put you over my knee for distractin' me while I'm drivin'."

"Is that a promise, sir?" I said coyly, and I reached over to unbutton his jeans. I slid my hand inside and grasped his cock tightly. He was hard, and it was an empowering feeling, knowing I had that much control over his body.

"*Roxanne*."

"Yes, sir? Would you like me to stop?"

The Jeep swerved when I squeezed. "Fuck."

Brand's quickened breath was the only sound I could hear except for the wind whipping past the SUV outside. I pumped his thick length, watching his face and the way his eyelids grew heavier, like they wanted to fall shut, but he couldn't let them because he was driving.

"This isn't behavior I'd expect from a law enforcement officer," he breathed.

As I unbuckled my seatbelt and leaned over his lap, his hand tangled in my hair and he pushed my head below the steering wheel.

Before I sucked his cock into my mouth, I whispered, "Then it's a good thing I'm not on duty."

"SO, THIS IS A YURT?"

"It is," I said, spinning in a slow circle in the center of the round, extremely fancy tent. "I don't think they're all this nice though. Ours has a claw-foot tub and a microwave."

The impromptu blowjob I'd given Brand had extended our driving time a bit. He pulled off the highway just short of Mad River into a little carved-out lookout cove, parked, and I sucked like my life depended on him coming.

It hadn't taken long, and then he calmly got out of the car and walked around to open my door and undress me from the waist down so he could finger me right there on the side of the road in the dappled daylight, and I came with my legs spread wide on the seat, his eyes on mine, and the mountain wind in my hair.

We ate an early dinner at a quirky little burger hut in Mad River, and then went to find our rental yurt.

"I'll draw us a bath." He set my suitcase and his backpack on a humungous round bed and went to fill the impressive tub while I sat and checked my messages on my phone.

I had been avoiding it. When I asked for a few days off work, Abey had agreed easily. Unless I was really sick, I wasn't one to take days off, so I had a bunch saved up. But she was definitely curious about why I wanted to take the time. I promised Brand I wouldn't tell her as long as he gave me his word that he'd come clean after we found Dixon.

He'd agreed again and sealed his promise with a kiss.

But I still felt hesitation coming from him. I knew he didn't want to keep his family in the dark. It was clear that doing so had been difficult and painful for him and that he was very aware of how much it would affect them, so I wasn't sure why he didn't want to come clean.

Finally, I opened my texts, and sure enough, there was an ongoing meme war in our group chat between my sisters and one from Abey waiting for me to open it:

7: 19 PM

If you and my brother are on some kinda sexcation, I don't want to know details. BUT if this is something else, you better fess up.

It's not entirely a sexcation. But why would you think it was something else?

She responded immediately:

Cuz Brand has been off lately. Idk why. Do you?

I didn't know the right thing to do. Answer with yes, but not tell her we were looking for Dixon? Or lie and say I had no clue what had been going on with Brand?

"The water's almost ready," Brand said, and he took my

phone and the decision out my hands, and then he pushed until I lay back flat on the bed. "How shall I punish you for earlier?"

"Mm. I thought you said you were gonna take me over your knee. I quite liked that threat."

"Later. Right now, I'm feelin' a little like gettin' even." He pulled my jeans down, kissing and licking as he followed the denim down my thighs. My pretty, frilly pink underwear went next, and then he stood and removed my sweatshirt and my Teton County T-shirt underneath. "Good girl," he praised when he saw no bra beneath.

When he said that, when he called me his "good girl," even though he was younger than me, it sent this rush of pleasure through my body, like a shot of dopamine. Maybe that was what hearing him say it caused inside me. Whatever it was, I loved it. It made me want to work hard to obey and please him.

It was a small bit of ease that took the edge off the loss of control I felt when anxiety and insecurity plagued me.

It wouldn't have worked with any other man, but Brand had a commanding way about him. And the look in his eyes, his utter devotion to my satisfaction made me *ache* to please him.

He played with my breasts for a few moments, licking my nipples and pinching with his fingers. He massaged and pressed my tits together and leaned over me to kiss me, but before I could claim his lips, he pulled them away and slid down to his knees between my legs.

"You are not to make a sound, do you understand?" He looked up my body. "You may answer this time."

"Yes, sir."

Grabbing his backpack, he yanked it to the floor and unzipped a pocket. My heart raced at the thought of what he might have packed in there. I squirmed, trying to see, but he gripped my throat to keep me still while he continued to search inside the bag. "Hands at your sides."

Well, that just made me wetter.

"If you move, you won't get what you deserve. Do you want what I have for you?"

I nodded eagerly. Whatever it was, I was desperate for it.

"Good," he breathed between my legs, and his cool breath washed over my hot pussy. "Look at you, beauty. Already so wet for me."

"Yes, sir. *Please*."

A loud *slap* rent the air and my inner thigh stung. "I said no talkin'." He set a short, black leather crop on the bed next to my hip, and I gasped and moaned while he continued to rummage in the bag a few seconds longer. Finally, he found what he wanted, and he stilled between my legs.

"You may answer my next question, and then not a word. If I have to, I'll gag you."

I kept my mouth closed and gritted my teeth to stop from moaning again.

"What's your safe word?"

"Basketball," I breathed, my whole body beginning to tremble with anticipation.

"Good girl. Now, from here on out, you may not speak or make noise, and my beauty, you may not *come* until I give you permission."

"Bu—"

The look in his eyes shut me up. He wasn't joking or fooling around.

"What was that?"

I shook my head. No way was I going to talk and lose whatever it was he was planning to give me.

With a nod and without warning, he leaned forward and

ate my pussy, licking inside my body and rubbing something small in the wet channel between my lips. I drove my hips into his face over and over, seeking the pressure I needed to come, but he refused to touch my clit.

After five minutes of that torture, I was sweating and ready to scream. Finally, he reached inside me and pumped his fingers, but there was also a foreign sensation, something kind of hard and round slipping through those fingers.

He pulled out of me and sat back on his heels, licking my mess off his mouth with an eager tongue. "I told you I want to fuck this ass." He pressed one finger against my hole and rubbed in a circle softly. "This *beautiful* ass. But you're not ready for that, so I'm gonna make you ready. Nod if you consent."

The back of my head hit the mattress so many times, I felt dizzy as he slipped a finger back inside my pussy.

"That's the right answer," he breathed, and it was the only warning before his finger slid out of one hole and pushed inside the other slowly. "Your cunt is so wet, I don't even need to use lube." But he pulled out quickly, and there was a really odd sensation left in my ass. "Don't move. Stay right here and get used to it."

As he walked to the sink to wash his hands, I wiggled my butt on the bed, trying to ascertain what he'd left in my body. I reached between my legs and felt some kind of bulbous silicone toy inserted shallowly.

"Anal beads," he said, walking back to me. He held out his hands and when I took them, he pulled me to my feet. "Is it painful?"

I shook my head.

"Good. Let's get you in the tub."

With his aid, I climbed into the hot water and sank down. The beads moved in my ass, and I moaned. Brand pulled the crop from his back pocket and slapped the space between my breasts once, then dropped the crop to the floor.

"No sound. Now, there are three connected beads. The one I slipped inside you is the smallest. I'm gonna undress, and I want you to watch me and finger your pussy. Do. Not. Come. And when you're ready, I'll give you the next bead."

Nodding like a starved puppy with a big ol' bowl of grub in front of me, I was practically panting.

"Start now," he said. "Fuck your pussy with those long fingers. Don't half ass it." He smirked and tore his T-shirt over his head.

He watched my hand beneath the water and the way my tits jiggled and my body tensed when I slipped my fingers between my pussy lips and rubbed my clit, and he smiled when I slid two fingers inside myself and my rigid muscles relaxed. I was already writhing, feeling an orgasm build, and then he unzipped his jeans and pushed them down his legs.

Brand's dick was majestic and supremely thick with arousal, his veins bulging as he wrapped his hand around it and pumped. The head turned purple as he twisted and squeezed himself almost violently.

Oh God. Oh no. There's so fucking way I'm not coming!

"*Roxanne*," he warned and I froze, as if his voice was the very neurons commanding my muscles and telling them to stop. "Not yet."

My eyes locked on his when he climbed over and straddled the curved edges of the tub, bringing his cock straight to my mouth. His balls dipped into the water, and I imagined sinking underneath and sucking them.

"Open."

My mouth popped open so fast, tongue flat and ready to accept his cock inside. It was probably funny, but there was no laughter on Brand's face.

Only lust.

"Good girl," he whispered as he scooted forward two inches and bumped his hardness against my chin. "I want to fuck your throat while you finger yourself.

"Tell me yes."

CHAPTER TWENTY-NINE

BRAND

ROXANNE NODDED, and she pumped her fingers in her pussy, feeling her slick arousal mixing with the bathwater. No woman had ever been so responsive to my words or the sound of my voice.

It took everything I had inside me not to pull her out of the tub and fuck her with the beads in her ass. But I wanted her prepared so I could slip my cock in that ass easily and she wouldn't feel pain.

"In a minute, you won't be able to speak, so you won't be able to use your safe word if you need it. Instead, if you want me to stop, you will pinch the outside of my thigh twice. Give me your hand, but don't stop touchin' yourself."

Her wet hand caressed its way up my thigh, and with a tight grip on her wrist, I led it to the outside and showed her where to touch me to stop me.

"Do it now so I know you understand."

Gently, she pinched twice.

"You can do better than that."

Her left eyebrow popped up, and she twisted my skin

between her fingers, digging her fingernail in. With her mouth still open, she blinked once and nodded.

"So eager to please," I praised, and I watched how the words transformed her face. She liked pleasing me, and when I told her, a light sparkled in her brown eyes. "But first, swallow my cock and push the beads further in your ass. Go up to the second bead."

She did what I asked, and I moaned when her warm tongue accepted and sucked my cock into her mouth. She pushed the beads in further, and her body hardened, her muscles tightening as she worked to accept the larger bead and acclimate.

God, just knowing her hand was between her legs made me ravenous for her. I wanted to own her. Every fucking part of her.

"Has anyone ever taken your ass before?"

Shaking her head carefully, she pumped her fingers in her pussy again, and the water reacted to her movement, sloshing around the rim of the tub and splashing over the edge and onto the floor.

I pushed to the back of her throat, but instinct closed it and my dick met resistance.

"Good girl, open up for me," I whispered through clenched teeth, the rough sound of my voice betraying me and showing her the struggle I was having, trying not to come. But her body followed my command. "Yes," I said, feeling her tight throat squeeze my cock. I thrust gently, and my eyes closed in ecstasy.

I felt her working hard to breathe, beginning to panic from lack of air, but she still wanted to obey.

"Swallow, Roxanne, and breathe through your nose. Let your body do what it wants to."

Her throat closed around my cock as she swallowed, and she inhaled deeply.

"Fuck, that's so goddamn good."

Moving over her, rolling forward and back over the tub, I took her mouth and throat slowly. She relaxed, getting into my rhythm, and she moaned again and closed her eyes, pressing her feet against the end of the tub behind me so she could fuck herself harder.

A sharp tug of my hand in her hair reminded her to keep quiet. She went silent again instantly, and she sucked harder. She liked the pain as much as I did. She couldn't lie to me. But it wasn't the reason I wanted her silence.

I wanted the pleasure to build inside her. I wanted it to be all she could think about so that when I gave her permission, she'd come so hard, she wouldn't need a window in a tent to see stars.

Demanding her silence and not allowing her to come would make her erupt on my cock when I gave the order, and all of it would make her pliant and make her tight ass ready for me.

"Make me come, Roxanne," I said between thrusts. "Keep your throat open so I can fuck it and my cum can coat it."

When she nodded, my dick slipped in deeper, and I groaned loudly. Threading my hands through her hair, I gripped it between my fingers so I could control her pace. She liked that. I knew she would, and she hollowed her cheeks, sucking as hard as she could, making me shudder above her and fuck her mouth faster.

Looking down at her, I saw her eyelids fluttering, cheeks flushing, and her whole body moving under the water as she finger fucked herself in rhythm with my thrusts.

I reminded her, "You do not have permission to come."

She was trying to hold out, but she was losing the battle. I could hardly blame her. What she was doing to me was the definition of sexy, letting me get off in her mouth while she fucked herself.

She trusted me to make the decisions. Trusted me to know what would make her feel good, and she trusted me not to hurt her, even though my dick was hitting the back of her throat and sliding further down. She let me choke her for pleasure, and the intimacy of the act and the trust she'd placed in me made me harder.

The bathwater licked at her breasts, rushing and flowing over her perfectly erect nipples, and it receded when she rocked on her hand.

Spit pooled at the edges of her lips and flowed down her chin, and still, she continued to finger herself, but she only needed one hand for that, so she reached beneath me and gripped my balls in her tight fist and pulled them down, rolling and smashing them together.

When she twisted them, sucked one more time as hard as she could, and swallowed, breath punched out of my lungs, and I cursed and groaned as the hot flow of my cum slid down the back of her throat.

"Good girl," I rasped as she swallowed her reward, and I released her hair and grabbed the edges of the tub to hold myself up.

I stood, then slipped into the water behind her and cradled her still needy body against mine. The warm water fused us together, letting her skin slip and slide over my mine, and already, need had begun to fill up my cock again.

"Keep fuckin' yourself," I whispered in her ear, rubbing my unshaven cheek against hers and loving how her wet hair stuck to my skin, but I slipped a hand over her hip and between her spread legs. My arms were long enough to reach the anal beads, and I used one finger to ease the last, largest bead inside her ass.

She gasped at the size and sensation, but I didn't punish her for the noise this time. She was ready. I nearly was too. My dick jumped behind her, hardening again easily with every wet, soft glide of her ass cheeks.

"Stop," I said, and she froze. "Now grip the sides of the tub. Hold on tight."

She complied immediately, and I lifted her with my hands beneath her ribcage.

"Keep rubbin' that beautiful ass along my cock and make me hard again."

She moved to kneel above me, then lowered her ass to do as she'd been told, but she leaned forward, trying to slip my dick between her pussy lips to steal some friction.

"Naughty Deputy, I didn't give you permission to come. If you keep doin' that, you will."

Whimpering, she released me and slid backward, rubbing my dick between her ass cheeks, and when I was hard again, I stilled.

My cock was positioned at her core, and with one fast stroke, I was inside her pussy to the hilt.

Her head rolled back on her shoulders, her mouth open but soundless just like I wanted. Goddamn, she felt so fucking good. If I wasn't rock hard before I entered her, her ready body cured me of that.

"Let me hear you now, beauty," I murmured in her ear. "Feel the beads in your ass rubbing my cock inside and come for me." I pushed a hand over her hip and between her legs, and this time all it took was one circle of my slippery finger around her clit, and she was screaming my name and shattering apart like tempered glass in the cold at the mercy of the head of my hammer.

ROXANNE DIDN'T SAY A WORD.

She couldn't. She could barely catch her breath after that orgasm. But that was okay by me, because I wasn't anywhere near through with her yet. Before I'd lifted her out of the bath, I pulled gently on the end of the string of anal beads, and her body released them easily, more proof she was ready for me.

"Don't move," I said softly when I carried her to the bed and lowered her onto her back.

As I dried her long legs with a bath towel, she laughed and rolled her eyes. "As if I could. You broke me. My whole body is in tatters."

"You're beautiful when you come, broken or not."

She blushed, and my dick pulsed with heat. I hadn't finished inside her in the bath, so I was still hard as granite and aching to fuck her.

"I don't understand, Brand."

"Don't understand what?" Reaching behind her, I grabbed a pillow and tucked it under her ass so it was lifted up and at the perfect angle for me to take it.

"What're you doin?" she asked.

"Answer my question."

"I don't understand why you call me beauty. I don't understand how someone like you wants someone like me."

"Someone like me? Roxanne, please explain to me why you seem to think you aren't worthy of my affection. How did you come to believe that about yourself?"

She shook her head, not wanting to admit her insecurities.

"This is all about trust. You know that, right?" I asked. "If you don't trust me, how the hell did you let me do to you what I just did?"

She grunted in frustration and threw her arm over her eyes. "No one has ever looked at me the way you do. Every relationship I've had has ended in disappointment. What I want never matters. What I need. And I'm not just talkin' about romantic or sexual relationships, although, sadly they're few and far between.

"But all my life, I've been the best friend. The middle daughter. The weird one. The sister without a husband or kids. In my family's eyes, it makes me less than. What I want out of life doesn't matter."

"It matters to me."

"But why? I know I'm different than the women you usually date."

"Yeah, you are. Very different. You're funny and kind, and you care for your friends in ways I haven't experienced in a long time. You care for me. You're smart and dedicated to your job and your role in your community.

"You are also the sexiest woman I've ever known, but it isn't about what you wear or how other people see you. Your beauty comes from inside you, and it shines so fuckin' bright, I can't see straight when I'm with you."

Lifting her arm away from her eyes, I placed her hand on my face, so she could see me and feel the words I needed her to hear. "The night of Merv's heart attack, when you held me and let me talk about hard things I'd never uttered to anyone, that was when I knew. My money doesn't matter to you. Status. Nice things. You don't care about any of that. When you told me you loved me, I didn't question it. I don't have to worry if you're lyin' to get somethin' from me."

"No, you don't. Never with me."

"That means more to me than I can ever say. So lie back and let me show you."

I kissed her, imagining a life I'd never dared to dream

before. Long walks through the woods. Laughter and nights spent wrapped up together in the house she'd imagined me building for her.

If I could fix things with my brother, I could be worthy of Roxanne and her love, and the life playing out in my head could be ours.

"Look at the stars above us, beauty. Tell me what you see."

She relaxed when I gave her direction and did what I told her to, and her trust in me made the need I felt for her inside my chest rage. Her head rolled back on the bed, and she gazed up at the night sky through the clear, plastic roof of the yurt, while I searched through my pack for the toy I'd brought with us, hoping for this exact occasion.

"I don't know," she said. "I never learned about the stars. I mean, I must have in science class at some point in my childhood, but I don't remember."

Crawling over her, I set the dildo, a condom, and a small bottle of lube between us on the bed, and I lay beside her. She tried to see what I'd brought with me, but I tilted her head back with my hand on her throat again and rolled to face her.

"Follow my finger," I said, releasing her and pointing up toward the sky through the window. "See that square cluster of stars that kinda looks like SpongeBob fallin' on his face?"

She laughed. "I think so."

"That's Pegasus. And below him is Aquarius."

I moved my finger lower, and she squinted, trying to make heads or tails of the constellations. Lifting her arm, she pressed it against mine and twined her fingers with mine, pointing with me.

I moved our hands together. "And I think this one is Cassiopeia. Looks like a zigzag."

She sighed. "So pretty. How do you know all this?"

"It got lonely at night when I left home. I stayed with friends for the first year, couch surfed, but then I rented this hole-in-the-wall studio apartment, and I was on the top floor with roof access. I was used to wide-open spaces on the farm, and the seclusion and small quarters started gettin' to me, so I spent a lot of nights up there, thinkin' about life. About the mistakes I'd made and how to fix 'em."

"Dixon," she guessed.

"Dixon."

"Are you scared to see him tomorrow?"

"Not scared, but I'm nervous, I guess. He says he's sober. I hope he is, but he hasn't been in a long time. I hated myself for thinkin' this, especially since it was partly my fault, but I didn't like the man my brother turned out to be. Just talkin' to him on the phone grated my nerves. I spent a lot of years wishin' he'd just buck up and get over his shit, you know? That's what *I* did."

"Maybe he didn't know how."

"Maybe, but it wasn't right for me to expect that from him in the first place. Men grow up thinkin' that havin' a hard head and manning up when things are down is what the world expects from us. And if we can't do that, then we aren't really men. It took me a long time to understand that that's just not fuckin' true. Dixon needed somethin' from me I didn't know how to give. And it wasn't money."

CHAPTER THIRTY

ROXANNE

"HE NEEDED MY CARE AND COMPASSION," Brand said, "but I didn't give it to him."

We lowered our hands, and I slid mine over his jaw, rubbing softly over the stubble there. I held him, looking into his eyes, judging what I found there. All I saw was love and regret. He still blamed himself for how his brother's life had turned out.

"You will now."

He smiled. "I will. Tomorrow, we'll find him, and tomorrow, if luck is on our side, my little brother and I will talk. But tonight under the northern stars, I have the most beautiful woman in the world in my arms. That ain't somethin' I'm willin' to waste, so spread your legs for me, Roxanne."

My entire body shivered at his command. The shakes started in my chest and moved to my arms and then my legs.

Brand moved between them, his big hands running up and down my ribcage, creating heat and anticipation. "I love you," he said. "I don't know how it happened so quickly, but it's this vast, tremendous thing inside my chest, and the only way I know how to stop it from breakin' me apart inside is to have you in every way that I can. In every way you'll let me. I need to be inside you, *every* part of you."

Lifting the mysterious accoutrements from the bed, he rose above me on his knees, and my eyes flared when I finally saw what they were. A gasp slipped between my lips, but my legs widened and my heart began to race, and I couldn't hold back the moan rushing out of my mouth.

He opened a condom packet that had lain hidden in the bedcovers and sheathed his cock with it, then slathered lube all over it with the palm of his hand, tugging his hardness and letting the lube ease the glide.

Heat flushed through me, and my asshole twitched at the sight. I was ready. He lubed the skin-colored dildo with a nifty little clit-massaging attachment, then lowered it between my legs and slid it inside me. When he pressed a button and the dildo began to buzz, I moaned and the clit attachment made me jerk in surprise.

Now who's a mewling bomb in his bed?

He pushed the dildo in and out slowly, the tickler doing its job quite nicely as it hummed and vibrated against my clit, and I braced myself for the impending invasion, but I already knew I'd love it. If Brand was the one filling me and making me come, it didn't matter how he accomplished it.

I wanted him, craved every single thing he needed to do to me, and I wanted to give every single thing he asked of me. He was right about the trust. I trusted that he wouldn't take too much and that he wouldn't hurt me, and he trusted me to accept him and his kinks and to tell him what I wanted and needed.

And now he was trusting me to hold his secrets safe.

"I need to fill your body completely. I need you to feel me everywhere, and I will make you come so many times, the stars in the sky won't compare to the light you see."

"Yes, baby," I said breathlessly as he leaned over me, his hands beside my arms on the bed, and he pushed the head of his cock inside my ass. I was relaxed, so turned on, and so in love with him that my body accepted what he gave me. There was barely any resistance. "Take me. Take everything you need from me. I belong to you."

A sexy smile curved the edges of his lips. "Forever found us, beauty. We weren't even lookin' for it, but the night knew what we didn't, and now she's guidin' us home."

MORNING CAME WAY TOO SOON.

My body ached in places I didn't know could ache. But the pain was delicious, and feeling the tightness and the well-used throb of certain orifices and muscles only made me want Brand again desperately.

Waking up beside him was delicious too. I hadn't told him, but I'd never done that with a man before. The motel didn't count since Brand hadn't had his own vehicle to get away in, but the men always ran, took what they wanted from me and then hit the road.

Not Brand. He wanted and needed me at his side, and that knowledge filled me fuller than his cock had last night.

I'd had no idea what I'd been missing by never allowing anyone to take my ass. The orgasms! Jesus. I had no clue I could come that hard that many times.

I tried to be quiet. I promised I would, but the entire yurt community was now quite aware of how much I liked butt sex, double penetration, and the feeling of being stuffed full of Brand's cock and a dildo at the same time. Everyone in a two-mile radius had to have heard me chanting and begging,

"Yes! Again. Fill me again, Brand. You feel so good inside me. Tap that ass!"

In fact, I'd probably screamed it loud enough for the entire state of California to hear.

Just thinking about it made me wet again.

Unfortunately, the impending, emotionally wrought conversation Brand needed to have with his brother kind of eighty-sixed that idea.

But when I rolled onto my back, eyes still closed in satisfied bliss and feeling with my hand for the hard, hot body I'd slept curled up against all night, Brand wasn't in the bed.

"I'm right here, good girl," he rumbled from the other side of the yurt.

Cracking an eyelid, I spotted him with his laptop open in front of him on the dining table. Coffee waited for me in an "I Love Yurts" mug, and a plate of what my nose told me was bacon and eggs sat opposite my boyfriend on the table.

"Is everything okay?" I nodded to his laptop.

"Yes," he said, and he lifted his "Golden State" mug for a sip of coffee. "Just checkin' emails while I waited for you to stir. I received an interesting one though. Someone heard about the job bid I won for the new housing development in Wisper, and they offered to take the contract off my hands for a very nice price."

"Really? Is that usual, for someone to email you out of the blue and offer somethin' like that?"

"It's not usual, I wouldn't think, but it's not *un*usual."

"Are you interested?"

He shrugged. "Dunno. Maybe." He laughed. "If I did sell it to this guy, he could work with Gina Scott. She'd *hate* that."

A wicked grin grew on my face. Oh, I liked that idea.

Brand chuckled, and I asked, "What time is it? Have you already showered?"

"It's eight thirty. And yes, though I hoped you'd hear me and wake up so I could take you in the shower, but you were dead to the world."

God. Why did everything that came out of his mouth have to be so sexy?

"Hm. I wonder why."

Morning light coming in the roof window bathed him in its buttery warmth, and it highlighted his face for a moment, drawing my eyes to his freshly shaven cheeks and chin and the smile lines around his mouth.

"Come eat," he said. "There's a small diner on the property, and they sent me back with fresh coffee and eggs for you. The woman workin' the grill said she thought you might need it this mornin'."

I sat up, groaning and covering my face with my hands. The blanket pooled around my naked hips, but I wasn't embarrassed to show my body to Brand. He loved it. He'd kissed and fucked all of it last night over and over again.

"Oh my God," I groaned. "I've never been so embarrassed in my life."

"There's no need for your embarrassment, Roxanne. You'll never see these people again. The important thing is that you enjoyed yourself." He closed the laptop softly and turned toward me still in the bed. "Did you?"

"Did I enjoy myself? Are you seriously askin' me that right now? Is it somehow possible you missed me screamin' your name and beggin' you to fuck me again?"

He rose slowly and crossed the yurt, his height making it feel small, when in reality, it was bigger than any hotel room I'd ever stayed in.

When he climbed over me on the bed, Brand murmured, "Would you like me to fuck you again now?"

He yanked the comforter away, letting it fall over the edge of the bed to the floor, and I lay back into the soft cocoon of the mattress and pulled him with me. He took my nipple into his warm mouth. He licked it, fluttered his tongue around it, and I ran my hands down his back and squeezed his ass cheeks, tugging him closer and feeling his hard cock rub my naked body through his jeans.

"Yes," I said. "I would, but I think we have more important things to attend to today." He dipped his head, lowering it into the crook of my neck and kissing me there. "Brand? What's wrong? Have you changed your mind? Do you not want to find Dixon? We came all this way."

"I haven't changed my mind. It's just that I have no control over what will happen today or the outcome, and if you haven't noticed, I kinda need to be in control at all times."

"Well," I said, lifting my hands and running my fingers through his still-damp hair, "if things get out of control today, I'll be there, and I will face it with you. Deal?"

He whispered, "I love you."

"WHAT WOULD you do if you sold your contract? I mean, would you just shut down Lee Construction?" I asked, trying to distract him as he drove us the few miles left until we arrived at the house Nesty had told us about.

"I would dissolve it, yes."

"Is that somethin' you've thought about?"

Filtered light broke through the treetops, and it flashed

across Brand's sunglass lenses, like a silent movie played on them.

"No. Not until very recently. But it's intriguing because lately I've been thinkin' about what my experience in business could do for the cabins and the ranch, for Bax and Rye and the family. So far, I've been pretty hands-off, but I don't *have* to be.

"Though, I have employees who depend on the income the jobs I provide earn them, and I could never stop bein' a builder. I love buildin' shit. So, I guess I'd need to figure out what I'd want to do. Money's not an issue, so what could I do that would better people's lives, let me still be a builder, and not take up all my time so that I could help on the ranch?" He slowed the Jeep. "I've got some ideas."

"Is this it?" I asked as we turned onto a gravel drive north of Mad River, twenty miles northeast of where we slept last night.

"We're about to find out," Brand said, his voice tight with nerves.

Small, wooden cabins dotted the property between Douglas firs and overgrown bushes, and so many ferns, I couldn't tell where they ended and the ground began. Clouds had moved in over us, and they made the mood in the Jeep sullen. A nervous and melancholic energy emanated out of Brand in a low pulse.

The whole place reminded me of summer camp from the eighties. I wouldn't have been surprised if Jason Voorhees ran out of the woods, mask on and machete in hand. Damn my sister, Maureen, for making me watch those stupid movies. Now I'd be looking over my shoulder all day. I should've brought my gun.

But when we arrived at the end of the drive in front of a white, rundown farmhouse, a short woman wearing a beekeeper's hat appeared around the side, and my thought seemed silly. See-through black mesh shaded her face, and she grasped a long pair of white gloves in her hand and a full-length, white beekeeping suit hung from her forearm.

"Can I help you?" she asked as we exited the Jeep, and the sound of her voice, weak and lacking strong breath support, told me she was older.

Brand seemed frozen, as if he didn't have the words to say the simple thing he needed.

I cleared my throat and grabbed his hand, leading him closer to the woman. "Yes, hello. I'm Roxi, and this is Brand Lee. We're lookin' for his brother, Dixon. We were told he might be here?"

The woman was nodding her head before I'd even finished my sentence, and she removed the hat and held it under her arm. "Yes, he's in the back field with the pups. He's a good kid. I hope you're not here to bring him trouble. He's had enough of that."

The woman was older, I'd been right, but she had shrewd dark eyes and long, thick, silver hair held back by a raw strip of black leather.

Finally, Brand snapped out of his trance. "No, ma'am," he said. "We're not here to cause trouble. I'd just really like to talk to my little brother."

"You got ID? One can never be too careful," she said.

Brand pulled his wallet from his back pocket and offered his license to her. She looked it over, glancing back and forth between it and Brand's handsome face. "I see the resemblance." She stepped closer, handed the license back, then held out her hand to shake his. "I'm Brenda. Brenda Coulter. My husband isn't here at the moment, but he'll be back soon. He just ran into town to run an errand."

"Nice to meet you," I said, shaking her hand too.

"Would you like a cup of tea? I was just about to make some for myself. It's a bit chilly today."

"Sure," I said, knowing that if I could get her talking, Brand might have a better opportunity for privacy with Dixon. It was a tactic I used all the time on the job. "Thank you."

"Alright then, follow me up to the house," she said, but her eyes never left Brand and she didn't move. Miss Brenda was a wise woman. She read him easily. "I s'pose you'll be wantin' to talk to your brother first. Roxi can come with me, but you go on now, straight back behind the house. Keep walkin' till you get to a fence. Dixon's back there, workin' with two of our dogs today. From the minute he showed up here, those damn dogs loved him. He's real good with 'em.

"But hear me now, young man, I won't tolerate any fightin' on my land, and I expect you to mind your manners. Your brother is hurtin'. He's here tryin' to find a path through a boatload of grief and to stay clean. Don't you say anything to him to rattle his cage."

Brand squeezed my hand in his and nodded. "Yes, ma'am."

CHAPTER THIRTY-ONE

BRAND

MY LITTLE BROTHER had changed since last I saw him.

No longer was he the scrawny teenager or the thin, heroin-addicted and malnourished man from my memories.

He looked like a different guy completely. He looked... healthy.

Logically, I knew he couldn't have grown in height, but it seemed that way because strong muscle and a clear head had transformed him. He stood tall in the middle of a field of grasses and meadow flowers. Was he taller than me? How had I never noticed that before?

A long, thin, silver dog whistle dangled from his lips as he faced away from my approach, his hand in the air, giving silent signals to two huge, fluffy, white dogs in the distance.

Whatever command he gave stopped them. They both sat where they'd stood a moment ago, waiting for further instruction.

I wanted to call out to him, wanted to see his face light up when he recognized me like he had when we were kids. I lifted my hand, but his name stuck in my throat.

Twenty years of separation and shame choked it right out of me.

I stopped at the gate, waiting for the right words to come, but the dogs spotted me before that happened, and they shot across the field, two white bullets of energy headed right for me. Dixon still hadn't seen me, so he cursed and blew the silent whistle again, but the dogs paid no mind.

Finally, he turned to follow them and try to bring them to heel, but when he saw me, he froze.

Thank God there was a fence between the dogs and me. Their deep, booming barks startled me, and they jumped at the gate, trying to get to me and nearly knocking the whole thing down. They seemed friendly, but they were still young, and they were huge, like two miniature polar bears, with black noses and deep brown eyes that seemed almost human.

The gate latch was a few feet away, so I walked to it, unhooked it, and inched through, trying not to let the dogs out, and was immediately bombarded with paws on my chest and lapping tongues trying to get to my face.

"Down," Dixon told them, and one dog sat, but the other raced around me in a circle, sniffing and whining, wanting attention. "This damn dog. Don't pet her yet. She hasn't earned it."

Nodding, I waited.

Dixon blew the whistle again, and I could hear it now, but barely because the sound was so high pitched, like a train whistle blowing miles away.

The silence between us was uncomfortable, so I asked, "What kind of dogs are these?"

"Great Pyrenees. Livestock guarding dogs. Usually, they're raised with the animals they're meant to guard, but these two are rescues. They've never worked a farm before."

I wondered if Rye and Bax back home could use a couple

of guardian dogs. We had Figaro and he did a good job, but as the ranch grew, we'd be raising more and more cattle and sheep.

The thought made me realize that the ranch and our family's land had become home again. I hadn't thought about Sheridan or considered it my home since I left it weeks ago.

"What're you doin' here, Brand? How'd you even find me? Didn't I just tell you not to bother lookin'?"

"Uh, well I called the rehab place."

"Miss Julie ratted me out?"

I shook my head. "No, though it wasn't for lack of me tryin', but she told me no over the phone, so we flew here. She still wouldn't tell me though. But there was a guy—"

"Nesty," Dixon guessed.

"Yeah."

"That tattletale."

"Listen," I said, stepping closer, "I…" What the fuck was I here to say? But I remembered my promise to Roxanne. "The family, Merv and Abey. Bax. They're goin' out of their minds with worry, Dixon. I think it's time we tell 'em what's goin' on. They need to know about Kel, but they want to know you're okay."

"I'm not ready."

"Okay, I understand."

"That's it?" he asked. "You took the time and paid money to travel here and find me, and you're just gonna accept it?"

"I don't want to, but I don't wanna push you. If you're not ready, you're not ready. But I wanted you to know before I admitted my involvement."

The dogs finally settled at Dixon's feet, and he reached down to pat their heads.

"How are you, Dix? You look really good."

"I'm not high, if that's what you're askin'."

"I wasn't. I can see that. I can see *you* again. You look so different."

Crossing his arms over his chest, a defensive move, he said, "Yeah? You don't. You look exactly the same."

"Oh, uh, Merv had a heart attack."

"What? You didn't fuckin' lead with that?"

"Sorry. Shit, I didn't think. She's okay. I promise."

"Truth?" he asked, and his face transformed into the one I grew up with, tan and freckled from the sun, blue eyes like mine questioning and trusting whatever his big brother said was true.

"Yeah. I swear. It was pretty scary for a minute there, but I drove her to Dr. Whitley. He helped, and he got her hooked up with a cardiologist in Jackson. Did you know she quit smokin'?"

"No shit?"

"Yeah, couple years ago. And now she's joined this exercise club in town to get healthy."

"Wow."

"So, yeah. Things're changin'. I moved home, and Bax just got remarried."

Pain flashed over Dixon's face, and he turned and signaled to the dogs to follow him. *Shit.* I'd forgotten how important Bax's first wife, Candy, had been to him.

"Bea's a great person," I said, following as he walked back into the field. "Bax's new wife. You wouldn't recognize our brother. She brought him back to life. She's kind and protective, and she's great with Athena and... Stuey."

That stopped him in his tracks, but he didn't turn to face me. Instead, he looked out at the dense tree line, and I could see him trying to compose himself. *Fuck. Way to go, Brand. In less than two minutes, you've mentioned the two people you swore you wouldn't.*

In a tight voice, he asked, "How's my boy? Is he happy?"

"Yeah. He is."

"They kept the name I gave him?"

"They did. We call him Stuey or Stu. Stuart if he's in trouble."

Dixon nodded. "And this Bea, she's the woman I saw last year when I... when I brought Stu home?"

"Yeah. She works with me. I'd sent her there to finish up the cabins we were buildin' at the time while I dealt with a court case in Sheridan."

"A court case?"

"Yeah, it's nothin'. It's settled now."

"And our little sister? How's Abey?"

"She's great. She's married now, too, and she's the local sheriff. Deputy Sheriff, but she's in charge of Wisper."

"Really?" He turned toward me then. "She's married? She found someone?"

"Yeah, Devo. Her name is Devona, but we all call her Devo. She's, uh... scrappy." I laughed, picturing my sister's five-foot-tall wife and her larger-than-life personality. "They're madly in love."

"God." He shook his head. "That makes me so fuckin' happy. Things weren't easy for her... before. With Dad."

"They weren't easy for you either."

Dixon dropped his hands to his sides. "Why'd you really come here, Brand? Just to hash out the past? I get it. Everybody's happy and movin' on. I'm the holdout. You didn't need to come here to rub it in my face. Trust me, I do enough of that to myself."

Facing him now, I couldn't tell him. I couldn't put all that weight on him. What if what I'd come here to say was the reason he relapsed?

"You got out," he went on. "Good for you, or you

might've ended up here with me, but I'm not ready to go back yet. I'm not ready to tell my kid his mama's dead. And I'm not ready to see Candy's replacement raisin' him. It's on me, I know. I left Stu there with Bax and his new girl, but that don't mean I'm ready to see it every day."

"It's not like that—"

"Why. Are. You. Here? Say it now and get it over with so I can go back to work. Listen, I'm grateful for what you did for me. Really, I am, but this job, this place is the only thing I have right now. It's the only thing keepin' me sober. I'm not leavin'. Not yet. So if you came here with all your money, thinkin' you'd swoop in and fix my life, you can turn right back around and go home."

"That's not why I came."

"So tell me why and get it over with already. Jesus."

"Fine." I took the bait. He was prodding me, trying to get a rise out of me. "I came here to tell you I ain't keepin' your secrets anymore. They're tearin' me up inside. I feel so fuckin' guilty! Every time I look at Bax. At Merv. At your fuckin' kid. I can't do it anymore."

"Fine. Just don't give them my location."

"Fine? It's fuckin' fine?"

"Yeah. Tell 'em. I don't care. But I'm not comin' home yet."

"Fine?" I repeated. All this time, and he was "fine" with it? "Fuck you, Dixon. I have protected you all this time the best way I knew how. I kept your damn secrets. I carried them and they're fuckin' heavy, man. I owed it to you, so I did it, but no more. I came here today because I wanted to earn your forgiveness. I wanted to deserve something I had no right to want. So thanks for makin' it clear that I *don't* deserve it. I don't deserve her."

I turned to go. What more was there left to say?

"'Her'?"

"Forget it. You don't need to carry my shit too. I'll see ya."

His hand on my shoulder stopped me from going any further, and the dogs jumped up and rushed around us.

He released my arm. "Sit down, you mangy muts. I'm not hurtin' him." To me, he said, "Brother, wait. What did you mean you wanted to earn my forgiveness. What's there to forgive? And who is 'her'?"

"I left you," I said without turning. "I left you with Dad after graduation. You didn't deserve that, and look what it did to you. I ruined your life."

The last thing I expected to hear was his laughter.

His loud snort cracked the air. "*You* ruined *my* life? Brand, you sure got some kind of superiority complex goin' on. Trust me, you don't have that kinda power. There are only two people responsible for my problems, and one of 'em is dead. The other one is standin' behind you, laughin' at the bullshit comin' out your mouth."

That had me spinning in a second. "What?"

He shook his head, chuckling, and it was the first time I'd seen a genuine smile on his face in years. "You didn't do this to me. *I* did this to me. Dad had a big hand in it, but it was my decision to pick up a bottle, and then pills and needles."

"You were just a kid."

"Yeah, and then I wasn't anymore. I'd been to enough therapy and rehabs to know there was help out there. I didn't ask for it. Thought I could handle my problems on my own, just like our old man said I should. We were both wrong."

"All this time… Twenty years."

"All this time, what?"

"I felt guilty. Shame. I thought if I'd done things differently back then, maybe you wouldn't have—"

"What else could you have done? You got out. You don't know how happy that made me. I'm not sayin' you were the best big brother. After you left, I didn't hear from you. But you were just a kid too. I never expected you to fix my life."

"Shit." My knees went weak, and I leaned on a dog. The silly beast stood next to me, guarding me and giving me strength.

"Yup. That about sums it up. You know, there's a program for the families of addicts. Al-Anon or Nar-Anon. You oughta look into that."

It had become painfully clear to me in the last two minutes that Dixon's disease hadn't only affected him. It had done a number on me too.

"These dogs, what are their names?"

He pointed at the dog still by my side, and I sank my fingers into its fur, letting its body warmth reach inside me.

"Your new best friend there is Tilly. She's a good dog. And Short Attention Span over here is Zephyr. They'll be good guardians for some farmer, but they're nowhere near ready yet."

"I want them. When they're trained and ready, I'd like to bring them to the ranch. We'll need dogs."

"I can't give 'em to you. They're not mine to give. I'm just the trainer."

"Who do I need to talk to? Brenda?"

He nodded. "Yeah, and her husband, Brooks."

CHAPTER THIRTY-TWO

BRAND

WE LEFT Tilly and Zephyr locked behind the gate, and they yelped and whined their displeasure at being left behind, but then they spotted a rabbit across the field and raced after it like fluffy, white bullets again. I hoped the rabbit had a safe place to hunker down until their attention waned.

"Listen," Dixon said. "I know I'm askin' a lot, and I heard you when you said keepin' my secret was tearin' you up, but can you keep it a little longer?"

"Dix—"

"Please, Brand. I wanna tell Bax myself about Stu's mama. And I need to have my shit together before I see Merv. She and I have a lot we need to talk about. I've been workin' with my therapist on it. My plan was to come home in the new year. It's only a few more months."

"Therapist?"

"Yeah," he said. "It's one of the Coulters' stipulations to stay and work here. I gotta go to therapy once a week and to AA or NA every day. There's a group that meets in Mad River four days a week that me and a couple of the guys here go to. The other times, I borrow Brooks's truck and drive over to Bridgeville. It's not far."

"I'm proud of you, Dixon."

Shrugging, he mumbled, "Thanks."

"You know," I said, trying to dismiss the feeling in my gut that he was playing me again, "you're like a tank now. How'd you get so damn big? I don't remember you bein' this fuckin' tall."

I wanted to believe he was on a healthy path, but history had jaded me. He had always been good at saying what his family wanted to hear.

He chuckled. "I got a lotta downtime these days, and usually, I'd drink or get high to pass it, so now I work out. Do odd jobs for people around here. There's lots of farms in the area, and it seems I picked up a few skills from the son of a bitch who raised us. I'm makin' money. Savin' it up for Stu."

He looked me over. "It's been a long time since I really looked at you. I was wrong before. You do look different." He cracked a smile that showed hints of the little boy he used to be. "Have you always been this ugly?"

"Oh, you're gonna pay for that," I said, and I had to jump to get my arm around his shoulder, but when I did, I bent him over and gave him a nuggie. Just like old times.

"He's not ugly," Roxanne said as she stepped onto the Coulters' back porch with a cup of steaming tea in her hand. Brenda followed, along with a tall, skinny man with salt-and-pepper-hair, who I assumed was Brenda's husband, Brooks.

"Roxanne!" I yelped as my brother took me to the ground and sat on my legs so I couldn't move. "This is my baby brother, Dixon. Arrest him for bein' a pain in my ass!"

"Wait. Shit," Dixon said, out of breath. "You didn't say your lady was a cop."

"Deputy, actually," Roxanne said. "And sorry, baby, I have no jurisdiction here. Guess you're screwed."

Brenda was smiling, but she said, "Get up outta the dirt. Get cleaned up and come on inside for dinner. Roxi says they can stay."

"Yes, ma'am," Dixon and I replied in unison.

WHEN WE BOARDED the plane home the next morning, after dinner with my brother and the Coulters and another amazing night in our yurt, Roxi asked, "So, when are you tellin' your mama? Abey's gonna be so excited Dixon's comin' home soon. I can't wait to see her. They're all gonna be so happy, Brand."

I cleared my throat, trying to buy a little time. "I'm not."

"You're not what?" she asked as we ascended the stairs onto the plane.

"Tellin' them. Not yet."

"I'm sorry. What?"

"Dixon asked for a little more time. He wants to tell our family everything himself when he gets there."

"Okay, and when will that be?"

"A few months."

Roxanne deflated, and she flopped down into a seat and fastened her seatbelt. "Oh, Brand. You agreed to that?"

"Yes." I left our bags in the aisle for the flight attendant and took my seat next to her. "He's healthy. You saw him. He's himself again. He'll keep his word."

"And if he doesn't? He's an addict, Brand. On the job, I've seen it time and time again. They make promises they don't know how to keep. Or they relapse, and their loved ones are left holdin' the bag."

"He's my baby brother," I said, letting the cracks in my armor show, the armor I'd kept so close to my chest all these years, but if I was going to let anyone see it, it would be Roxanne. "Please understand."

"I do understand. Truly, I do. But it's a mistake."

No. She didn't get it. Keeping my promise to my little brother was all I had to prove me worthy of *her*. Didn't she see that if I went back on my word, my integrity, my loyalty, and my right to everything I'd earned in my life weren't worth shit?

"I'm not discussin' it with you, Roxanne. Dixon gave me his word and he'll keep it. End of story."

"And what about your word? You promised *me* you'd tell your family."

And now my armor hardened around me, like cured concrete, and I broke into pieces beneath. But I couldn't let her see the devastation. I loved her for questioning and challenging me, but on this matter, my decision had to be final. My family's happiness, their love for me, and my fucking self-worth depended on it.

"And I will. When Dixon's home, we'll tell them everything together."

"Did it occur to you how this might affect me? I have to face your sister every day, which now means I'll have to lie to her every day."

She looked at me for a long while, silent. But I couldn't look at her because she was right. If I kept Dixon's secrets one day longer, I would be letting her down.

"You said this is about trust." She motioned with her finger between the two of us. "Trust between you and me."

"It is. I trust you. Don't you trust me?"

She didn't answer. She crossed her arms over her chest, closing herself off.

"Roxanne, answer me."

"No. You don't get to do that anymore. I'm not your toy. You can't wind me up when you want me and expect me just to sit around waitin' for the next time if you won't give me anything back."

"Pardon me," the flight attendant said as she approached us, "I'm sorry to interrupt." Her smile seemed forced, but she'd probably heard us arguing. "We'll be taking off soon. Can I get you anything?"

Roxanne shook her head, looking out the window.

"No, thank you," I said.

"Very well. Please buckle your seatbelt, sir," she said, and she waited while I complied. "Thank you. We'll be in Wyoming soon, but once we're in the air, let me know if you change your mind."

"Thanks," I said as she dragged Roxanne's suitcase and my backpack behind her to stow before takeoff.

As soon as she was out of hearing range, Roxanne turned toward me. Her beautiful brown eyes flashed with hurt, and I wanted to fix it. I wanted to tell her what she wanted to hear but—

"I'll answer your question," she said, "but not because you expect me to or demand it of me."

"Okay."

"I *don't* trust you, Brand. Not in this moment, because you're choosin' to put your faith in someone who has repeatedly lied to you and taken advantage of you. You have no faith in *me*, in my knowledge of this kind of situation, and you're settin' yourself up to fail and stay miserable."

"Roxanne, he's my *brother*."

"Yeah, he is. Your baby brother, and you love him, and you want everything to be okay, but he's also an addict. You have this idea in your head that you have some kind of control over the situation. Hear me when I say *you do not*. You can't control Dixon any more than you can control the change of seasons.

"What you *can* control is how the rest of this flight is going to go. The next three months. I'm your girlfriend, or I was twenty minutes ago, but just like every other man I've ever dated and my family, what I want doesn't matter to you. What I need doesn't matter. Because I need to not be tangled up in this lie with you, but now I am. And you don't care."

"You're puttin' me in an impossible position, R—"

"No, actually, I'm not. You've put yourself in an impossible situation, and no one can get you out of it but you. It seems so obvious now, but all this time, you thought you'd tell your brother what you wanted him to do and he'd just do it. But there's a lot of work you both need to do in your relationship. You can't just 'man up' and expect things to be hunky dory.

"I'm so stupid. It wasn't another woman or an ex I needed to be worried about. It was you. Your entitled belief that everything should just go the way you want it to. You can control me in bed. It's fun and sexy, but out here in the real world, things just don't work that way.

"And you need to learn the difference."

My mouth gaped open. She'd put me in my place, just like when she bit me and I bled for her.

Roxanne was absolutely right, but I had no idea how to bridge the divide between what I needed and what she did.

A chasm grew between us on the plane. I felt her icy distance now and it burned me inside.

"I'm sorry," I said. "I know you're right. I hear you, Roxanne, but I need to believe in my brother. I *need* to have hope. If I betray him now, what was it all for?"

"That's for you to figure out," she retorted. "When we get

back to Jackson, please drive me home, and then you can be on your way. Bein' with you these last few weeks has taught me somethin' about myself. I *am* worthy of love and I deserve it. But not just from you. From myself, too, so you can go be miserable over the holidays without Dixon, but I won't be around to watch. I cannot and will not lie to your sister again, not about this. It's way too important."

"Are you... breakin' up with me?"

"Yep. How you like them apples? Mr. Important Rich Guy who can snap his fingers and demand whatever he wants gets dumped by the weird, small-town cop." She laughed, but there was no humor in her eyes. "Forty years it took me to find what I wanted. *Who* I wanted, and I lost him before I ever even had him. It fuckin' figures."

The pain in my chest squeezed around my broken pieces. They shattered further into jagged shards, and if I wasn't sitting upright, breathing and feeling my heart pound, I would've thought those shards had sliced up my lungs and cut all my arteries. It felt like I was bleeding out right in front of the woman I loved, but she refused to see it.

I whispered, "What will you do?"

"That's none of your business anymore."

"Will you— Can you just give me a little time?"

"Time's up," she said, looking away and trying so hard to keep up her bravado, but it was killing her just like it was me. It was clear in the way she held herself, trying to hold her hurt inside, trying not to let me see her shaking. "Even if you walked into a therapist's office the second we stepped off this plane, you can't process twenty years of co-dependency and trauma in five minutes. And I'm too damn old to wait around until you do."

CHAPTER THIRTY-THREE

ROXANNE

MY SISTER'S name and her kids' faces flashed on my phone. It was a picture her husband Drew had taken of them at Disney World. She said the kids had pooped out after that picture, and all hell had broken loose in the middle of the "Happiest Place on Earth" with meltdowns and tantrums and blood sugar plunges.

She wasn't the oldest of my sisters, but Maureen had always tried to mother me. She was only two years older than me, but it was just her nature.

Answering the call, I tried to put on my usual chipper, happy front. "Hey, sis. How are you?"

"What's wrong? We haven't heard from you in the group chat for a while. Are you okay?"

I sighed. My fake happiness lasted, like, three seconds. I'd known one of my sisters would be calling soon to demand I tell them everything about my life. Sisters were like that.

"Yeah, sorry. I've just been busy with work and... you know."

"No," she said, "I don't know, so tell me. What's up with you?"

"It's nothin'. I broke up with a guy. I'm just a little down, is all."

"Oh, Riri, I'm sorry. Was he a jerk?"

No. No he's not a jerk at all. He's everything*, and now he's gone.*

Technically, he wasn't "gone." Brand was still in Wisper. I heard his sister over the last few weeks talking about him and their family. She'd said he'd chosen the plot of land he wanted to build his house on. *His* house. The house he'd told me could be *ours* when we'd lain in bed all night, fucking, dreaming, and planning our imaginary future.

But now I knew Brand was moving on. He hadn't liked that I'd challenged him about his brother and the disease their relationship had nurtured in them both, and it seemed he wasn't prepared to change or do anything different than he had been doing for years.

Where could I even fit into that?

I couldn't, and Brand must have realized it, too, and that was why he hadn't come banging on my door, asking for my forgiveness. And just like all the other men in my past, maybe Brand had realized that the fucking was all he really wanted from me anyway.

Who builds a house for a woman he's known less than two months?

The one-two-threes had come back with a vengeance, and I tapped the side of my leg now so hard, I probably left bruises.

I had avoided conversations with Abey at all cost. She demanded to know what had happened between her brother and me, but I told her it just hadn't worked out. When she prodded for more information, I said it was too painful, which was the truth, and that I needed time.

Even after he broke my heart, I couldn't bring myself to

betray Brand's and Dixon's confidences, but it was eating away at me.

To avoid further questioning, I took a week off work after Thanksgiving and did nothing but ingest dangerous amounts of carbs and sodium while I binge-watched all five seasons of *Yellowstone*, every *Jurassic Park/World* movie ever made, and *Little House on the Prairie* episodes until I started considering getting rid of my TV and phone and living like Teton Tom or Laura Ingalls.

"No," I said, "he's not a jerk. It just didn't work out."

As much as I wanted to be with Brand, I knew the trust was gone. If he hadn't lived up to his promises in the short time we'd been together, how could I expect him to do it in the future?

Had I asked too much of him? His family's issues were big, and they'd been building for a long time. Was it wrong to ask him to face them for me? For us?

Was there ever really an "us?"

"Riri, come home for Christmas. I know you've got work, but we all miss you. Can't you just take a few days? You haven't hugged the kids in two years. Let your family love and support you. Sounds like you need it this year."

But Maureen didn't understand. She had the perfect life with the perfect little family and a perfect husband. If she made a mistake, everybody forgave her and moved on. But I didn't have a man to absorb my shock, so when I made a mistake, it became fodder for my sisters, their husbands, my parents, and even some of my older nieces and nephews.

I was tired of showing up at home with my tail between my legs, having failed once again at finding anyone to love me. And it was too painful to pretend it didn't matter, that being alone was all hunky dory and happy dances. It fucking wasn't.

When I wasn't in love, it had been hard enough. But now…

"I don't know," I said. "I'll think about it."

"Okay." Maureen sighed. "Honestly, that's more than I was expectin' from you, but I really hope you come. I'll give you a big hug, and you know bein' around the kids would lift your spirits."

"Yeah." She was right about that. I missed their cute, smiling faces, all fifteen of them.

"I have to go," she said. "Someone's knockin' on my door, but call me if you decide you wanna come home. I've got some airline points you can probably use."

"Thanks."

"Love you, Riri. Bye."

"Love you too."

The person at *my* door didn't bother to knock. She just barged in like she always did.

"Hey, Aubs," I said, clicking off my phone and flopping onto my couch, watching her lug two bags from the Food Mart into my kitchen. "Whatcha got there?"

"Pick-me-up food," my best friend said, and she disappeared behind my fridge door.

"Thanks, but I'm not really hungry."

When she emerged from the depths of the old appliance that probably needed a good scrubbing out and the door slammed shut, the new bottle of whiskey on top of the fridge rattled, and it reminded me of the old bottle that used to be up there, until Brand had poured it over me and sucked it from my body.

Gah! Roxi, quit it! He's gone, and he's not coming back. He's not your prince. He's not your anything.

When she walked into the living room, Aubrey had a bottle of red wine in one hand, a bag of white cheddar popcorn tucked under her arm, and her favorite dark chocolate quinoa crisps Rye had introduced her to.

"Gimme," I said, holding my hand out for the popcorn.

She tossed me the bag and flopped onto the couch opposite me, lifted her short legs, and rested them over mine.

"Shitty day?" she asked, eyeing the tent-sized pajamas I'd changed into after work and the greasy hair framing my face I hadn't bothered to wash this morning.

"Yep. And my sister just called. She wants me to go home for Christmas. Said she has travel points I can use if I want."

"Why don't you? You never do anything nice for yourself."

I snorted. "You think showin' up at my parents' depressed and still husband-less is *nice*?"

She crunched her crisps and swigged the wine right from the bottle. "You know what I mean. Go somewhere, get out of your head."

"Gimme those," I said, holding my hand out for the bag of crisps. When she tossed it onto my lap, I grabbed a handful and stuffed four or five of the crunchy treats in my mouth.

Aubrey shuddered. "Ew. Dark chocolate and cheddar popcorn do not go together."

Actually, now that she mentioned it, the combination kind of tasted like puke in my mouth. I threw the crisps back to her and held out my hand for the wine.

As I took a chug, she said, "I saw Brand today," and I almost choked on it.

Wiping my mouth with the back of my hand, I asked, "Where?"

"At the ranch. He was with Bax and Rye."

"Oh. Well, how'd he, you know, look?"

"Haunted and miserable," she assured me definitively.

"I know you're lyin', but thanks."

She smiled. "He looked the same as he always does. But I will say that it felt like somethin' has changed with him. I couldn't tell what it might be when I talked to him, but—"

"You talked to him?" I asked, pulling my legs out from beneath hers. Her feet fell to the floor, and we both sat up.

"Yeah. Well, I yelled at him, actually."

"What? Why?"

"Because, Roxi, he broke my best friend's heart."

I wanted to pummel her, but she was the best damn friend I could ever hope to have.

"What did you say? What did he say?"

"He didn't say much, but *I* said a lot. I told him you were the best thing to ever happen to him and that he's an idiot for lettin' you go."

"And?"

"And he agreed with me."

Somehow, that made me feel worse. If he was oblivious as to why he'd lost me, at least then I could blame my heartache on his stupidity.

But Brand was anything but stupid, so I felt certain he knew exactly what had gone wrong between us. I'd been pretty clear back on his friend's jet, and he'd heard every word.

So if he was admitting to Aubrey that he'd made a mistake, then why wasn't he doing anything to fix it?

CHAPTER THIRTY-FOUR

BRAND

"I HAVE SOMETHIN' to tell y'all," I said, watching my family's faces as they gathered in Bax's kitchen.

They had no clue the shit I was about to dump on them, but when I texted and asked them to meet me, they'd all agreed.

Maybe they expected good news about Lee Construction and the projects we'd been building on the property, or maybe they expected news about Roxanne and me. Every single one of them had badgered me for information over the last month, even Athena. *Especially* Athena, and even Stuey asked, "Where Ro?"

But I couldn't talk to my family about Roxanne, because if I did, the need I felt for her would rise up and rage, and it wasn't time yet. I wasn't quite ready.

"Can we sit?"

"Sure," Bax said, and we all took a chair at his kitchen table. "What's up?"

"The kids aren't here?" I asked. "There's no chance Athena's listenin' in?"

My brother's eyebrows dipped, and his head tilted in

alarm. "They're outside with Rye and Aubrey, like you requested."

Wincing internally, I tried to shake off the "talking to" I'd received from Roxanne's best friend. She'd chewed me out thoroughly after Roxanne told her she'd dumped me. Roxanne hadn't told Aubrey why, not the full truth anyway.

Even after I'd let her down and broken her heart, Roxanne had kept my secrets safe.

But it was time to set the truth free because Roxanne had been right about me. Aubrey too.

Dixon's sickness was like a virus, and I'd caught it years ago.

I tried to get ahold of him again, called the Coulters since he didn't have a cell phone, but I hadn't heard back from him, and whether it worked for his timing or not, I needed to come clean to my family.

For Roxanne, for Stuey and Merv, Bax, Bea, and Athena.

And for me.

"What's goin' on, son?" Merv asked, looking worried across the table. Abey and Devo had just arrived, and they pulled up chairs between Bax and Merv.

"I talked to Dixon."

Merv gasped, and Bax narrowed his eyes.

"When?" Abey asked.

"I don't have exact dates, but let me start from the beginning so you can understand. I won't ask for your forgiveness. I'm not sure I deserve it, but here goes…"

Bea cried for Stuey's mama. Merv looked relieved her youngest son was still breathing, and Bax looked like he wanted to murder me for keeping the truth about Stuey's birth mother from him and Bea. And Abey looked ready to start a manhunt.

"When you saw him," Merv said, "he looked good? You're sure he wasn't high?"

"As far as I could tell, no. He seemed to have landed in a good place with good people, and he said he'd been seein' a therapist once a week and goin' to meetings."

Relief oozed out of Merv, and she nodded.

"If he's sober, why hasn't he come home?" Abey asked. "What did he say about that?"

"Just that he wasn't ready, but his plan had been to come home in the new year."

"Thanksgiving was last week," Merv said hopefully. "That's only a month away."

"Yes, but Mama, I tried to call him this mornin' before I got here, to tell him it was time for me to let you know what's been goin' on. I promised him I'd let him tell you about Stu's birth mother himself.

"But the people he's been stayin' with, Brenda and Brooks Coulter, said he wasn't there and they didn't know where he'd gone. They haven't seen him in a few days. He didn't show up for a job he'd been hired to do at a local farm, and his clothes and the few possessions he had were gone from his cabin when Brenda checked."

The disappointment hearing Brenda tell me Dixon had run again had been crushing. My chest felt heavy when she said it, like there was a brick on my lungs not letting me take a full breath. I'd had to force myself to see that the knowledge wasn't any different than the heartache I'd been carrying all these years, and that my brother's actions didn't have to affect my life the way I'd been letting them since I was eighteen years old. But I had to work to not let the lost hope I felt wreck me again.

"Well, maybe he decided to come home early," Merv said.

"Maybe he's on his way, but he didn't wanna say goodbye to those people. He never did like goodbyes."

"It's possible," I admitted. I'd had the same thought, but Dixon's history said otherwise. "But there's no way for us to know because we can't call him directly. He doesn't have a cell phone, at least not one I know about."

"You'll see," Merv said. "He'll show up. He's a good boy."

"He's not a *boy*," Abey said. "That's part of the problem, Mama. You know this. If he does come home, you cannot keep treatin' him like your baby."

"Listen," I said. "I found a therapist. I've been talkin' with her for a couple weeks. And yesterday, I went to a support group for families of addicts. I think y'all should check it out. Even after just one meeting, I've learned a lot. And it's nice to know I'm not the only one who struggles with how to relate to my brother and how not to let his illness run my life."

Bax had been quiet, but now he asked, "Why?"

"Why what?"

"Why'd you keep his secrets? Why didn't you come straight here to tell us Dixon was alive when every day we worried and wondered?"

"I..." Here was the hard part. The part I'd been dreading. I didn't want to rip open old wounds. Didn't want to remind my family about the hell Dixon had to live through. I still didn't think Bax had any idea how bad things had gotten with our father. "I felt guilty. I thought it was my fault."

"What, son? What was your fault?"

"When I graduated high school and left home, I also left Dixon, and I thought it was my fault that things with him turned out the way they did. I thought I should've done more to protect him."

"From what?" Merv asked.

Looking her straight in the eye, I confronted her with the truth she'd been trying to hide from since her husband died. "From Dad. He hid the worst of it from Bax, Mama, because he wanted Bax workin' the farm with him, but Abey and I saw the monster that man had become. You justified his behavior or you ignored it or dissociated from it. But when I left, Dixon was alone here. None of us can know how bad it got."

"*I* was here," Merv said. "I would've seen if…"

"You were here," Abey said, "but you weren't out there in that barn with them every day. You worked and you ran your household. God, I remember you sayin' that all the time. Like made beds and a clean kitchen and bathrooms were more important than all the stuff that went down with Dad."

Bea and Devo had been mostly silent, but it was clear they were uncomfortable. This—our mom and dad and the dynamic between them and us—had been the heart of the matter for years. But now, everything had come to a head, and we had to face it.

I did. If I wanted Roxanne in my life, the truth needed to come out and I needed to be free of my brother's secrets.

And I wanted Roxanne like I'd never wanted anyone or anything in my life.

I loved her, and I missed her so much. I woke from dreams of her, sobbing. In the dreams, she still loved me, and we were together, building our house and making love in the stupid yurt again.

And the therapist helped me see that I needed to come clean for Dixon too. I'd thought all this time that protecting him showed I loved him, but in truth, it was the opposite. Me keeping his secrets only helped him stay sick.

Merv began to shut down. I watched it happen; her body

became rigid in her chair, muscles tightening, face pinching. This was hard for her too.

"Why, Mama?" Bax asked. "Why did Dad hate Dixon? Why are we in this mess now? What did he do to his own son? You have to know. You may've been distracted, but you *were* here."

"I don't know."

"Mama," Abey said softly. "Please don't get defensive. No one is blamin' you or judgin' you. It was hard for you too. We know that, but we need the truth so we can help Dixon when he comes home."

Merv looked around the table. She relaxed a fraction, loosened her arms at her sides, but I could see in her eyes she wouldn't tell us what we wanted to know.

"It… What you're askin' isn't somethin' a mother talks to her children about. You're right that you deserve to know, but I'm not prepared to discuss it today. Besides, this is about your little brother. Don't you think he should know before all of you? When he comes home, I'll be ready and I'll talk to him."

She stood and smoothed her sweater over her hips with shaking hands.

"*If* he comes home," I said. She still wasn't hearing us. She was still trying so hard to see only what she wanted. "Mama, the therapist I've been talkin' to is really nice. I'd like you to talk to her too."

She scoffed. "You want me to go to *therapy*?"

All eyes were on me and Merv now. This was something my siblings and I had discussed for years, but Merv had always been insistent that she could handle her issues on her own. Just like I had. Like Dixon had. Which *was* the reason we were all in this mess.

"Yeah, Mama," Bax said. "Brand's goin'." He looked at

his wife. "Bea and I will go to help us process what happened with Stuey's birth mom and how to handle that as he gets older." Bea nodded, grabbed his hand, and held it on the table. And then Bax looked at Merv. "So, why can't you?"

"Because," she said. "Because in my day we didn't spill our guts to strangers and pay them to listen to our sorrows."

In a rare flash of anger, Abey's chair slid out behind her as she pushed away from the table and to her feet. "It's not 'your day' anymore, Merv. Things have changed. You may not like it or be comfortable with it, but that's reality. And this family needs help. We can't keep goin' like we have been. It's too important.

"If you can't do it for yourself or for your own children, you *will* do it for Athena and Stuey. And if you ever want to have a relationship with Dixon, you better get your shit figured out before he comes home, or he'll just run again."

Merv didn't react. She just stood there and took it. Finally, her eyes cast down to the floor, she said, "Okay."

"MAMA," I said, opening the door when I heard her on her porch. She'd just gotten back from a walk through downtown Wisper in the flurrying snow with Clay and her walking group, and she reached her arms high in the air, stretching out the muscles.

"Son?"

More than three weeks had passed since our family roundtable, and the weather had turned. We already had a foot of snow, and more would come.

Things had been strained between Merv and the rest of us, but she wasn't shutting down like she would have in the past. And still no Dixon.

Bax and Bea were irritated with me, but preparing the ranch and the animals for winter took up most of our time, and Bax seemed to work out his anger as he worked the farm. Bea chewed me out nearly every time we talked, but her temper had died down some.

I hadn't spoken to Roxanne since the week after Thanksgiving, when she had to drive out to Abey's house for some work-related task. She said "Hi" and walked away from me, and I died inside at the lack of connection between us, but it wasn't gone. It had just gone into a dormant state. I hoped.

She'd said I couldn't work out my issues in five minutes. That was true, but I could at least get started. So that was what I did, and I would keep doing it until Roxanne was back in my arms and my brother's illness was his alone.

Abey told me last week that Roxanne had decided to fly home to Oklahoma for Christmas, and I knew that would be hard for her. I had a plan to make it better, but I needed a little moral support.

"How was your workout?" I asked Merv, judging her mood.

"Good. That Clay's a talker. I barely have to say anything. It's kinda nice since I'm so out of shape." She watched me. She could probably feel the energy buzzing under my skin. "What's goin' on with you?"

"There's somethin' I need to do. Will you come with me? It would mean missin' Christmas mornin' with your grandkids."

"Is it important?"

"The most important thing I'll ever do."

"Then yes. I'd be glad to go with you."

"Pack a weekend bag," I said. "We leave tomorrow mornin'."

Her eyebrows lifted in question. "A bag? Where we goin'?"

"Oklahoma."

Understanding dawned in her eyes, and she nodded.

"I need to sweep someone off her feet."

"Better pack a sweater then," she said. "There's a big winter storm predicted across the Rockies for Christmas."

"Yes, ma'am, but ain't no storm gettin' in my way."

WE FLEW from the private air strip in Jackson on the same plane Roxanne and I had taken to California. I owed my buddy, Mason, for the use of his jet, and I knew he'd come to collect at some point.

When we touched down in Oklahoma City, Merv and I headed straight for a rental car company in the small regional airport, grabbed a car, and then I dropped Merv at our hotel's spa while I made my preparations.

A friend of Evan Moran's from back in his rodeo days lived south of the city on a horse ranch. The guy, Billy Wilson, agreed to transport two of his draft horses into Choctaw with an old-fashioned sleigh. I spent the afternoon decorating it with Christmas lights, and I stocked it with whiskey and champagne and blankets. Billy said he'd stay close in case I needed him, but Evan told him I had experience with horses, so Billy agreed to let me loose on my own.

I didn't let on that my experience with horses didn't quite extend to recent times, nor did I tell the man that I'd never been around a draft horse. The animals were huge! But the two mares he'd transported up in a trailer seemed docile enough, and he said they had been trained to work around city traffic.

When the sleigh was ready and the horses had been fed and watered and were hitched and itching to get going, I lifted the reins and kissed the air twice, and they walked on, out of the deserted city park I'd used to prepare.

It was only a mile to Roxanne's parents' house, and I spent that long mile trying to slow my racing heart and practice in my head what I wanted to say to her.

Merv sat next to me, her hair shiny and her skin glowing from her spa treatments. I'd called the hotel manager and asked her to drive my mama out to Choctaw so she could be a part of this with Roxanne and me.

I had no idea what I'd do if Roxanne said no the question I planned to ask her. Merv was there to pick me up off the floor if she did.

Roxanne was it for me. She was everything.

Merv was over the moon about being included in my life, and the hotel manager had been happy to drive her, especially when I tipped her probably the equivalent of a month's salary and wished her happy holidays before she drove back to work.

"Are you nervous, son?" Merv asked as she rubbed her hands together.

Christmas Eve in Choctaw was a crisp thirty-four degrees and dropping at eight p.m. When we landed in OK City, the temperature hovered in the mid-forties, but snow was expected tonight, and I hoped for it. Snow would make everything perfect with the twinkling lights and Christmas decorations smattered everywhere through town.

Roxanne's parents' middle-class neighborhood had been decked to the nines, and a huge blow-up Santa waved at us from someone's front yard as I guided the horses onto Forest Cove Road. Traffic was non-existent. Everyone was home with family and loved ones, celebrating the holiday.

"Yes," I answered. "I'm more nervous than I've ever been in my life. I feel like I might be sick. If she says no…"

"She won't. How could she? You love each other. I don't have to know what happened or what you said to upset her, but you just say you're sorry and tell her all the ways you love her, and she'll say yes."

Merv nodded to herself, trying to convince us both she was right. I hoped like hell she was.

"I asked Roxanne to keep Dixon's secrets for me. She said no and she broke up with me."

Merv harrumphed a laugh. "I knew I liked her."

"I'm sorry he didn't keep his word, Mama. I really thought he would this time. But now I know that it has nothin' to do with me or you or anybody else. If Dixon ever comes home, it will be because he's ready and because he wants it, not because we do."

The Coulters had called me back to ask if we'd heard from Dixon. He'd taken off from Mad River without a word. No one in town or at his NA group had heard from him, and he'd skipped out on his weekly therapy sessions. Brenda had wished us a happy holiday and said she had faith Dixon was on his way home to us, that maybe he had gotten waylaid, but she knew in her heart we'd see him again.

But I knew he had run just like every time in the past when things got too hard. I had no way of knowing if he was using, but if he was, it had no bearing on my life anymore.

He had been right that his decisions were his alone and that I shouldn't feel guilt or shame about them. I'd done everything I knew to help my brother. If he ever came to terms with his demons, he could come home. His family would always be there, waiting to welcome him back.

"Here we go," I said as I pulled the horses to a stop in front of the second house on the right. The mid-century brick home had a long curved driveway, great for the horses, but I could see the cracks needing to be filled in and resealed.

"Wait, Brand," Merv said before I disembarked. She held onto my forearm with a strength that would rival a pro ball player's grip on his bat. "I never said thank you. You're right about Dixon, and I'm learnin' to live with the choices your brother has made.

"Dr. Tammy says I have to move on. I can't stop livin' just because one of my sons is sick. When she said it like that, it made sense. If you or Bax or Abey had an illness, I wouldn't stop livin'. Why should addiction be any different? But I know how hard you tried to help Dixon, and I'm grateful. I know you didn't do it for me, but I'm still proud of you and grateful for your generosity."

"Thank you, Mama. But you're wrong, it was for you. Part of it anyway. I'm just sorry nothin' I did for him worked. But you and Dr. Tammy are right. It's time we move on. It's time we live. It's time all that pain from our past takes a backseat to happiness."

Merv nodded, and she leaned over to kiss my cheek.

Taking a deep breath, I climbed down, patted the horses and thanked them for their hard work, and then I helped Merv down from the sleigh, and she followed me to the Fittses' front door, where a wreath had been hung, decorated with dried oranges, berries, and deep red bows. When I pushed my finger to the doorbell, a bell chorus of "We Wish You a Merry Christmas" rang out.

Thirty seconds later, the door swung open, and I could hear little kids squealing in delight. Somewhere inside the house in a room I couldn't see into, a TV played *Miracle on 34th Street,* and it sounded like another TV in a different room was playing a football game. Glasses clinked together and more than two women were arguing about something animatedly and laughing.

Roxanne's parents' house was a busy, happy clatter of Christmas sounds, sights, and scents. The smell of warm cinnamon wafted out to me on the front porch, and balsam and cedar hinted in the air.

Finally, I focused on the person who'd opened the door, and it was a man with a bit of a beer gut under an Oklahoma Sooners T-shirt, a trimmed, graying beard, and a hint of laugher in his eyes.

"Duuude," the man said, eyeing me, my cowboy hat, my mama, and then the sleigh. "You're gonna put all these women in an uproar."

I straightened my coat and my sweater beneath. "Excuse me?"

"We were just lookin' you up online, and all five of Riri's sisters, including my wife, said they'd leave their husbands for you."

My face flushed Christmas red. "Uh. Well… sorry?"

"Drew," he said, chuckling and extending his hand to shake mine. "You're a brave man, Brand Lee. Good luck." He stepped back from the door to allow Merv and me inside and jabbed his thumb over his shoulder. "Go on then," he said, "go get your girl. She's in the kitchen."

"Thank you. Uh, this is my mama, Mervella."

"Come on in, Merv. May I call you Merv?" Drew asked with faux formality.

"I wish you wouldn't," Merv said with her usual sneer.

Drew laughed. "I think you'll fit in just fine around here."

We entered the small foyer, I removed my hat and tucked it under my arm, and a little girl appeared from the living room. She reached for my hand and held it. "Are you Aunt Riri's boyfriend? She told my mommy you were fifty shades, but you look like one color to me. Like my tan crayon."

A woman came charging at us, her face the same shade as the red bulbs on the huge fir tree behind her, and her hair was the same color as Roxanne's, light brown with hints of wheat and shiny flax. "Oh my God, Maizie. Leave the man alone. I'm so sorry," she said to me, embarrassed, and pulled Maizie away by her hand. "Maizie, get your cousins. Grandma said y'all can open your Christmas Eve gifts now while Aunt Riri and the nice man talk."

Maizie, who couldn't have been more than seven, pumped her fist in the air, smiling and flashing a missing front tooth. Her white sweater had a knitted Christmas tree on the front, with little light-up bulbs sewn into it and tiny, multi-colored pom-poms for the ornaments.

"Present time!" she screeched to her cousins.

A scurry of children poured out of every room and headed straight for the tree, some near Maizie's age and others older and in their tween and teenage phases. They all knelt or sat cross-legged around the tree, staring at the opening that led to the kitchen.

An older man and woman appeared through the rounded arch, each carrying a mug, and the woman, Roxanne's mama, held a third mug. She nodded at Merv and me and handed the extra mug to Merv. I could see the shape of Roxanne's eyes in her mama's, and she had her dad's height and regal stature.

I assumed Roxanne's sisters were the five women now huddled up by the fireplace, watching me and whispering to one another, and their husbands were the men plopped on a sofa, in a small den off the living room, all of their eyes fixed on a huge flat-screen TV showing a football game playing at a low volume. Drew threw me a thumbs up over the back of the couch, and the other men peeked occasionally, trying to appear uninterested but clearly curious about the unexpected Christmas Eve drama.

"Hello, Brand. I was hopin' we might get to meet you. I'm Doris, and this is Ed, Roxanne's parents."

Ed reached out to shake my hand and then Merv's. "You're both very welcome," he said with an easy smile.

"You can meet everybody else later," Doris said, and she shooed me toward her kitchen. "Mrs. Lee, please join us, won't you, while your son and my daughter talk?"

Merv looked up at me and I nodded. What I needed to say to Roxanne didn't really warrant a peanut gallery, so I left Merv there with Ed and Doris and took the last steps to their kitchen and my destiny.

When I saw her, Roxanne stole the breath from my chest without even touching me.

She stood in front of the kitchen counter, her hands planted on it to hold her up, watching me coming toward her, breath heaving in her chest, fire-lit eyes glued to mine. The look in them was curious but wary, and I saw a little hurt still there too.

"What are you doin' here?" she asked, breathless, and the sound of her voice reminded me how much I'd missed it.

I'd missed her more than I could ever say, missed her laugh and her willingness to try to see the good in everyone. I missed the way I could feel her heart slow and her body relax when I touched her. I missed the gentle way she touched me, even when we were in the throes of hard sex.

She'd only said it twice, but I missed the way her eyes had flashed with forever when she told me she loved me.

Her name came out of my mouth like a plea. "*Roxanne*, if you'll permit me, there's some things I need to say to you."

Her fingers began to tap the counter. "Here? Now?"

I nodded. "Will you listen? Tell me yes."

CHAPTER THIRTY-FIVE

ROXANNE

BRAND DROPPED to his knees in front of me and reached up to set his hat on the counter next to me.

I'd heard his voice at the front door, talking to Drew, and I panicked. My sisters all saw the look on my face and the way my hands began to shake, and instantly they knew who had paid the Fitts household a visit.

When I saw him for the first time in almost a month, he was so handsome that it took me a minute to remember how to speak to ask him what the hell he was doing at my parents' house on Christmas freaking Eve. And now his hands clutched my hips, his breathtaking face and excited sky-blue eyes tipped up and trained on me, and it felt like he'd infused me with some kind of calming juju.

Instantly my heart slowed, and I felt like I could breathe again.

My nieces and nephews were all in the living room, oohing and aahing over the gifts Mama let them open early, but my sisters and some of my brothers-in-law peeked around the doorway, watching Brand. He didn't seem to know or care that he had an audience.

"I'm *sorry*, Roxanne," he said. "You were right back on that airplane. You've been right all along. I didn't believe it then, but I do now. I'm sorry I let you down, and I'm sorry I betrayed the trust you put in me. I told my family everything. Dixon's gone again, but that's not why I finally told them. I'm in therapy, and I've been goin' to a Nar-Anon family group. I started journaling and—"

Despite my resolve not to give in too quickly, my hands lifted to his hair, and I smoothed soft strands away from his face, realizing just how much I'd missed his touch on my body, the feel of my skin on his, and the possessive love he couldn't help but show me. "I know. Abey told me."

He nodded. "Can you forgive me? Please say yes," he whispered, and he laid his cheek against my stomach and wrapped his hands tightly around my back. "I don't know what this is, this thing inside me that makes me crave you the way I do.

"Maybe it's 'cause you're the only person on the planet who knows me like this. I've never let anyone in the way you're inside me, Roxanne. I don't know where you came from, but now I can't picture my life without you in it.

"I love you," he declared loudly.

My sister, Molly, swooned with the back of her hand pressed to her forehead, three of my sisters had their hands pressed to their chests and hearts in their eyes, and my youngest sister, Cecily, stood to the side, rocking little Jessica in her arms. My brothers-in-law all looked miffed, like Brand was winning some game I didn't know they'd been playing.

My mama had tears in her eyes, and my daddy smiled from ear to ear beside her. Merv was there, too, watching, and she smiled and nodded when we made eye contact.

He couldn't know that I'd already forgiven him before

he'd even shown up at my parents' place, but he hadn't given me the chance yet to tell him.

My family made me see that I had been a little unreasonable about Dixon. "If it was one of us," Maureen had said, "and you'd been keepin' our secret, would it be so easy to let it go?"

And she was right.

"You can submit to me," Brand said, "or I can submit to you. It doesn't really matter to me, beauty, as long as you're with me."

I cleared my throat, my face heating with embarrassment. "Um, Brand, that might be a conversation for another time. We kind of have an audience right now."

"I don't care," he vowed. "Let them see and hear how much I love you. I can't live without you. I will kneel here at your altar till the end of time if that's what it takes. Say you'll forgive me."

"Baby, seriously, this really isn't the right time."

"Yes, it is. Don't you remember what you said to me?"

"No. When? What did I say?"

"When Merv was in the hospital, and I came to your house and you held me and loved me all night long—"

Maureen let out some kind of cry-squeak, and she slapped her hand over her mouth, tears collecting at the corners of her eyes.

Cecily elbowed Maureen in the ribs, rocking side to side to keep the baby asleep. "Shhh. I can't hear over all your blubberin'."

Brand paid no attention to them. "You said you wanted the man who'd win your heart to be head over heels in love with you, and he'd propose in front of your whole family, and then you'd ride off into the sunset with him.

"Well, the sun has already set, and I don't have a valiant

steed, but I love you more than my own life, and I've got two draft horses and a Christmas carriage outside waitin' for us, and—"

He reached into his jacket pocket and pulled out a box.

My mama gasped loudly, and Daddy wrapped his arm around her shoulder. Everyone else stood speechless, watching my dreams come true in real time, and the kids all began to filter in from the living room, poking their heads around the adults wherever they could to get a good view.

But my eyes stayed fixed on Brand. No one else existed anymore.

He reached for his hat, and I watched silently as he placed it on his head. His hair had grown longer since we'd been apart, and the thick ends showed beneath.

He was exactly the man I had been in search of my whole life, but it wasn't the hat or his money or a ring; it was the love in his eyes.

"I planned to do this on the sleigh under a warm blanket and the falling snow, but right now feels perfect."

Suddenly, the front door opened and shut loudly, a deep, brusque voice interrupted the most important moment of my life, and then it really was perfect.

My uncle Al's head popped around the corner, his gray hair cropped short as usual and a sixer of Coors dangled from his fingers. "What's goin' on here?"

Daddy whispered, "Brand's about to propose to Riri. Be quiet."

"Who?"

Exasperated, Drew pointed to Brand on his knees on the kitchen floor in front of me. "*That* guy." He rolled his eyes at Uncle Al. "Now shhh. They're just gettin' to the good stuff."

Uncle Al smirked at me and pretended to zip and lock his lips.

I looked at Brand and saw utter devotion on his face.

"Roxanne Rhiannon Fitts. Roxi. Riri." He inhaled deeply and smiled. "I love you. You are the kindest, most open and honest person I've ever known. Your deep sense of loyalty and the way you love disarm me. I want you. And I need you. You will never again have to question or doubt me. To this I swear."

Somebody could have dropped a grain of sand on the floor and we all would've heard it.

Mama and Merv clutched each other's hands and held their breath, and my daddy beamed with pride.

Brand lifted one leg and planted his boot on the kitchen floor to steady himself as he pulled a massive diamond ring from the little black box. He stuffed the box back in his jacket, took my left hand in his, and isolated my ring finger.

"Will you marry me, Roxanne? Will you love me forever as I do you?"

Pins and needles rushed through me from head to toe. My breath hitched in my lungs. And was I bawling? Yep. Completely blubbering now. I held my breath to stop the sobs, and when they died down to hiccups, he pushed the ring to the root of my finger.

Even the house seemed to be holding its breath.

I couldn't look away from Brand's eyes, not even to admire the ring. So many things flashed across his face: hope, joy, excitement, pain, regret, submission and dominance at the same time. But all of it boiled down to one thing.

Love.

"Yes," I breathed. "Yes, I will marry you, and yes, I will love you...

"Forever."

EPILOGUE

BRAND
A Year and a Half Later

MY PHONE RINGING on my desk jerked me out of the daydream I'd been having about what I wanted to do to my wife in our kink bed when she got home from work.

I answered and listened to Billie Cade deliver unpromising news.

"Hey, Brand. I've got an update on the search for your brother. I tried calling Abey a couple times today, but she's been busy. I can wait to talk to her at book club later this week if that works better?"

"No," I said, my heart racing, "please go ahead. What have you found?"

Abey hadn't decided to look for Dixon again because the family was worried. I mean, we were, but Bax and Bea wanted to adopt Stuey, and they had been coming up against roadblocks because the local courts wouldn't accept the nota-rized paper relinquishing Dixon's parental rights he provided the day he'd abandoned his son.

They'd found a death certificate for Kellie Gale, Stu's birth mother, but not one for Dixon so the judge had contended that until he could speak to Dixon and make certain he was in the right frame of mind to make such a big decision, he wouldn't grant the adoption.

But we still had no clue where Dixon was. It had been a year and a half since he'd disappeared from the Coulters' place in Mad River, and now we needed to talk to him but hadn't had any luck finding him. That was when we brought in Billie again.

"Unfortunately, not much. Look. I'll keep my auto searches set to alert me if the dude comes back online, but from what I can tell, Dixon's still off the grid. He either doesn't have a cell phone or he's using a burner. That's not unusual for addicts though.

"But I can tell you he's alive. There's no John Doe cases or death certificates I can find matching his description. The floral tattoo you gave me a picture of helps with eliminating him when a case pops up with a similar description."

"You weren't able to find him in a rehab facility anywhere?"

"No, but that doesn't mean he isn't in one. But I can't hack every single rehab in the US. If we had a clue as to where he might be, it would be a start. I've looked through the rehabs in the area of California where he was before, in and around Redding, and there's one other place in Idaho I caught a short trail of him, but that's a dead end.

"I can't find him."

I sighed. I couldn't help it. The hope I'd had dissolved inside my chest like there was a leak in my lungs.

"I wish I had better news for you," Billie said. "Look, I'm not usually one for pep talks, but Abey and Roxi are family to me, which I guess means you and Dixon are too. Don't give up hope. He's got something to live for. He has a son. I used to be a jaded bitch, and I would've told you that didn't always matter to an addict, but I'm about to pop out a munchkin myself, so I finally get it. It does matter. It doesn't mean your little bro's addiction won't win, but I know he's fighting, wherever he is."

"Thank you, Billie. That means a lot. Can I pay you something? I know you said you're doin' this as a favor to Abey, but I don't feel right knowin' how much work you've put into this."

"I won't take your money, Brand. I don't need it. But you can make a donation to Ace's House or to a rehab here in Wyoming or something. That'd be cool."

"I'll do both," I said, "in your name. Thanks again."

Bax and Bea had a good lawyer, a Wisper local, Brady Douglas, and he said he could try to find a way around Dixon's absence so they could adopt Stu. Bax didn't feel right about going forward without at least notifying Dixon, but even if we couldn't find him and they weren't able to go ahead with the adoption, it wouldn't change Stuey's role in their lives, in mine or Merv's.

But Dixon's story still ate at me. Not because I wanted to fix him, but because it was an ending I couldn't control, an unfinished life. A loose thread that tickled my neck.

But I had better ways now to deal with my control issues. Much sexier ways.

A mile and a half away from Bax's and Merv's houses, the log A-frame I'd built for my wife sat nestled between the trees on a bluff, and the front door opened and closed softly, so I left my study and rushed to our living room to greet Roxanne after a long day's work. Her uniform was rumpled, and she looked tired, but she seemed happy to see me.

She smiled at me as she hung her hat on the hook by the door, and all the rest of my worries floated away.

Through therapy and meeting and talking with other families of addicts, I knew that I might never see my little brother again.

But I still had hope.

Roxanne

"WHAT IS THAT?" I squeaked. "It looks like one of those crocheted plant hangers from the seventies, but gargantuan sized."

"That, my beautiful wife, is a suspension system."

After work, my husband led me to the secret room in our home only he and I knew was there.

I supposed my sister-in-law, Bea, knew it was there because she had been the only other person Brand allowed to work on it when he built it, but she didn't know what was *in* it. Bax, Rye, and Clay had all seen the plans too. They poured the foundation and helped frame our house, so they knew *something* was there in the room behind our bedroom in the loft of our gorgeous mountain house with fabulous counter space.

But I was betting not one of them could guess what Brand had transformed the room into.

I hadn't even seen it, not since we'd painted the walls and Brand asked me to trust him to outfit it with new toys for us to indulge in. We'd started out with white walls and rudimentary tools and toys—dildos, crops, nipple clamps, which I found I loved—but we were moving up in the world. My devilishly handsome other half had finally convinced me to let him go to town.

The deep, dark, dusty-blue color of the walls calmed my nerves. And I had *a lot* of nerves right about now. Some of the items I saw when he led me to our newly decked-out playroom looked medieval.

He pointed to what looked like a folding table, but it was black and padded. "See, here's the table. It's portable, so I can lay you down and tie you up, and then I push this button"—he stepped to the wall and lifted what looked like a small, flat flap next to a light switch, pressed a button the size of the pad of his thumb, and the ropes hanging from the ceiling began to lift in the air—"and move the table out of our way, and I can fuck you up in the air. Or I can take you with my mouth while you dangle in front of me.

"Ain't it great? Oh, and this over here is your very own pleasure throne." He rushed to the corner of the room and pointed to a short contraption. It kind of looked like a camping chair, but King Aurthur style. "It's just a stool you sit on, but it's got this opening here, and I lay beneath you like the queen you are and eat you out."

"Oh my God, Brand."

"Yeah, I know, right? I can't fuckin' wait to taste you like that."

It still amazed me to see the man Brand had become. No longer was he a closed-off CEO. All the different parts of him had blended into the excited, generous man who had become my husband. And the boy could get down and country like the best of them.

Therapy had helped him tremendously, and learning not to keep secrets had been freeing for him. And for me.

Turned out, I was in fact neurodivergent. The doctors tried to prescribe medications, but I refused. I was learning to manage my anxieties naturally, through breathing and sensory coping mechanisms, and by talking through my thoughts with Brand and Aubrey and my therapist. My family was supportive too. My mama cried when I explained my diagnosis and said it was a relief to hear because it made so much sense and explained so many things she'd never understood about me.

As I turned to survey the rest of our new toys and the king-size bed in the middle of the room, my eyes began to bug out of my head. Something had been crisscrossed over our mattress.

"Those are bed restraints," he explained. "They go under the mattress when we're not usin' 'em, but they keep your arms and legs spread for me so I can fuck you and torture you however I want."

"Um."

I hated to ruin the excitement seeping out of him like he was a kid in a candy store for the first time, but I might have been at the beginning stages of a panic attack.

"You don't like what I picked out for us?" He stepped in front of me, angling his head down to look in my eyes. "If you don't like it, it all goes."

"No, I… I mean, I don't know if I like it. I've never done any of this before."

"Me either," he whispered, stepping behind me. "We'll find out together, okay?"

"Okay," I said as he moved me toward the bed with his body pressing behind mine.

He laid me down and crawled over me, and his warmth eased my anxiety. He lay next to me, and I lifted my head so his arm could slide beneath.

"But the most important thing in this room, besides you and me, is that." Pointing to a huge, framed photograph taking up a third of the back A-shaped wall, Brand said, "From the day you married me and made me the happiest I've ever been. Remember?"

As if I could forget one second of our wedding day, halfway across the world near the coast in Maremma, Italy. Both of our families had traveled all that way for us, and it was the most joyous time of my life.

And the happiness was doubled when Rye proposed to my bestie again at our wedding dinner after the ceremony, and Aubrey cried and screamed, "Yes! Okay? I'll marry your sexy ass. Happy now?"

Brand murmured in my ear, "When that picture was taken, you were laughin' at somethin' Athena said. You were so fuckin' beautiful that day in the middle of Tuscany, surrounded on all sides by wild sunflowers and our families. All I could do was stare at you. I look like a lovesick fool in that photo, but you took my breath away, Roxanne. You still do. Every day."

"You don't look like a fool," I said, blinking and trying to stop the tears from coming.

When he reminisced about our wedding, which he did often, I always teared up. I'd never heard a man talk so much about his wedding, but Brand did all the time.

We had already begun planning a trip back so we could see more of Italy and France. Anywhere we wanted to go, really. He wanted to take me everywhere. He wanted us to live our lives like an adventure when we could because we both worked hard. We played pretty hard too, and this secret room was definitive proof of that.

Brand hadn't sold his contract for the new housing project or dissolved Lee Construction. Instead, he made structural changes. His foreman Tweety now ran the commercial contracts division of Lee Construction, and Bea and Clay handled the single-family home builds so Brand could be at home more and work the ranch with his brother and Rye. But the thing he'd become really excited about was a special, nonprofit plan he been working on to build homes for veterans in the area and their families.

Tab worked with Tweety, Bea, and Brand, but most closely with Brand and his new nonprofit. She'd turned out to be a bloodhound when it came to finding funding and donors to contribute money and resources. And she was a very good friend. She'd even joined my book club, and she and I spent way too much time texting and giggling late into the nights about the sexy things we read about in our books.

And just like that, my new family had welcomed a new, fresh iteration of Lee Construction. It was now one more business we all contributed to, alongside Spitfire Ranch, Lee Valley Cabins, and Abey and Devo's CSA farm, Two Girl Veg.

When my eyes strayed from our way-too-big wedding photograph, they landed on some kind of huge X-shaped contraption just inside the door that I'd missed when we came in. It took up nearly the entire wall, but it wasn't attached to the wall; it stood on its own, with a heavy metal base and leather-covered planks crossed in an X.

Brand saw me gaping at it. "That's a St. Andrew's Cross, or an X-cross. It's hot, right?"

I whimpered. I was terrified of that thing.

"I built it for us. It's kinky as fuck. It even spins, but don't worry. We'll take it slow."

He crawled over me again and began unbuttoning my uniform shirt. "But not tonight. Tonight, my beauty, I wanna feed you and fuck you on this bed." He reached above us and pulled a mattress restraint to my wrist and tested the fit. My clothes came off slowly, but his stayed on, and when he had me completely naked, my wrists and ankles strapped down, he stood at the foot of the bed and stared. "Do you have any idea how goddamn beautiful you are?"

I blushed. He still had the power to bring me to my knees with just a few words and the look in his eye, even after a year and a half together.

"No, I don't think you do," he said. "So let me show you. Tell me yes."

"Yes," I breathed, still in awe of the way my man loved me, like it was his one true mission in life.

The restraint cuffs fit snugly, but they didn't pinch. He'd made sure to buy comfortable, supple leather gear with soft, padded linings. And they spread me open for his taking.

Without warning, and still fully clothed, he lunged at me and dove between my legs, sliding his hands under my ass, and ate my pussy like a starving man.

"Brand!"

"Yeah, beauty," he rasped between licks. "Tell me your safe word."

"Basketball!" I yelped when he sucked my clit into his mouth and jammed at least three fingers inside me. "Yes!"

"Good girl. Scream all you want. Only the mountains can hear you."

I moaned so loudly, I felt the vibrations run through my whole body, and I tried to ride his face, but he held my hips to the bed with a strong hand placed expertly on my stomach. Nothing turned him on more than holding me down and forcing orgasms out of me.

Like I was going to complain about that?

"Come for me, Roxanne. Quickly, so I can feed you the dinner I made for you and then my cock, and then I'm gonna fuck you like I did in our yurt. By the way, I bought one for us."

His hands and mouth were relentless, and my question came out in breathless shudders. "You... b-bought... what?"

"I bought us a yurt to camp in. I set it up on the back forty near the woods. We'll go out there this weekend. It even has a claw-foot tub."

His touch left my stomach and inched up to my breast, and he pinched my nipple tightly before his hand slid up my chest and around my neck. He cuffed my throat and curled his fingers inside me, reaching and massaging the spot he knew would set me off like a bomb.

"Brand!"

"Come."

And I did.

His commanding voice was all I needed, and I called my pleasure to the stars in the window above us, the stars that would forever shine and find us here, together, loving and living for each other.

If you liked *Forever Finds Us*, please consider leaving a review—even just a few words would help—on your favorite bookseller website, Goodreads, or BookBub. Self-published indie authors rely heavily upon reviews to get our stories out to the masses. And thank you. I know it takes time to do this. I appreciate the time out of your day and the effort.

DEAR READER,

Thank you for reading Roxi's and Brand's story!

I have to admit that when I met miss Roxi, I had no clue she'd get a book. In my head, she was weird and quirky, but she stayed in the background. That was until I got to know Brand better. I still didn't know how and why they'd fall in love until I thought about Roxi's handcuffs. Then the whole story just bloomed in my brain and I couldn't stop myself from writing it.

I hope you enjoyed it, and stick around cuz there's one more Lee brother, and he deserves a comeback, don't you think?

Turn the page for a peek!

Or you can sign up to receive my newsletter and be the first to know about upcoming releases and get sexy teasers, updates, and probably cat pics.

Learn more at gretarosewest.com.

XOXO,

Greta

From internationally bestselling small-town western romance author, Greta Rose West, *Scars Forget Us* is a story of redemption, of second and third chances, and of a love that perseveres in the face of adversity.

Dixon Lee doesn't think he deserves a comeback, but he wants one desperately. He's done things in his life he can't excuse, things he doesn't have hope he'll ever be forgiven for. Leaving his family when they needed him most should probably earn him a one-way ticket to Hell.

The scars he wears won't let him forget his mistakes, but he has to try.

His purpose after a long, self-imposed exile is to make things right with the only person who matters: his five-year old son. The shame he's felt, the blurry picture he carries in his wallet, and the torn piece of Stuart's baby blanket in his front pocket tried to break his resolve to stay clean, but the memory of a girl he used to know, laughing in a western meadow, played in his head every day, and the echo of her voice has gotten him through countless sleepless nights.

When Dixon hitchhikes back into Wisper, Wyoming, planning to finally face his past, the last person he expects to run into is his memory girl.

Avery Jane Harlowe's not just a small-town girl.

She's a woman, and her only dream has always been to run the floral shop her gran started when Avery was a baby. She let a man get in her way once, and her heart barely survived. She won't give it away so easily again, but when Dixon shows up back in town and she gets the urge to love him like she did when they were kids, she refuses to be that naïve girl this time around.

Dixon's certainly not little anymore, and as much as he tries to make her believe he's irredeemable, Avery knows it's not true. He's beautiful and strong and desperately broken but learning how to love himself. She wants to risk it, to help him see himself the way she sees him, but Dixon has heartbreak written all over his back, even has it tattooed there.

Falling in love with Dixon Lee would be a messy complication, and it would set her world on fire, but something tells her the burn might just be the very thing she needs.

In the shadow of the Grand Teton Mountains, *Scars Forget Us* is the second chance that might break your heart, but the mending is the good part, and it will leave you breathless.

Turn the page for a sneak peek!

DIXON

"D, why don't you start us off today?" Mo said.

It looked like he'd showered and combed his hair, brushed his teeth, but he was probably three cups of coffee deep this morning, so there was a discolored tinge to them. Drugs and drinking hadn't left them pearly white anyway. His button down was rumpled, as usual, and his khakis weren't the wrinkle-free kind by any stretch of the imagination.

I asked, "We're tellin' memories? Good or bad?"

"What comes to mind?"

But Mo was a good guy. Maybe the nicest person I'd met since I got sober. He always had a kind word, even if his day had gone to shit. He had real, true belief in his fellow man, and if you needed it, he'd give you the shirt off his back even though he didn't have a pot to piss in.

A memory? I had to think about it. I had lots of those. The therapist told me to let the bad ones come, that I couldn't avoid them forever if I wanted to stay clean, but today had been a good one up till now, as far as memories went, and I didn't want the bad ones to sour my stomach quite yet. I'd just eaten shitty diner bacon and eggs, and if I let the bad memories flow, I'd chuck.

If I thought about Candy and my brother's baby, what I'd done to them, what I didn't do...

No, today, I wanted to think about something good. Something sweet.

Memories of my brothers and sister from when we were kids hit me like a bullet train. My oldest brother, Bax, was off limits, though, because he was attached to the memories of Candy and their baby. He wasn't safe. My other brother, Brand, was a good man. Maybe a little self-centered, but I loved him. I always had. And I wouldn't be clean if he hadn't flown down from Wyoming to California and paid up front for rehab.

I loved all my siblings, and maybe Brand had his own demons to wrangle and that was why he'd always been a little standoffish and stiff.

My sister, the youngest in our family, Abey... What a beautiful soul.

I ached for her. She'd gotten the worst of our dad. He'd made her feel like she didn't even deserve to live—

No. My brothers and sister were out of bounds this morning if I wanted to keep my day on track, and I sure as shit wasn't going to give myself permission to remember Kel, the dead mother of my kid.

Stay positive.

"There was a girl."

The tired, beat-down group of men around me mumbled their agreement. Didn't it always start with a girl?

"Yeah," I said, "but this girl was a kid. I was a kid. She didn't have anything to do with why things got dark for me. She was a light. Her grandparents lived near our family farm, and she used to stay out at their place during the summers.

"Her hair was the color of cornsilk. The sun made it that way. And she had this tinkling laugh. Her name was... I don't remember. It won't come to me. There's too much bad and hurt between now and then." The hurt made the good memories blurry and out of reach. "But I remember that laugh.

"She loved flowers, was always picking the wild ones, even picked 'em from her grandma's prized garden, and she'd make these bouquets for the squirrels and birds, deer and elk. Now, I knew they didn't give a shit about flowers, but she insisted on leavin' 'em for the animals. She made beds of flowers and strung the stems together to make strands we'd hang from tree limbs. She said when the wind blew through the trees, she thought her flowers made the animals happy."

Next to me, Nesty chuckled. He thought shortening his real name, Ernesto, to Nesty sounded like Posty. He was always doing that, comparing himself to celebrities, even though he was the scrawniest, least-famous dude I'd ever met. He was strong though; he punched me once when we were high after I called him Ernie. Most guys didn't, but I hoped if he stayed clean this time, he'd rethink the nickname.

"Don't think I've ever seen you smile like that," he said.

I elbowed him. "Shut up. Mo said good or bad memories. This is my good one.

"Anyway, I think about that girl when I can't sleep. I always told her she should take over her grandma's flower shop. I wonder if she did. I wonder if she's happy. If she still laughs like that, like a wind chime."

Or was she like me, broken and sorry and scarred?

I prayed like crazy I'd stay clean, like it wasn't up to me.

But it was. And this time, I had the best reason to beat my demon into submission.

A son.

A beautiful, soft, perfect baby boy.

He had a family, people better than me to look up to. My brother and his girls were raising my Stuey. He had love around him. Before my car died, I'd driven up to check on him, to make sure my family had come through for me this time.

They had. Stuart was happy and healthy. He was up on my family's land right this very minute, and when he grew big enough, he'd run free like I had when I was his age, laughing and learning, maybe picking flowers with his own memory girl.

But he needed his dad in his life. Even if my brother

would always be Stuey's *daddy*, his father figure, and I could only be his friend, if it was all I could give my son, I would.

I'd be his best friend if that was what was healthiest for him.

I loved him enough to do that for him, no matter that just thinking about him never knowing the real me made me ache like I'd never ached before.

And I'd known plenty of fucking ache in my life.

But my baby boy didn't need to know anything about that.

He needed smiles and tinkling laughs, mountain air, dirt to dig in, grass to roll in. He needed birds singing to him from the trees and evenings spent around a happy dinner table. Nights filled with stories from books with silly cartoons on the front and bubble baths.

My son deserved good dreams and good memories, and I intended someday to give those to him.

But I still had to make it through these first thirty days. And after that?

Well, I wasn't sure. I didn't have a pot to piss in either, or any kind of direction about the path my sober life would take.

But I was goddamned determined to figure it out.

The last book in the Wisper Dreams series, Scars Forget Us.

EXTRA CONTENT

Join my newsletter for a FREE short story, *Wild Heart: Welcome to Wisper*. This is where you can get all the Wisper news and sexcapades—naughty little interludes for my subscribers ONLY!

Sign up on my website: gretarosewest.com/VIPS

LETS CONNECT!

You can also join me in my Facebook group, Wisperites Unite. We get up to a lot of fun there. Mostly we drool over sexy cowboys, but we do other things there too, I promise, like giveaways and fun games, and my Wisperites always get new book news first, teasers, and we chat about books. We'd love to have you!

Go to: https://www.facebook.com/groups/wisperitesunite

I would love to hear from you. Email me at greta@gretarosewest.com. I'll reply. Or find me on Facebook and Instagram.

@gretarosewest

ABOUT THE AUTHOR

 Greta Rose West was a floundering artsy flake until cowboy Jack Cade showed up, knocking on the door of her brain, pounding on it, and then he just plain kicked it down. She's a boy mom to a grown freakin' man, who has recently gifted her with the title of GRANNY! She comes from the "Region" of NW Indiana, but Greta, her husband, and her two precocious kitties, Geoff Trouble and Sally Mae Midnight, now reside in the Denver, Colorado area, where she often makes her husband drive her into the mountains so she can look and dream. When she's not writing, she's reading and devouring music. She enjoys indie films no one else likes, and her favorite food is Aver's Veggie Revival pizza.

You can find her on Instagram @gretarosewest, in her Facebook group, Wisperites Unite, or on her website.

gretarosewest.com

f facebook.com/gretarosewest
⊙ instagram.com/gretarosewest
BB bookbub.com/authors/greta-rose-west
g goodreads.com/gretarosewest